ROBERT B. PARKER'S

SHOWDOWN

THE SPENSER NOVELS

Robert B. Parker's Showdown
(by Mike Lupica)
Robert B. Parker's Hot Property
(by Mike Lupica)
Robert B. Parker's Broken Trust
(by Mike Lupica)
Robert B. Parker's Bye Bye Baby
(by Ace Atkins)
Robert B. Parker's Someone to Watch Over Me
(by Ace Atkins)
Robert B. Parker's Angel Eyes
(by Ace Atkins)
Robert B. Parker's Old Black Magic
(by Ace Atkins)
Robert B. Parker's Little White Lies
(by Ace Atkins)
Robert B. Parker's Slow Burn
(by Ace Atkins)
Robert B. Parker's Kickback
(by Ace Atkins)
Robert B. Parker's Cheap Shot
(by Ace Atkins)
Silent Night
(with Helen Brann)
Robert B. Parker's Wonderland
(by Ace Atkins)
Robert B. Parker's Lullaby
(by Ace Atkins)
Sixkill
Painted Ladies
The Professional
Rough Weather
Now & Then
Hundred-Dollar Baby
School Days
Cold Service
Bad Business
Back Story
Widow's Walk
Potshot
Hugger Mugger
Hush Money
Sudden Mischief
Small Vices
Chance
Thin Air
Walking Shadow
Paper Doll
Double Deuce
Pastime
Stardust
Playmates
Crimson Joy
Pale Kings and Princes
Taming a Sea-Horse
A Catskill Eagle
Valediction
The Widening Gyre
Ceremony
A Savage Place
Early Autumn
Looking for Rachel Wallace
The Judas Goat
Promised Land
Mortal Stakes
God Save the Child
The Godwulf Manuscript

For a comprehensive title list and a preview of upcoming books, visit PRH.com/RobertBParker or Facebook.com/RobertBParkerAuthor.

ROBERT B. PARKER'S

SHOWDOWN

MIKE LUPICA

G. P. PUTNAM'S SONS
New York

PUTNAM
— EST. 1838 —

G. P. Putnam's Sons
Publishers Since 1838
An imprint of Penguin Random House LLC
1745 Broadway, New York, NY 10019
penguinrandomhouse.com

Title page photo by ronstik/Adobe Stock

LIBRARY OF CONGRESS CATALOGING-IN-PUBLICATION DATA

Names: Lupica, Mike, author.
Title: Robert B. Parker's Showdown / Mike Lupica.
Other titles: Showdown
Description: New York : G. P. Putnam's Sons, 2025. | Series: A Spenser novel |
Identifiers: LCCN 2025019991 (print) | LCCN 2025019992 (ebook) |
ISBN 9798217045297 (hardcover) | ISBN 9798217045310 (ebook)
Subjects: LCGFT: Fiction | Detective and mystery fiction | Novels
Classification: LCC PS3562.U59 R656 2025 (print) | LCC PS3562.U59 (ebook)
LC record available at https://lccn.loc.gov/2025019991
LC ebook record available at https://lccn.loc.gov/2025019992

Printed in the United States of America
1st Printing

The authorized representative in the EU for product safety and compliance is
Penguin Random House Ireland, Morrison Chambers, 32 Nassau Street,
Dublin D02 YH68, Ireland, https://eu-contact.penguin.ie.

This book is for my children:
Christopher, Alex, Zach, Hannah

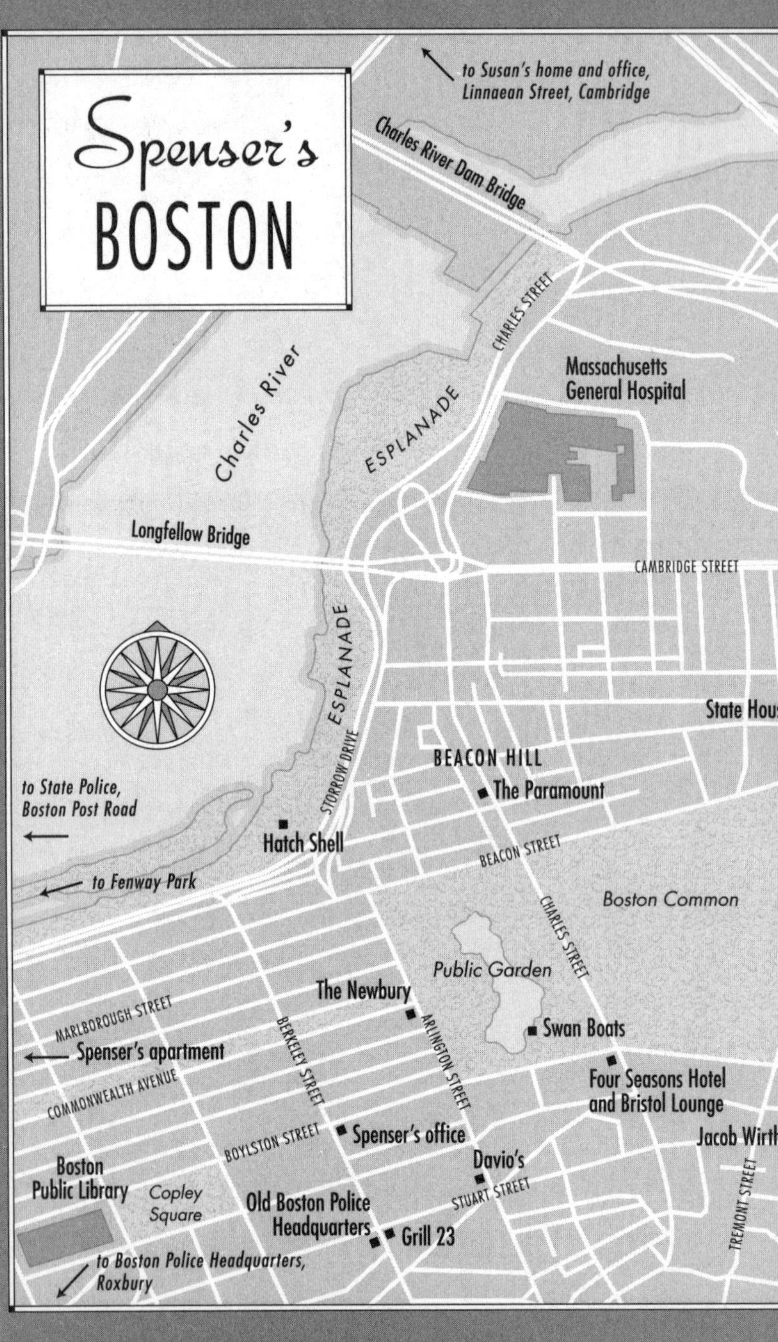
Spenser's BOSTON
to Susan's home and office, Linnaean Street, Cambridge
Charles River Dam Bridge
CHARLES STREET
Massachusetts General Hospital
Charles River
ESPLANADE
Longfellow Bridge
CAMBRIDGE STREET
ESPLANADE
State House
STORROW DRIVE
BEACON HILL
The Paramount
to State Police, Boston Post Road
Hatch Shell
BEACON STREET
to Fenway Park
CHARLES STREET
Boston Common
Public Garden
The Newbury
MARLBOROUGH STREET
BERKELEY STREET
ARLINGTON STREET
Swan Boats
Spenser's apartment
Four Seasons Hotel and Bristol Lounge
COMMONWEALTH AVENUE
BOYLSTON STREET
Spenser's office
Jacob Wirth
Boston Public Library
Davio's
Copley Square
Old Boston Police Headquarters
STUART STREET
Grill 23
TREMONT STREET
to Boston Police Headquarters, Roxbury

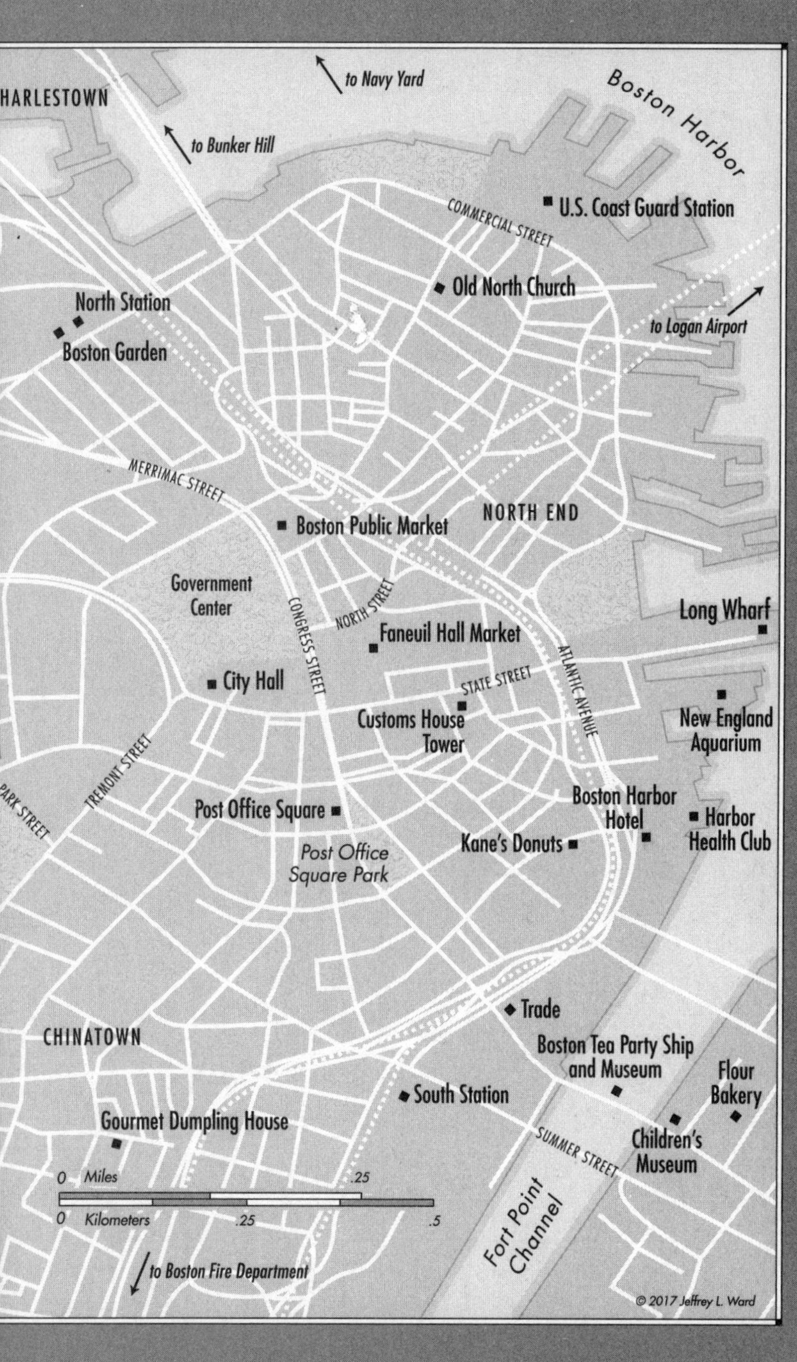
CHARLESTOWN
to Navy Yard
Boston Harbor
to Bunker Hill
U.S. Coast Guard Station
COMMERCIAL STREET
Old North Church
North Station
Boston Garden
to Logan Airport
MERRIMAC STREET
Boston Public Market
NORTH END
Government Center
CONGRESS STREET
NORTH STREET
Faneuil Hall Market
Long Wharf
ATLANTIC AVENUE
STATE STREET
City Hall
Customs House Tower
New England Aquarium
TREMONT STREET
PARK STREET
Post Office Square
Boston Harbor Hotel
Harbor Health Club
Kane's Donuts
Post Office Square Park
Trade
CHINATOWN
Boston Tea Party Ship and Museum
Flour Bakery
South Station
Gourmet Dumpling House
Children's Museum
SUMMER STREET
0 Miles .25
0 Kilometers .25 .5
Fort Point Channel
to Boston Fire Department
© 2017 Jeffrey L. Ward

ONE

Hawk was stretched out on the couch in my office, where I sometimes thought he had been since right after the Puritans had arrived.

He was wearing black exercise pants, Hoka sneakers with more colors in them than the Pride flag, and a Caitlin Clark T-shirt.

When I'd asked him about the T-shirt, he'd said, "Just my way of showing solidarity with that bad, bad girl."

The book he was currently reading—*The Wingmen*, about the friendship between Ted Williams and John Glenn—was currently closed and bookmarked across Caitlin Clark's No. 22. I'd long since accepted the fact that Hawk, when the spirit moved him, viewed my office as his personal reading room. Out of friendship, I felt it more flattering than calling him a squatter.

I pointed at his book now and said, "You don't even like baseball."

"Not reading it for the baseball shit, reading it for the war shit," he said. "I always thought I would have been the ass as a fighter pilot."

"You're assuming the Marines would have gotten past your rap sheet?" I said.

"Only if they wanted to win," Hawk said.

I sipped more coffee from the temperature-controlled mug Susan

Silverman had bought for me, having figured out just this morning how to keep the coaster charged, and already knowing that I probably wouldn't stay with it for the long haul. When I'd phoned to tell her that I finally did have it working the way it was supposed to, I'd also mentioned that it was a good thing, since I liked my coffee the way I liked my women: hot.

Susan had said, "The twenty-first century just called, big boy. They're still holding a table for you."

I didn't get the chance to ask what she was wearing, as I so often did, because she'd already ended the call.

To Hawk now I said, "You're at least aware that Ted Williams was considered the greatest hitter of all time, right?"

"Only reason I am," he said, "is on account of it having sunk in after the first thousand damn times you told me."

"They called him the Splendid Splinter, you know," I said. "Also the Thumper. And Teddy Ballgame."

Hawk turned slightly toward me on the couch, his eyes looking so hooded I thought he might be on the verge of a nap even though it was only midmorning. But he'd pointed out on more than one occasion that baseball talk from me often acted as a powerful sedative for him.

"And down the rabbit hole we go," he said.

I had finally given in to peer pressure from him, even though Hawk constantly told me he had no peers, and purchased a longer couch, mostly so his feet no longer had to hang over the edge when he was reclining the way he was now. To my way of thinking, that made me at least as good a wingman as either Ted Williams or John Glenn had been. In my dreams, a larger couch also might be more functional in the future if I could ever again talk Susan into us using it for a midday flight of heavenly transport.

Or a reasonable facsimile thereof.

I had been slowly making my way through *The Globe* while Hawk had been reading his book. I still liked having a newspaper in my hands. But then, I was someone who considered texting to be the devil's handiwork.

I looked over at Hawk, whose eyes now seemed to be all the way shut, and felt myself smiling at my own wingman as I did, thinking about all the wars the two of us had fought together. In almost the same moment, he turned back to me as if reading my mind, and we'd already begun our next conversation. He could do that with alarming ease, much the way Susan Silverman could. It was concerning to me, if only because it chipped away at my notion of being a man of mystery.

"How long you figure we been doin' this, you and me?" he asked.

"By *this*," I said, "I assume you're referring to us doing our own patriotic bit to make the country a better and safer place."

Hawk smiled then, the smile coming up and out of him slowly and finally brilliantly, the way the sun did when it came up over the Harbor.

"Not necessarily better," he said, "for the ones we keepin' it safe *from*."

"You make a solid point there," I said.

"As I so often do," he said.

"But being the trained detective that I am," I said, "I sense that you're about to make a larger point."

"As I so often am," he said.

"Don't make me come over there and beat it out of you," I said.

He was smiling again. "If you do," he said, "and I find out about it . . ."

He sat up then, placed his book on the end table behind him, and walked over and poured himself a cup of coffee. I had offered to get him a temperature-controlled mug of his own. He had taken a hard pass on that, saying it would only make him drink more coffee. I told him that was the point.

"What I'm getting at," he said, "is if you ever wonder how long we're gonna keep doing whatever it is we've been doing for as long as we've been doing it."

"It sounds like you've been wondering about that very thing."

"Uh-huh."

"Are you considering a career change?" I said. "Because I'm thinking it might be a little late in life for you to do the *Top Gun* thing."

"Turn and burn, like my boy Tommy Cruise says," Hawk said.

"Good God, Watson," I said in a British accent that wasn't nearly as good as the one Hawk liked to use when he switched conversational gears. "Are you actually considering retirement? I still see you as being in your prime, my dear man."

"Ain't never been anywhere *but* my prime," Hawk said. "You're the one needs to be the late bloomer, not me."

"There *is* that," I said.

"Just been thinking lately about all the fighting you and me been doing, in the ring and out the ring, and for such a long-assed time," he said. "And wondering if you ever get tired of fighting."

"I do," I said. "The problem is, I have no other skills."

"Got to have at least one other," he said, "or Susan staying with you this long makes no sense whatsoever."

"It's sweet for you to have noticed," I said.

"We both know you didn't just buy this couch for me, even though you say you did," he said.

"A man can dream, can't he?" I said.

He stared at me now, face both serious and solemn at the same time.

"Any asshole you wouldn't be willing to help they came through the door asking you for it?" he said.

"Asking for help, you mean?"

"Uh-huh."

"Other than a New York Yankee?" I said.

"Other than that," Hawk said.

"It would have to be one raging asshole," I said. "And even then, you know me." I slid into my Bogart impression then, just to amuse myself. And because sometimes I couldn't help myself. "Trouble is my business, *schweetheart*."

"Told you never to call me that," Hawk said.

His face was still serious as he looked down at his book, all the usual irony and smart-ass completely absent, tapped the cover of his book with his index finger, looked back at me.

"Since I'm asking the questions today, here come one more your way, ball down the middle you could probably hit out the park like Ted Williams," Hawk said. "You think there's anything in this world could ever *stop* us from being wingmen?"

"Not a chance," I said. Then winked broadly and added, "*Schweetheart*."

I was wrong about that, as it turned out.

And nearly dead wrong.

Wasn't the first time.

TWO

After Hawk left for what I suspected might be his own flight of heavenly transport, I immediately began thinking about lunch.

Occasionally I am thinking about lunch before I've had breakfast. You have to get out ahead of these things, or risk being run over later on. Susan had suggested recently that I thought about food more than I thought about sex, understanding the scope of that statement better than anyone.

I told her I was still looking for a graceful way to do both at once.

"You know how much I love you," she said, "but there really are several screws loose here."

"Do you think a good therapist might be able to help?" I asked.

"It might be too late for that, in which case you're screwed," she said. She smiled wickedly at me. "See what I did there?"

My two finalists for lunch this morning were Billy's Sub Shop on Berkeley Street or the Flour Bakery + Café on Clarendon. I was weighing the pros and cons of each, not that there were many cons to speak of, when Rita Fiore called.

"What's going on with the Incredible Hunk?" she said.

"I'm trying to decide where to have lunch," I said. "Which means that if you need me to save your life again right now, it's going to have to wait."

"You didn't save my life," she said. "You were tireless in finding out who tried to take it."

It was last year, and some very bad men had come after her because she'd had a very bad boyfriend, a politician who in the end made George Santos look more truthful than Honest Abe. She had been gunned down on the street where she lives in Beacon Hill. But with some help from my friends, I had found out who shot her and why, and made Rita's world a better and safer place this time around.

"A distinction without a difference," I said.

"May I stop by?" she said. "There's someone I'd like you to meet."

"A potential client?" I said.

"Perhaps," Rita said.

"Okay," I said, "but if so, he can't be a raging asshole. Hawk and I decided just this morning that I need to draw the line there once and for all."

"He's not," she said.

"And who, if I may ask, might this potential client be?" I said.

"He says he's Vic Hale's son," she said.

"Speaking of ragers," I said.

"He happens to be a son nobody knew Vic had," Rita said, before adding, "At least until now."

If Joe Rogan was the biggest podcast personality around, Vic Hale, Boston guy, was in the conversation about who might be the next biggest. And loudest. I wasn't a fan, even though I had once boxed with his late father, and had considered the father a friend. Now the son, a former pro wrestler and local radio host and even standup comic the way Rogan still was, had become one of the most powerful and popular media personalities in America.

His America, anyway.

Vic hated just about everybody who didn't look like him, his audience loved him passionately for it, and he had the downloads and page views and streaming numbers and all the other ways success was measured in his world to prove it. These were data points I knew as much about, really, as I did needlepoint. Mostly because I wasn't a podcast guy, something else that stamped me as being out of step with the modern world. Susan said it was just one more thing to add to a list that was starting to run longer than a Harry Potter novel.

Vic Hale didn't really hate everybody and everything. He liked cops. He absolutely loved the Second Amendment the way children loved their first puppies. He apparently still talked about Ronald Reagan the way young girls mooned over Taylor Swift.

In the America where just about everybody with a microphone, on radio or TV or in the podcast world, was shouting at us and one another more and more, Vic Hale now had one of the loudest voices in the bullhorn media. Vic Hale, Boston's own, as he was so frequently described.

And we sure were proud to have him.

"King of the mouth-breathers" is the way Hawk described him. Susan just called him that "awful, awful man."

Hale had achieved his earliest fame being on the front line of defending our borders, in what he described as the ongoing war between Them and Us. On the rare occasions when I heard a clip from his show somewhere, he always made it sound as if there was some kind of invading army of migrants and immigrants who'd already made their way to *Old Ironsides*.

And no matter how many politicians, all over the country, got in line after that, Vic Hale liked to brag that he had been there first.

"So why did Vic Hale's son come to you?" I asked Rita.

"It'll be easier for him to explain when we get to your office," she said.

"Can you at least tell me who the young man's mother is?" I said.

"A migrant from Guatemala," Rita said.

"Oh, ho," I said.

THREE

Daniel Lopez was nearly my height, a lot leaner, and handsome enough to be in the movies, and had lost his mother, Marisol, when she was shot to death six weeks ago in Miami Gardens after withdrawing cash from an ATM not far from where they lived near Hard Rock Stadium. This all happened in his final semester at the University of Miami, by which time he'd already been accepted at Harvard Law.

He told me all of this quickly and dispassionately after taking one of the client chairs across from my desk. Rita Fiore was in the other chair, wearing a tight green dress that showed off the amount of leg she generally showed off in my presence. She'd told me once that she knew she had great legs and wasn't afraid to use them.

After Rita's near-death experience on Joy Street, Susan had softened her position on Rita, who, she believed, had consistently done everything except hire a skywriter to let me know how available she was to me, even knowing that nobody had a more significant other than I most significantly did with Susan. It didn't stop Dr. Silverman from occasionally mentioning how nice it was that Rita, even at her age, was still shopping at the come-and-get-it department.

Once they had settled into their chairs, Rita laid out and allowed

Daniel Lopez to tell his story, at least the preamble to it, at his own pace and in his own way. As did I. You had to. He didn't know me and I didn't know him and this was at least the beginning of us knowing each other. Daniel already knew that I had a rough outline of an idea as to why he was here. He clearly wanted me to know how he got here before we all began talking about where he might go from here.

At one point when he had paused to take a breath I said, "Did the police ever have a suspect in your mother's murder?"

"They did not and do not," he said. "There have been a series of crimes a lot like it in the Miami area this spring. They think it might be the same person doing the robberies and the homicides, but they're not sure. And might never be. My mother was just one more person in America at the wrong place at the wrong time and at the wrong end of a gun."

He really was a good-looking kid. I thought he could easily have played one of those *Top Gun* flyboys.

"She died because of two hundred dollars, Mr. Spenser."

I said, "A kid over in Blue Hill got shot in the head a week or so ago over a pair of sneakers that cost less."

He shook his head and looked out the window before his dark eyes returned to me.

"At first I thought it might be some sort of retaliation against me," he said.

"Against you?" I said. "What in the world for?"

"I've become a bit of an activist for immigration reform during my time at the U," he said. "And an increasingly more vocal one. I even see myself described as a media darling occasionally. There's one reporter who's taken a particular interest in me and my story and has been putting my name out there every chance he gets."

"Ironic, isn't it?" Rita said. "In light of who the young man thinks his father is."

"But the police are convinced it was just a robbery gone wrong," Daniel said. "My mother was always a fighter. They think she fought back and her assailant shot her and ran." He smiled bitterly. "Assailant," he said. "It sounds so much more benign than 'stone-cold killer,' doesn't it?"

There was nothing for me to say to that and nothing for Rita to say. Nothing any cop was ever going to say to make things right for a moment when the kid's life had gone this wrong, never to be the same ever again after the loss of his mother this way, no matter who his father was. It was like he took a bullet, too, that day. He just survived.

We all sat there in awkward silence until I finally said to him, "So tell me why you think Vic Hale is your father."

And he did.

"It has come to my attention, Mr. Spenser, that a lot of my life story turned out to be a lie," he said.

For his entire life, Daniel said, he had been told that his father had died when he and Marisol were trying to cross the Usumacinta River, which forms the border between Guatemala and Mexico, in a sudden storm that had hit the Lacandon Jungle and swept him away along with a few others in their group.

"She even showed me the pictures of him she had been able to preserve," Daniel said.

Marisol told Daniel she was pregnant with him by the time of the crossing, and because Daniel was born in America, that made him an American citizen, a status it took his mother, he said, years to attain, not becoming a citizen herself until her son was in the eighth grade.

He said he had never pressed her on her timeline of the events that brought her into Texas as a young woman, just had trusted her version of things, about how she had found her way to Miami from Texas with another friend who had been part of the crossing that night on the river. How she had managed to support herself by taking housekeeping jobs for other immigrants in South Florida who had enough money to provide her room and board.

"Did you ask who she'd worked for?" I said.

"I did," he said. "She would just smile and shake her head and say that they were people who wanted to hold on to as much of their money as they could, which meant not paying taxes for people like her."

"You didn't press her for more details?" I said.

"I didn't think it mattered," he said. "She was my mother, and those days were not happy ones for her, even though she had finally made it to America. I had no reason to doubt any part of her story." He closed his eyes and shook his head. "I never even knew she'd lived in Boston after she got to America. And because my mother was unwed at the time of my birth, she just elected to leave the father's name blank on my birth certificate in Miami."

"One more lie baked into the bigger one about who Daniel's father really was," Rita said. "But it was just the two of them, there was no other family."

"She was my mother, and I believed her," Daniel said.

Marisol Lopez eventually started what became, he said, a moderately successful tutoring business. And began to build a real life for her and her son.

"We didn't live a lavish life," he said, "but a good one. And we never seemed to have to worry about money when I was growing up." He shrugged. "It wasn't until after she was murdered that I found out why. Maybe I should have asked sooner how we lived as well as we did on what she was making as a tutor. But I read somewhere that when you're growing up, however you're growing up seems normal. Whether you're rich or poor."

I said, "You said there was no other family back in Guatemala?"

"Her parents were killed in the earthquake of 1976 in Los Amates," he said. "She was at her grandmother's house when theirs was destroyed. Her grandmother raised her until she left for America. She passed away when I was ten."

It was when he was packing up Marisol's things after her death that he found a box in one of their closets in which he discovered years of bank statements that showed a separate savings account at the Truist bank in Miami Gardens, even though his mother had done all of her other banking at Wells Fargo. Ten thousand dollars deposited every month electronically from the Shawmut Bank in Boston, the first deposit having been made a couple months after Daniel was born. Nearly $2.5 million in total, all-in.

"Single mothers can create their own reality," Rita said. "I should know. I had one of those myself."

"I did some checking at Truist, saying I just needed to clear up my mother's finances now that she was gone," Daniel continued. "One of the women at the bank was quite nice to me, and did some checking, and said that the money had come from an LLC in Boston with the name 'Tommy's Boy Inc.,' which was the first time Boston came into play."

I looked at Rita.

"Vic Hale's father was named Tommy," I said.

She said, "How do you know that?"

"Because he was a friend of mine," I said.

"So the name fits?" Daniel asked me.

"It does," I said. "Not that it proves anything."

"But one more piece that seems to fit the puzzle," Rita said.

"There are others," Daniel Lopez said.

He turned to look at Rita, then back to me.

"It was right after I found the other savings account that I found the letter," he said.

"From Vic Hale?" I said.

"It would be easy enough to check that it came from him with a little handwriting analysis," he said. "Written in script. Signed 'V' at the end."

The writer of the letter said that he hoped that someday Marisol could forgive him but hoped, even after all this time, that she understood how devastating it would have been to his show and to his career if their secret had come out, and that he had honored what they'd shared by taking care of her, and Daniel.

"The letter was dated at the time of my graduation from the U," he said. "He said he wanted to write to her just this one time to tell her that he wished things could have been different. He even had the nerve to put 'love' at the end before his initial."

"Maybe," I said, "that was all his idea of showing it, if he does turn out to be who you think he is."

"Evidently," he said.

"I know you think there's a lot here," I said. "But it's still not proof of life. The life being yours, in this case."

"One more reason why I'm here," he said.

"Do you have the letter with you?" I said.

"It's locked away in a safe place," Daniel said. "But I took a picture of it with my phone."

He took his phone out of the pocket of his jeans, tapped at it briefly, handed it to me. He was right that the handwriting was difficult to decipher. But it was as he described. The writer of the letter, V, never came out and said that he and Marisol Lopez had conceived a child together. It was almost as if it were written in code. If this had been written by Vic Hale, it was like he had adopted the defensive crouch *his* father, the boxer, once used in the ring.

I reached across my desk with his phone.

"You're going to need more than this, even if that is Vic Hale's handwriting."

"I told him you always find out whatever it is you need to find out, and then do whatever needs to be done after that," Rita said. "Daniel knows what you did for me last year."

"I'm not saying you're wrong about this," I said to Daniel. "It goes without saying that a terrible thing happened to your mother, and to you. Now you're having your life turned upside down all over again because of the contents of that box. But even Rita will tell you that what we're really talking about is a case built on circumstantial evidence. But there's a lot of things that already don't make sense here."

"Think how I feel," Daniel Lopez said. "But you didn't let me finish."

"So finish," I said.

"My mother kept a copy of the DNA test," he said.

FOUR

I happened to know that the small hospital at which the DNA test had been conducted, Stuart Medical in Milton, had closed down a long time ago, back when a wave of hospitals a lot like it were shuttering across Massachusetts.

The mother was Marisol Lopez, age twenty-seven at the time, six months pregnant. The father's name was listed as "Halgvist." No initial.

"But then I did some checking with public records," Daniel said.

I finished the thought for him.

"And you found out that Vic Hale's real family name was that," I said. "His old man thought it was better for him to be an Irish boxer. He told me one time he had it legally changed first chance he got. Told me that he thought Tommy Hale had a nice ring to it, at least before he made a career out of getting his bell rung, and repeatedly."

Daniel had taken a screenshot of the report. At the top of the first page was DNA PATERNITY, and a line right underneath that said that the father had submitted saliva taken from a cheek swab, called a buccal swab, and that the mother had taken an NIPT, which Daniel informed me was a blood test that analyzed fetal DNA in the mother's bloodstream.

Then came three columns with the headings MOTHER and CHILD and FATHER. Finally, there was a box at the very bottom that read this way:

"Mr. Halqvist is in fact the biological father of the male fetus. This conclusion is based on a full match for the father and the unborn child."

"Obviously this report would never stand up in court for five seconds," Rita said, "depending on how far down the line Daniel wants to take this. The hospital is long gone and the mother is now dead and to know conclusively that Vic Hale is Daniel's father, he'd have to submit to another DNA test."

"Which I suspect will occur right after pigs fly," I said.

"Well, he *is* kind of a pig," Rita said.

"Kind of?" I said.

"You need to talk to him," she said.

"Under what pretext, if you don't mind me asking?"

"You'll think of something," she said. She smiled. "Just as you have so many times in the past."

"And then pull his hair and bring you back a sample of it?" I said. "And by the way? Isn't taking DNA from someone without their consent against the law?"

"Oh, don't be a sissy," Rita said.

"Not sure you can say that anymore," I said.

"Just did, sissy boy," Rita said. She looked over at Daniel then and said, "Don't worry, this is all part of the process."

Then she uncrossed her legs and crossed them, as if she thought somehow that sweetened a deal to which I hadn't yet even agreed.

She said, "Just tell him you want to talk to him about his father and the old days or something along those lines. Bullshit, bullshit, bullshit, like you do."

"So you want me to lie to him," I said.

"As you have so many times in the past," she said.

"I'm not saying yes," I said. "And that's the truth."

"But you're also not saying no," she said.

"You're leading the witness," I said.

"Bet your ass," she said.

"Why did Daniel reach out to you?" I said. "I probably should have asked that already."

"One of his law professors at the U in Miami is an old friend of mine," she said.

"Define *friend,*" I said.

"Shut up," she said.

We again sat there in silence. Rita uncrossed and crossed her amazing legs one more time. Daniel Lopez checked his phone and then put it away.

"I have to ask you this because, well, I have to," I said finally. "Is this going to be nothing more than a shakedown in the end, Daniel?"

"This isn't about money," he said.

"There was an old football guy I used to know," I said. "And he said one time, talking about one of his players, that when they say it's not about the money, it's always about the money. And that was when there was a lot less of it around in sports than there is now."

He shook his head. "It's not, Mr. Spenser," he said. I'm telling you straight up, it's not. I just want him to acknowledge that I'm his son. And maybe, because of my own vision of the future for people like me, acknowledge that maybe people like my mother and me really aren't the devils he makes them out to be, even at a time like this in this country."

"Daniel basically just wants him to do the right thing, whether the acknowledgment comes in the public square or not," Rita said.

She smiled at me, eyes full of fun and mischief and perhaps even malice.

"Or else," she said.

"Or else what?" I asked.

"We go to Plan B," Rita said.

"And what might that be?" I asked.

"That would be me," she said.

FIVE

Susan and I were having dinner at Mistral, on Columbus, my midday sandwich from Billy's by now a distant, if fond, memory.

Mistral was one of our favorites, as I told Susan it should be, its website promising an experience of both taste and elegance.

"And here I was under the impression it was because of how much you like the whole roasted duck," she said.

"With exotic mushroom risotto," I said.

"Let's put the sex-versus-baseball discussion aside for the moment," she said. "Here's a good one from me: Do you think more about food or baseball?"

"That's easy," I said. "Sex."

She sighed.

"Now ask me a hard one," I said. "So to speak."

"Sigh," she said.

She was dressed in black tonight. I loved her in black. But then I liked her in clothes of any color. Or out of them. The dress was new, from Miss Mia on Newbury Street, and she was wearing the new strand of pearls I'd given her for her birthday. When I told her how wonderful they looked, she said I was spoiling her. I said I saw the pearls in particular and the spoiling in general as an investment in my future.

"He that leaveth nothing to chance will do few things ill," I said, and then quickly added, "That's George Savile. English statesman and writer. I knew you secretly wanted to know."

"Sigh," she said again.

"In case anybody ever asks you about George," I said, "he was raised to peerage in 1668."

"That fact will probably kill at parties," she said.

She ordered a Kir royal. Not all restaurants, even the tasteful and elegant ones, carried crème de cassis. Mistral did. I ordered a dirty martini, having already picked out the cabernet I wanted for when the duck was served.

I then told her about my meeting with Rita and Daniel Lopez.

"How is the red-haired hellcat?" Susan asked.

"I thought you two were pals now?"

"Still a work in progress," she said. "Rita continues to remind me of an old Bette Midler line when she was still doing concerts. There was a point in the act when she'd tell the audience that she called them her backup girls because she was always saying, '*Back up*, girls.'"

"She's just trying to do right by this kid," I said.

"I'm fine with that," Susan said, "as long as she stays on her own side of your desk."

Our drinks were served. I tried not to reach for the martini before the waiter had set it down. Then drank, quite happily.

"So are you going to try to do right by the young man, and help him out?" Susan said. "Or is that a rhetorical question?"

"Even though he's the one who wants to do this right," I said, "there's probably no way for him to get to Vic Hale. But I probably can."

Susan smiled then, with enough ice in it to fill a highball glass.

"Don't go see him without having your shots first," she said.

"All I want to do is talk to him," I said.

I took another healthy swallow of the martini. Once the glass was back on the table, I looked sadly at how close the olives already were to the bottom of the glass. I resisted the urge to pluck one and lick the vodka off it now.

"Why are you even thinking about getting involved?" she said. "You just met Daniel Lopez."

She had her elbows on the table and leaned forward now, if only slightly. Her focus in moments like these, as if I were one of her patients, was so intense I was occasionally surprised I didn't go over backward in my chair.

"Vic's father was my friend," I said. "I liked him and he liked me, even though he was getting up there, and I mean way up there, when I met him and I was young and stupid."

"I can't imagine you were ever stupid, even when you were young," she said.

"You're just saying that because I'm picking up the check," I said.

"Well," Susan said, winking at me, "I can't say it isn't a contributing factor."

"Tommy Hale had hung around way too long as a clubfighter," I said, "and knew it was too late to do anything about his brains being scrambled. He didn't want the same thing to happen to me." I drank the last of my martini. "He passed away several years ago."

"Do I even need to ask how?" Susan said.

"Parkinson's first, like Ali," I said. "Then dementia. The real retirement home for old boxers."

"But not for you," I said.

She reached across the table and covered my hand with hers.

"So far, so good," I said.

I started with escargots tonight, Susan with tuna tartare. The entrées arrived not long after we finished with our appetizers, the service at Mistral was that good. We ate in silence for a few minutes until I said, "There's one other thing I didn't mention about Tommy Hale, when I first met him."

Maybe it was the tone of my voice. But Susan put her fork down and waited.

"He saved my life one time," I said.

It had been in an alley outside a bar called Street Lights in South Boston that used to have the nickname "Street Fights." I might not have been young and stupid on the night in question, but I was definitely young and drunk. There were a couple boxers in Street Lights even drunker than I was, and one of them accused Tommy Hale of having taken a dive in one of the last fights of what was already a forgettable career. Tommy laughed it off, because at that point in his career he didn't care one way or another what people thought, he was just going from one tiny purse to another.

I wouldn't let it go, however, and one thing led to another, as they so often did in dumb saloon moments like this, and I told one of the guys drunker than me that we needed to take the whole thing outside.

Now, it wasn't just the whiskey in me, it was adrenaline, and a high singing sound in my ears, and steam coming out of them and out of me.

Out we went.

What I didn't see was the other boxer, more overserved than all of us, come up from behind me with a knife once I had thrown a left hook and put his buddy on the ground.

"Do you think the man with the knife was going to use it on you?" Susan asked.

Her eyes were big and dark and lovely. I wasn't sure why I had never told her this story. But then I'd never told it very much to anyone.

"I'll never know," I said. "Because the guy with the knife never saw Tommy Hale come up from behind *him*. Tommy almost politely tapped the guy on the shoulder and turned him around like the knife wasn't even in the guy's hand and threw a much better left hook than I'd just thrown. It not only broke the knife guy's nose, I was surprised it didn't break his head. And that, as they say, was that."

I told Susan that Tommy and I went back inside as if nothing much had happened in the alley. But I told Tommy Hale that night that I owed him.

"He just hugged me," I told Susan. "And told me that maybe someday I could look out for some kid, maybe even his kid, the way he'd just looked out for me."

"The kid who grew up to be Vic Hale," Susan said.

I grinned.

"That awful, awful man," I said, "to quote this hot woman I'm sleeping with."

She sighed again, with even more vigor than before.

"Some people cannot be rehabilitated," she said.

"I have to at least try," I said.

"I know," Susan said. "Oh, don't I know."

SIX

The conversation about Vic Hale didn't end with dinner. Susan's choice, in this case, not mine. I then did what I so often had done in the past with the girl of my dreams, in conversations even more nuanced than this one:

I went along to get along.

Mostly because that policy was still working for me.

We paused the conversation, once we'd both walked Pearl the Wonder Dog in the Public Garden, only for lovemaking back in my apartment, an event that I felt once more raised the bar for both of us, and not just because of the noise level.

I pointed that out to Susan once the festivities had concluded. She was on her back next to me, under the covers, dark hair splayed in all directions on the pillow, a sheen of sweat just barely visible on her forehead, eyes closed. Smiling contentedly.

"I wasn't *that* loud," she said.

"I believe you scared the dog," I said.

"If I did," she said, "I was just trying to encourage you. Somewhat like an in-game pep talk."

"I don't need encouragement," I said. "Though I am considering a defibrillator at the moment."

She sat up then, but covered herself with the sheet. One of the things I loved about Susan Silverman, one of the countless things I loved about her, was how quickly she could make the transition from immodesty, in the extreme, back to modesty.

"Now, as I was saying," she said.

"Uh-oh," I said.

"Hush and listen," she said.

I did.

"I'm not trying to tell you what to do," she said.

"Never," I said.

She punched my arm.

"But even though I know you're telling yourself you're just trying to do the right thing by this young man," she said, "I think you should be very cautious before voluntarily walking through a portal and into Vic Hale's world."

"In college football they now call it the transfer portal," I said.

"Good to know," she said.

"And by the way? You make it sound as if I'm walking through a gate to hell," I said.

"You said it, big boy. Not me."

"I've walked into more dangerous situations," I said. "Voluntarily and involuntarily, and lived to tell about it, at least so far."

"His loathsome ideas are what are dangerous this time," Susan said. "Ideas that make reasonable people feel as if they're shedding IQ points just listening to him."

"I *don't* listen to him," I said. "Until today, I really didn't think all that much about him. And by the way? Nobody is forcing anybody to listen to his podcast."

"But far too many people do," Susan said. "In almost frightening numbers. Worse than that, they believe him."

I wanted to change the subject. But when Susan was dug in this way, it was somewhat like trying to turn a battleship around.

I still felt as if I did have to try, before this turned into an all-nighter.

"This may sound crazy," I said, "but even postcoital talk like this is beginning to make me hot for you all over again."

"So does opening a window," she said. "And I'm being serious."

I turned so she could see me smiling at her and said, "Oh, don't I know."

"I've got a bad feeling about this," she said.

We could hear Pearl whimpering softly from the other side of the closed bedroom door.

"I'm just going to talk to the guy," I said.

"That's the way it always starts for you," Susan said, "and before you know it, there's a bad moon on the rise."

"I never made you for a John Fogerty fan," I said.

"There was a time when my younger self had a huge crush on him," she said.

"Look at me," I began to sing, *"I can be centerfield."*

"Now you're the one trying to scare the dog," Susan said.

"Many people think I have a very nice singing voice," I said.

"Name two," Susan said.

Then she turned so she was facing me and said, "Don't do this."

"I have to, Suze," I said. "Not just because Rita asked me, but also because it may turn out to be the only chance I ever get to pay back Tommy Hale, depending on how this thing plays out."

"I can't make you reconsider?" she said.

"There's one way you could try," I said. "If you're game, I mean."

She got up then and walked across the room, more than somewhat immodestly, giving an exaggerated swing to her hips, opened the door, and we both saw Pearl come bounding in and jump on her end of the bed before Susan got back in next to me.

"I'll take that as a no," I said.

SEVEN

Even though I explained my history with Vic Hale's father to Todd Jakes, who was not only Hale's producer but his gatekeeper as well, I still had to go through Jakes if I wanted to get to Hale.

I had done extensive reading about both him and Vic Hale before even making the call, and learned that Jakes was often referred to by the media as "Vic Hale's brain."

It was Jakes who had first seen the potential for Hale to be something more than just another host at a local FM talk station, when talk stations like that were still the rage, back before podcasts swallowed most of them up the way sharks swallow up bluefish. In the rare interviews that Hale himself did, he gave Jakes more than his due for spotting the potential in him, helping to shape not just the show's content but its sound, and being what Hale called "foxhole loyal."

In addition, Vic Hale often said, "Todd's the nice one."

Their station in those days was WTKK, and before long the show was growing in popularity the way Vic Hale was. And growing. Going off much of what I had read online—something I knew was as potentially more harmful than greenhouse gases—it had now become abundantly clear that everyone on Hale's team, him and his lawyer and Jakes, were about to become even richer than they already were once the new deal with his parent company was concluded.

It was, I thought, just another indication that far too many people had far too much time on their hands to be as outraged as they were. Which might have been the biggest outrage of all if I thought about it, which I frankly tried not to, at least not too often.

I had also learned in my research that *All Hale*, the name of the podcast, was broadcast from Hale's home in Newton, which sounded more like some kind of fortress. But the offices for All Hale Productions, I had likewise discovered through intrepid online detecting, were located on Guest Street in Brighton, half a block from WGBH, Boston's legendary public broadcasting television station, and around the corner from the building that housed the radio station, WEEI, where the majority of the outrage was limited to the local sports teams.

So the next morning, I found myself seated in the office of Todd Jakes, dressed as if I were about to sit down for a job interview. I wore a Brooks Brothers blazer, a Brooks Brothers button-down shirt with the traditional roll to the collar, charcoal-gray pants, and my new Ralph Lauren driver loafers, black with brown tassels. Susan called it my sincerity outfit. I would remind her when she did that that nobody faked sincerity better than I.

She and Pearl had still been at the apartment before I left for Brighton, Susan having made one last-ditch attempt to get me to call the whole thing off.

"Unfortunately, at this point," I said, "we'd need to call the calling-off off."

"Cole Porter, am I right?" she said.

"Indeed."

"I was afraid of that," she said. "At least you knew who John Fogerty was."

"Take the win," I told her.

Jakes was fifty years old, I knew, but looked younger than that, by a lot. Gray hair worn long, sweater with the sleeves rolled up, better to show off a watch that looked big enough and complicated enough to be worn by astronauts, along with oversized and old-school black glasses that seemed to have once again caught the fashion curve.

"Thanks for seeing me on such short notice," I said.

He grinned and gently pushed the glasses back up his nose. "Before we start," he said, "gotta ask you something, because I always find that useful: How political are you?"

"Not," I said.

"Not at all?" he said.

"Not so you'd notice."

"Does that mean you don't listen to the show?"

I grinned back at him. "Not if I can help it."

"But you know where Vic is coming from?"

"That I can't help," I said. "By now even people in outer space know where he's coming from, which sounds to me like somewhere around 1862, around the time things began to turn to shit for the Confederacy."

Jakes laughed. It sounded sincere, but then he could have been faking it. He was a media guy, after all.

"Whatever the boss is doing, it's working for him, wouldn't you say?" Jakes said.

"Fuckin' ay," I said.

He laughed again.

"Just so you know," he said, "I'm not him. I'm actually one of the good guys."

"I saw somewhere where they call you his brain," I said.

He held up his hands. "You know who never says that? *Me.* And you know why? Because I like this job."

"I'll bet," I said.

"Who was it that said all the world's a stage?" Jakes asked.

"It was either Bill Shakespeare or Bill O'Reilly," I said.

"I keep my own politics to myself," he said, "even though Vic knows they don't always align with his."

"Do his ever bother you?" I said.

"Not at these prices," he said.

"I heard you guys are about to shoot the moon with this new deal," I said.

"No comment," Jakes said, "other than perhaps this: God is good."

He had offered me coffee. But I'd had plenty already while reading up on Hale and him and their history, and didn't want to run back to my office quick as a jackrabbit once we had concluded our business.

Jakes was sipping something or other from the straw stuck into one of those Yeti tumblers. Susan had replaced plastic water bottles with so many of them, there was a cupboard at her house I referred to as a Yeti farm.

"So what do you want to talk to Vic about?" he said. "All you said is that it was a personal matter."

"It is," I said.

I smiled. He smiled. We just sat there smiling at each other.

"Care to share?" he said.

"Not so much," I said.

He nodded.

"When I told him it was you who'd called, he told me that we should talk, you and me, because of the history he says you had with his father," Jakes said. "But I really do need to know what you want to talk to him about."

"You mean other than the basics?" I said. "The border. Deportations. White replacement theory. If the country really was better off when everybody liked Ike."

"Wait," Jakes said. "I thought you said you didn't listen to the show."

"I was just being ironic," I said, "as risky as I know that can be."

"No shit," Todd Jakes said. He took another sip of whatever it was he had in the mug. "Nobody is better living proof of that than me. If you don't mind me asking, who do you listen to?" Jakes asked.

"Dave O'Brien," I said.

"Huh?"

"Dave's the voice of the Red Sox on television," I said. "I used to listen to Joe Castiglione on radio, but he retired."

"More irony?" Jakes said.

"Not when I'm talking about the Red Sox, there isn't," I said.

He leaned forward and put his elbows on his desk and tented his fingers underneath his chin.

"We gotta get past this," he said.

"Get past what?"

"You, uh, being less than forthcoming about why you want to see Vic," he said. "Because if we can't get past that, you can't get past me." He tapped his fingers together. "I just have to get some sense of where we're going with this."

"*We* aren't going anywhere, not to sound obstreperous," I said.

"Obstreperous," he said. Grinned again. "I'd be worried about you using big words like that in Vic's presence, even though it's starting to look as if you're not going to end up in his presence."

"Listen," I said. "You actually do seem to be a good guy. But all you need to know is this: Vic would rather hear from me what I have to say. Because if he hears it somewhere else, you're going to be unironically in the shit with him."

"Anything you have to say to him you can say to me," Jakes said.

"Somehow I doubt that," I said.

He sat back in his chair, either surprised or amused or both. Maybe he wasn't used to hearing that word from anyone other than the host of the show.

"For the last time," he said, "you have to go through me to get to him."

"I *am* going through you," I said, "which is why I dressed up like this. But if that fails, then I will go around you, and I will get a face-to-face with him, even though you probably think that couldn't happen on a bet."

"He's Vic Hale, Mr. Spenser," Jakes said, as if that explained everything except the theory of relativity.

"And I'm me," I said. "And would now like you to call him and tell him I want to talk about Marisol Lopez."

The air in the office changed in that moment, not the kind of electrical charge you feel in the air before a summer storm. But something, not just in the air, but in his eyes.

"You seem to know the name," I said.

"I do," he said.

He stood then, reaching for the phone on his desk before he did.

"Give me a minute," he said, and walked out of his own office with me still sitting in it.

I was going to tell him to take all the time he needed, but being a trained detective, I had already intuited that before I heard the door close.

EIGHT

It took until the next morning for Jakes to set up the meet with Vic Hale.

I had offered to go to Hale's home in Newton, a place that really did appear to have everything except a moat from the pictures I saw of it online. It actually resembled another castle-like home in Newton, known as the Winslow-Haskell, built by one of the rich guys who had owned the *Boston Herald* in the late nineteenth century, which meant in far better times for the newspaper business than these.

But according to Jakes, Hale wanted to meet in a more public setting, just the two of us.

"Well, it will be the two of you and his security," Jakes said.

I told him I completely understood.

"Fortunately," I said, "my own security detail is me."

The place Hale selected, or Jakes selected for him, was the Fenway Victory Gardens, one of my favorite natural wonders in all of Boston, ranking just slightly below the Public Garden and Boston Common, but still on the medal stand.

It was seven and a half acres of truly gorgeous land at the north end of the Back Bay Fens, designed in the late 1800s by Frederick

Law Olmsted, part of what was known as the city's Emerald Necklace, and had become particularly famous during World War II, when people who lived in the neighborhood grew vegetables there because of food shortages caused by the war.

I happened to know that Olmsted and his partner Calvert Vaux had also designed Central Park in New York City, something I didn't hold against them, having to admit that as much as I loved our parks, theirs was bigger, and better.

These were things I pondered while I waited for Tommy Hale's son and whatever kind of bruiser entourage he might be bringing with him.

Susan said that my endless curiosity about even trivia that did not include baseball was often heightened, especially in the morning, when the caffeine started to wear off and my mind began to wander.

Hale was late and I had long since finished the large Dunkin' with which I had arrived at the designated spot near the entrance to the Fens. And when Hale finally did arrive himself, it turned out he hadn't come with an entourage, just two rather broad bruisers bookending him as they all walked toward me on the path.

One bodyguard was Black, the other white. The white guy was bald with almost no neck. The Black guy was taller, and even broader, and wearing a green Red Sox hat, something I had always considered mildly sacrilegious. Both of them looked strong enough to bench-press the Kennedy Library if asked.

Tommy Hale, even passing for Irish, had been blond and blue-eyed. Vic Hale, I knew from pictures, had the old man's blue eyes, but with darker hair and complexion. He currently had the hair covered underneath the hood of an Everlast sweatshirt that looked almost ancient enough to have belonged to his father. He was wearing baggy blue jeans that bunched up over white sneakers that looked as if they had just come out of the box, and walked with a noticeable limp that I knew from my research was the result of having had both hips replaced. It made his gait resemble that of someone walking out of a bar after last call. All in all, he looked nothing like someone routinely described as one of the baddest media personalities on the planet, punching his way up into Rogan's weight class, a bear that even popular politicians on the other side of the issues were wary about poking.

When I got up off the bench on which I'd been sitting, one for which Jakes had nearly used latitude and longitude when he'd described its location, Hale grinned and stuck out a big hand.

"You must be Spenser," Hale said.

"There is no substitute," I said. "Somewhat like a Porsche."

"Hey, I got two," Hale said. "A red one and a black one."

"Only two?" I said.

"My old man said you were a wiseass," he said.

"Look who's talking," I said.

He turned to the bald white guy then, who upon closer inspection did have some neck showing, if not much, covered with tattoos.

"Pat him down, Bobby," Hale said.

"Seriously?" I said.

"Not my first rodeo, dude," Hale said, "whether you were pals with my old man or not."

"Wow," I said. "And it might be a small point, but I'm not your dude."

"Huh?" Hale said.

"But it is good to know people still say that about rodeos with a straight face," I said.

"Whatever," Vic Hale said.

Bobby had crouched down in front of me and was working his way up my own jeans, having arrived at my thighs.

"No inappropriate touching," I said to the gleaming top of his head.

Bobby responded with a grunt. When he finished he said, "He's good, Vic."

"Wait till you all get to know me better," I said.

Vic Hale told his guys they could give us some room. He and I sat down on the bench. If the people passing us, walking dogs or speed-walking or jogging or pushing strollers, recognized him now that he'd pulled the hood back, they were managing not to cause a riot. But then it was still fairly early.

"I like this place," Hale said. "You can't say *Victory* without Vic, right?"

I told him I'd never thought of it exactly that way.

"My father really used to say how much he liked you when he'd see your name in the paper for some case you worked on," he said. "He got pretty upset that time when they wrote in *The Globe* that some guy had shot you dead and dumped you in the Charles until you did that Lazarus shit." He shrugged. "That was before the old man couldn't find his way to the bathroom or remember what he wanted to do once he got there."

"Reports of my death," I said.

"And so on and so forth," Hale said.

I said, "He came out of the time, your father did, when taking a punch was a badge of honor, and a way of showing everybody how tough you were."

"Too tough, in his case," Vic Hale said, "for too goddamn long, until he didn't even know his own son at the end." Hale turned to me suddenly. "Even though there are plenty of people who'd probably see that as a blessing now."

"You said it," I said.

"Beat you to the punch," he said. I saw a grin work its way across his face. "The old man took them. Now I throw them."

"Roundhouses, apparently," I said.

"Hell, yeah," he said. "Or as I say on my show, *Hale, yeah.*"

"Clever," I said.

"You bullshitting me, Spenser?"

Now I grinned. "Hale, yeah," I said.

He nodded. "Yup," he said. "Clever bastard, just like the old man said."

We momentarily sat in silence. I looked up the path at the two bodyguards, trying to appear as unobtrusive as possible, even looking like bouncers hired to guard all the flowers around them.

Finally Hale said, "You want to stop feeling each other out like it's the first round of a fight?"

"I thought you'd never ask," I said.

"What's this about Marisol?" he said.

"Thought you'd never ask," I said again.

NINE

Before I began to tell him Daniel Lopez's story, Hale told me that he was aware of Marisol's death. Jakes had told him about it almost as soon as it happened, having seen a story in the online edition of the *Miami Herald*.

"He's always looking for crimes involving migrants, though we're mostly only interested in ones they've committed, of course," Hale said. "But then he kept reading and found out that this time it was Marisol, and she was the victim. Isn't that the balls?"

"The balls," I said.

"She was my housekeeper back in the day," I said.

I nodded.

"So you had a migrant working for you."

"That a question?"

"More an observation."

"You trying to be funny again?"

"You decide," I said.

"She didn't like *migrant*, by the way," he said. "She preferred *immigrant*." He put his hands out. "Tomato, to-mah-to."

I said, "You didn't have any qualms about hiring an illegal?"

"She was a good worker," he said, "and hot as a firecracker."

He stared past his bodyguards and out across the gardens. There were more people walking the path now. It was a beautiful morning here. But then this was always a beautiful place, despite the subject matter.

"Anyway," Hale said, "she was living in the house. I was single." He gave a little rap on the bench with his knuckle. "And what can I say, one thing led to another, bada boom bada bing."

"As it so often does with these things," I said.

"That a judgment?"

"Call it another observation."

"You're aware that I'm only here because my old man was your friend," he said. "And not here to take your shit indefinitely."

"So there's two things we have in common, Vic," I said. "Your old man is one. Not taking a lot of shit is another."

Now he nodded.

"You told Jakes you wanted to talk about Marisol," Hale said. "So talk."

I told him then what I knew about Daniel Lopez. I told him about his mother's second savings account, and the checks going into it, year after year, starting right after Daniel was born, more than two million dollars in the end. I told him that Daniel had traced the deposits to back here, and to an LLC called Tommy's Boy. I told him about the DNA test submitted in the name of a father named Halqvist.

Finally I showed him the copy of the letter that Marisol had kept, signed with a great, big *V.*

He read the letter, frowning, then gave me back my phone, but said nothing.

"I have this theory about coincidence, Vic, one often stated," I said.

"What's that?"

"That God wouldn't leave nearly that much to chance," I said.

He nodded. "I hear you," he said. "But I've never believed her kid was mine."

"Then please explain her having a DNA result that says he is?" I said. "One with your family name on it, I might add. It says the father submitted a saliva sample back in the day."

"I didn't submit it," he said. "She did, even if she didn't tell me about it until afterward."

"How did she get it?"

"I snore like a champion," he said. "She used to make fun of me for not only sleeping the sleep of the dead, but with my mouth wide open. What can I tell you? She managed to swab me without waking me up."

"So she knew how to get a sample out of you and got it tested and she got tested and told you that, lo and behold, you were the father after all," I said. "By the way? Why didn't she save a lot of trouble and just ask you to give a swab or blood voluntarily once she knew she was pregnant?"

"Because I wasn't the father and told her there was no fucking point!" Hale snapped. "The math and the timing just never fucking worked, whatever her piece of paper said after she got tested, and not just because I'd been touring the show for three or four months right before that. I'd stopped fuck— I'd stopped with the sex part even before that, finally having woke up to it being a zero-sum game, at least for me. And you know what they say, even about somebody as hot as she was: Somewhere somebody's tired of her."

"Is that what they say?" I said.

"What, you're gonna start that woke shit?"

I said, "It would be easy enough to settle this once and for all if you and Daniel voluntarily submitted DNA samples now."

"And please explain how that would help me, now that I'm a hell of a lot more famous, and a hell of a lot richer, than I was twenty years ago?" he said.

"You'd know with certainty whether or not he is your biological son," I said.

"How many times do I have to tell you I never believed that he was, or is?" he said. "And if that shit could be screwed around with once, which I believe it was, somebody could do it again, right? Happens all the time in the movies. What do they say about statistics? You torture them long enough, they'll tell you anything you want them to."

It was like arguing with someone asserting that the earth was flat.

I took a deep breath and went back at him one more time.

"So you sent that kind of money, over more than two decades, to a woman who had not only been your housekeeper, but one with whom you now admit you'd had a sexual relationship," I said. "All to help support a kid who you maintain isn't your own, one whose mother is of a group—or was—that you consider to be as bad for this country as terrorists, now more than ever."

I gave the bench a couple raps with my own knuckle.

"Is that what you're trying to tell me?" I added.

He was looking out at the flowers again. But I was certain that Hale was not struck by the expanse of beauty stretched out all around him, not at the moment, anyway. Even though he didn't seem the existential type, perhaps Vic Hale was asking himself the question of why he was here.

"Not what I'm trying to tell you," he said. "What I *am* telling you."

"Then maybe you can finally make me understand why you sent Marisol Lopez all that money," I said.

"Because my old man, who you've probably already figured out was much more of a stand-up guy than I am, told me it was the stand-up thing to do," he said, "at least when he still had all his marbles."

I saw him look over at his man Bobby now, who pointed to his watch. Hale shook his head.

"Vic, you have to know what a ridiculous version of things this is," I said.

"It's not a version," he said. "It's the way it was, and fuck you whether you think it's ridiculous or not."

"All that money, all those years, to help support a son who you keep saying isn't your son," I said. "How does that make sense?"

"Hey," he said, turning back to me, grinning and raising his eyebrows. "There's a lot of people out there who think I make no sense at all five days a week, but you may have heard I still get paid pretty fucking well to do it. Like, money to die for."

"When did you find out she was pregnant?" I asked.

"She was just starting to show," he said. "At first, I figured she was just putting on a few. But then she told me, maybe four or five months in. And then, like I told you, I did the math."

"Because you'd been on tour and because you say you'd previously stopped sharing a bed with her before that."

I just wanted him to know I was trying to keep up.

"I just assumed there was another guy," he said. "But when I asked her about that, she swore she'd only been with me, and now she had the test saying I was the father, even though at the time I thought she knew as much about DNA tests as citizenship tests."

He rubbed his forehead with stubby fingers as if he felt a headache coming on. I knew the feeling, having spent even this short time in his presence. I could only imagine what it would be like to listen to his show every day.

"Did you ever raise the subject of an abortion?"

"That was never going to happen, the abortion part, she was more Catholic than the Pope, even though we'd been doing what we'd been doing in my bed like cats in a sack," he said. "And whether there was a chance it was my kid or not was frankly irrelevant at that point. What was relevant was the optics for me if any of this shit got out, something I should've considered from the start if I wasn't thinking with my dick. Bottom line? It was bad for business any way you sliced it. So I told her she had to go away and I'd take care of her."

"Where was the child born?" I said.

"Miami," he said.

"And you were already sending the checks?"

He nodded. "Listen, I could've just had her deported," he said, "if I thought she was setting me up for some kind of shakedown. But when I told the old man, he said that it was clear that I had feelings for her and should take care of her, whether the kid was mine or not, it was the best way of handling the situation. So I had my lawyer draw up an NDA." He snorted out a laugh. "NDA. DNA. Same letters. Funny, right? She'd relocate, I'd make sure her and her kid were taken care of, and pretty goddamn well. In a lot of ways, it was win-win."

"Problem solved!" I said brightly.

"Talk shit all you want," Hale said. "Like I said, it was business. I didn't have the heart to call ICE on her. But I had a brand to protect, and what I paid her, in the long run, was pennies on the dollar if you look at the big picture."

He put out big hands that looked as big as his father's had looked when he took the gloves off.

"She made a good deal for herself in the end, and so did I," he said. "But part of the deal was that she didn't contact me once she moved to Miami. Goodbye, farewell, amen."

"Did you write her that letter?" I said.

He said, "Yeah, I got into the Irish whiskey one night and wrote the letter. Old school. And decided to send it even after I sobered up."

He stood, grimacing slightly as he did, as if deadlifting himself.

"And now," he said, "we're done here, you and me."

"Almost," I said.

"You don't give up, do you?" he said.

"Not even as a last resort," I said.

He looked down at me, waiting.

"You need to know this kid isn't going to go away as easily as his mother did."

"He and his mother already got fucking paid," Hale snapped. "And since you seem to be pretty good at math, you know how much."

"He doesn't want money from you."

Hale said, "So what the hell does he want?"

"He wants you to acknowledge him as your son, because he believes he is."

He sighed as if all the air had come out of his body at once, to the point that I expected him to start flattening out like a pool float.

"He's. Not. My. Son."

"But there is a possibility, no matter how slight, that he could be," I said. "Even you have to admit that."

"You haven't been listening to me," he said. "At this point, I don't give a shit, one way or another. I upheld my end of the bargain and now he has to hold up his mother's and get the fuck out of here."

"What if he's unwilling to do that," I said, "and decides to go public?"

"In that case, I will bury his ass," Vic Hale said.

"Even though he's Marisol's son," I said.

"Hale, yeah," he said. Then he said, "I got a question: What's in this for *you*?"

I said, "I'm starting to ask myself the same question."

He began to walk away then.

"Vic," I called after him, and saw him turn around.

"You do know how much talking in circles you just did, right?"

Hale was about to pull the hood back down over his face. But stopped, so I could see him smiling at me.

"Hey," he said. "It's a living." And turned and kept walking.

TEN

When I called Rita to give her an update, I was told by her top associate, Benjamin Walsh, that she was in out-of-office meetings with clients all morning, presumably doing extremely billable Rita-type things.

So I told Walsh to tell her that I myself would be in meetings with Hawk for the next couple hours, and that when I was finished and she was back I could describe my meet-and-greet with Vic Hale in full.

I had walked to the Fens from my apartment and now walked back, before getting into my car and driving to the Harbor Health Club.

Hawk was finishing his weight-room work when I arrived, just part of a regimen for him that I always felt would make Navy SEALs look for another line of work. He asked if I wanted him to spot me in there, but I told him I was on my way to what was left of the boxing club that had once been Harbor Health's reason for being before going all Pilates and yoga and Peloton bikes and barre classes and juice bars.

"Make sure you don't pull nothing with all that speed-and-power shit," Hawk said. "Not that you're much for the speed part these days."

I gave him the finger.

"I can still lick any man in the house," I said.

"Not my house," Hawk said.

"You know who said that, right?" I said.

Hawk sighed. It was a sound I frequently heard from him, not exactly mournful, more one of resignation at this point. I think Susan had learned it from him. Or vice versa.

"Another damn quiz," he said. "But I got the answer, on account of all the other times you asked the question. Was John L. Sullivan. Only difference is that unlike you, he really could lick any man in the house, least until Gentleman Jim Corbett come along."

This time I gave him a thumbs-up and headed for the ring room. The sequence that had evolved over time was one of the most rigorous boxing drills I knew about. I did start out with speed work, one hard minute of it, lefts and rights, feet planted, weight distributed evenly. Then a minute of rest before two minutes of hooks. Another minute of rest after that. Then full range-of-motion hooks, low to high, really turning my body to get into them, the way I had with the hook to the head I'd thrown that night in the alley before Tommy Hale saved my ass, and probably my life.

Another minute of rest then, as if I were between rounds. Then three minutes of combinations, low to high and high to low again, the punches coming more quickly now, hooks followed by left jabs and straight right hands, telling myself throughout not to worry about power here as much as maintaining balance, knowing that balance was one of the things that went first when you got older. One of many.

The last one was a step-back drill, a flurry of rights and lefts, no real pattern to them, my hands doing the thinking for me as I threw the punches. I stepped away from the bag then, but only briefly, before moving right back up on it, blinking sweat out of my eyes, feeling all of the power here come all the way from the feet up, feeling as much burn in my legs as I was feeling by now in my arms and shoulders and core, trying to ignore the chronic pain in my bad left knee, now only marginally worse than the other one.

I gave myself a five-minute rest and then went through all the drills again, the sweat pouring off me in waves by the time I finished for good, feeling as if I'd gone fifteen rounds, the way we'd gone fifteen when Hawk and I were young.

Hawk had been on one of the bikes in the Peloton room while he waited for me. When he came back, I was still out of breath, chest heaving. He was not out of breath, of course. But then I'd always felt Hawk could have run all four legs of the 4x100 relay by himself without breaking a sweat.

"How's the knees today, John L.?" he asked, tossing me a towel.

"Shot," I said. "Just not *shot* shot."

"You ever think about getting them replaced?" he said.

"Next question," I said.

He drank some water out of the liter bottle in his hands. "So how'd it go with the shitbag?" he said. He grinned. "Different kind of heavy bag, if you get my meaning."

I told him.

"You believe him?"

"I think some of what he told me was true," I said. "I just don't know which parts."

"Why don't you walk the fuck away from this while you still can?" he said. "'Fore you get in too deep, like you do."

"You sound like Susan," I said.

He smiled now, brilliantly. "Hale, yeah," he said.

"Aha!" I said. "So you do listen to Vic Hale."

"Only did yesterday on account of you going to see his ass, like a refresher course for me," Hawk said. "And come away feeling like I did on the other occasions when I listened to him, mostly by accident."

"Enlightened?" I said.

"Waterboarded," he said.

Henry Cimoli came walking into the room then, still looking as fit and as trim as he'd been in his own boxing days, still strutting like a rooster and looking full of piss and vinegar, though I told him every chance I got that he was older than both.

At which point he would generally tell me to piss off.

Now he said, "You ever consider how much money it's costing me keeping this space reserved so the two of you can cling to a dying sport?"

"Hawk and I still consider it to be the sweet science, Henry," I said.

"That so?" he said. "Name me the current heavyweight champ."

"That Russian," Hawk said. "One that beat Tyson Fury."

"Or was it the other Russian?" I said.

Henry was wearing old-school satin boxing pants, black with a white stripe down the sides, a tight Harbor Health T-shirt, black-and-red Air Jordans, maybe just to show he wasn't the one clinging to the past. He still had a lot of white hair, and the T-shirt showed off abs that looked hard enough to serve as body armor. His eyes were the color of a robin's egg. In his day Henry had always fought bigger than he was, and somehow, even with all the scarring around his eyes from the punches he took, he looked younger than he should have, and younger than I knew he was.

And still had all of his marbles.

"Hawk says you went to see Tommy Hale's kid," Henry said after motioning for us to make room for him between us on a bench he'd kept from the old Boston Arena. "You got business with him?"

"Indirectly," he said.

"The kid know that Tommy saved your ass that time?" Henry asked. "Even though he ain't no longer a kid."

"He does."

"Tommy tried to get the kid into the Golden Gloves up in Lowell when he was a teenager," Henry said. "I went up there to watch him, as a favor to Tommy. But I could tell after just one fight he didn't have the heart for it."

"He have any talent?" I said.

"He could hit okay," Henry said. "Not a bad left hand, the way I remember it. But he liked throwing punches a lot better than taking them."

Hawk snorted. "Shocker."

Henry ignored him. To me he said, "So Tommy's kid has some kind of problem?"

"In a manner of speaking."

I bumper-stickered Daniel Lopez's version of things and then Vic Hale's.

"You believe this guy Daniel?" Henry said.

"I do," I said. "Even knowing that he might have an angle that he didn't mention, and one of which I'm not aware. Or wasn't telling me everything."

"Yet," Hawk said.

"What are you going to do about it?" Henry asked.

"Henry," I said, "I'll tell you what I told Vic Hale: Beats me."

"You could always beat it out Vic Hale," Hawk said.

I said to Henry, "Whatever happened to Tommy's wife? Vic's mother?"

Henry shook his head no. "Best of my recollection she took off not long after the kid showed up. Far as I know, Tommy raised the boy himself. Don't know how he did it, frankly, around his boxing. But he did."

"You ever meet her?" I asked Henry.

"No," he said. "But Tommy and me weren't that kind of close, even after I stopped training him. The only thing we really had in common was the fights. The last time I ever remember asking him about the mother, he just said something like, 'She's no longer in the picture.' Come to think of it, I'm not sure I ever heard him mention her name."

Henry popped up then and said he needed to get going, there was a barre class he needed to supervise.

"'Supervise' another way of saying you going to check out ass?" Hawk said.

"Piss off," Henry said.

Hawk and I showered then and changed and went downstairs for smoothies in the juice bar that Henry had just expanded for the second time. Or maybe the third. We were at a table there when Rita called and, as she so often did, skipped the preliminaries after telling me she was back at her office.

"I hate the media sometimes," she said.

"Wait," I said. "Only sometimes?"

ELEVEN

Because I was already at Henry's place and because it was nearly lunchtime, I met Rita at the Boston Harbor Hotel at Rowes Wharf, and a restaurant there I liked a lot called the Sea Grille. But Susan told me one time that I liked any restaurant that didn't have a drive-thru window, and I wanted to know what she had against drive-thru windows.

When I arrived, Rita was halfway through a Bloody Mary as tall as the sailboats outside the Sea Grille's picture window, one loaded with olives and a celery stalk and what I knew from experience might very well have been a jalapeño pepper down at the very bottom of the glass, lurking.

"I'll have what she's having," I said to the bartender.

The dining area of the big, sunny room, the walls featuring a lot of nautical art, was starting to fill up a few minutes after twelve o'clock. Rita was at the far end of the bar from where you walked in, her leather-backed chair turned sideways, so diners had a view of the water if they looked one way, but a view of Rita if they chose to turn their heads.

When I leaned down and kissed her on the cheek before settling into the chair next to her, I thought a good-looking young guy at the opposite end of the bar from us looked like a puppy suddenly on the verge of dying of heartbreak, probably kicking himself for having waited too long to settle into the chair next to Rita himself. I thought about going down to ask if he needed a hug.

When the bartender put my Bloody in front of me, I raised my glass to Rita and said, *"Slainte."*

"Slainte this," she said gloomily.

"Well, despite that display of attitude, I'm still planning to enjoy my drink," I said. "Not to mention the company."

"Men are so selfish," she said.

I took a sip, put my own tall glass down, and immediately plucked an olive and ate it. No time like the present. I was saving the celery stalk. I'm not an animal. I would deal with the jalapeño later.

"You want to hear about my meeting with Vic Hale, or would you prefer to tell me your problems?" I said.

"Give me the highlights," she said, "if there were any."

"Okay," I said. "He freely admits that he and Marisol had a sexual relationship. Admits that he's been paying her all these years. Says his father's the one who talked him into taking care of her and the boy when she told him she was pregnant."

She started to interrupt. Or object. I held up a hand to stop her, even knowing that could be like trying to stop the ocean.

"Got her to sign an NDA before she left town, just to head off his public thinking that someone he was supposed to hate was his lover. And last but certainly not least, he says the DNA test is wrong or a fake or somehow both, and that he's not the father."

"Says him," Rita said.

"Actually, it's *says he*," I said.

Her eyes narrowed, but she managed to hold her fire.

"Did you by any chance suggest we could clear this up if he took a DNA test now?" Rita asked.

"I did," I said. "He declined."

"Let's face it, the reality is that as much as the kid thinks he's got on Vic, it's largely circumstantial," she said. "Or supposition. But we've gone over that."

"So we have," I said.

She gave a toss of all that red hair then. Rita had a lot of hair tosses, depending on her mood. Often a form of punctuation for her. This one seemed to be all about frustration, or exasperation, or a combination thereof.

She drank. I drank.

Finally I said, "You said something about hating the media earlier?"

"So I did."

"A problem with your *Globe* subscription?" I said. "I know the former editor, I could call him."

"You're not funny," she said.

"Am so," I said.

"Sooooo," she said, "our problem with the media, or potential problem if Daniel decides to go forward, is a very ambitious and extremely cute young reporter and podcaster from Miami named Ricardo Baez."

"Cute?" I said. "Relevance, Counselor?"

"None," she said. "The observation was more descriptive in nature."

"Is he the reporter Daniel says has been putting his name out there?" I said.

Rita nodded. "He works for an increasingly popular and well-trafficked website in South Florida called *Libertad*. It's owned by a rich expat Guatemalan named Mauricio Estrella, who's becoming more and more of a power broker for the entire Latino community down there." She drank. "Want to hear more about Mr. Estrella?"

"I do," I said.

"He started with one cable TV station, now has stations scattered all over Florida," Rita continued. "*Libertad* was originally a weekly paper, but Estrella didn't get rich by not seeing which way the media wind was blowing, and went online hard. He's now become the loudest voice down there for immigrant rights. Ricardo Baez is his star. But Baez sees Daniel as a future star, too, and has hitched his wagon to him, as we used to say in the old days."

"*Really* old days," I said.

"Shut it," she said.

"I can do that."

"Baez and Daniel have gotten pretty close," Rita continued. "The story Daniel referred to is actually a podcast series on Daniel's life, one that starts with his mother's journey across the water, them ending up in South Florida, Daniel's growing activism, the future of the movement."

She finished her Bloody Mary and waved at the bartender for another one. But I had no concerns about her getting drunk in the middle of the day. Rita had always been able to drink Navy Week under the table.

"Obviously everything changed when Marisol died," Rita said. "Baez was still just putting the project up on its feet, but then she died with answers about both their stories that only she could answer, because Daniel clearly could not."

Rita took in some air, let it out, as if even she could run out of breath occasionally. "Too much information?"

"In your case, I've never believed there's any such thing," I said.

"Screw you," she said, then smiled. "Theoretically speaking, of course."

I gently asked if we might be staying for lunch. She said no. Only then did I give in and take my first bite of my celery stalk. Man's gotta eat.

"So Baez started asking more questions on his own," she said. "Including in Boston. And asked enough that he became aware that Marisol had worked as Vic Hale's housekeeper not long after she got to Massachusetts. But you already know that."

"So I do," I said.

"So now we all know that Marisol was doing more than the sheets," Rita said. "Not to sound cynical."

"You?" I said. "Never."

"Screw you," she said again.

The young guy who'd been eyeballing Rita when I arrived stood up now at his end of the bar and laid some tip money near his glass. As he walked out, he took one last look at her over his shoulder. When he did, I gave him a broad wink.

"Anyway, and in conclusion," Rita said, "I met with Baez in my office right before I came over here. The guy is so ambitious, I thought he might spontaneously combust."

"And he knows his story has perhaps gotten a lot more combustible," I said, "and not just because Hale, the migrant hater, had an illegal immigrant working for him, and living at his house."

"You *think*?" Rita said.

"Has Daniel told Baez his theory about Vic Hale being his father?" I asked.

"Baez is a little pissed that he hadn't shared that with him," Rita said, "but that's irrelevant now. Once Baez found out on his own that Marisol had been Hale's housekeeper, he didn't exactly have to be Stephen Hawking to do the math. Now he's even more of a man in a hurry than ever. He wants to do a stand-alone podcast on this as soon as possible, post it, expose Hale for being one of the great phonies of the Western world, have Daniel call a press conference, worry about the series later. And just so you know? I feel as if the reporter knows a lot more than he was telling me."

"As is so often the case," I said.

"Anyway," Rita said, "Daniel told Baez to stand down for the time being. Slow his roll. Told him he's not going forward until he—Daniel—meets with Hale face-to-face."

"Good luck with that," I said.

"You can make it happen," she said. "The face-to-face piece, I mean."

I said, "Is it at all worth me pointing out that Daniel Lopez isn't my client and is barely yours?"

"Don't start," she said.

"Hale threatened to bury him if he goes public with any of this," I said.

"And I'll bury him if he tries," she said.

She waved the bartender over then and handed him her credit card, which I thought should give off a beam of light. The bartender was back at warp speed.

"It's not as if taking this kid on as a client is going to be a big moneymaker for you," I said, "even if it does put you smack-dab back in the middle of the headlines. So why is this so important to you?"

She took out her wallet, stuck the credit card back in it, tossed the wallet into her purse, gave one more toss of the red hair. Turned to look at me, her face almost solemn.

"Because I spent a lot of my life trying to find out who my real father is," she said.

Then she was the one placing a cash tip next to her glass, standing, smoothing out imperceptible wrinkles in the tight dress. I felt as if all eyes in the place were on her, as they so often were, whatever the place, day or night.

"Did you?" I said. "Ever find out?"

"No," she said.

When we were outside, I asked if she wanted me to drop her back at her office. She said she preferred walking off the vodka. But I had the feeling it was more than the two drinks she'd had that she wanted to walk off.

I drove to the apartment, parked in back, walked to my own office from there.

The podcast guy was waiting for me.

Two podcasters in one day.

Had to be some kind of record.

TWELVE

Ricardo Baez was in the hall, sitting cross-legged next to my office door, staring at the phone in his hand as if the secret to a happy life were on his screen.

"I would've called first," he said when I got to him, "but I wasn't sure if you'd see me."

He effortlessly rose up out of the position he'd just been in, as if he'd mastered a movement like that. I used to be able to do it. Now Susan kept urging me to try yoga. I told her that would happen right after the Rapture.

"Why would you think something like that about a welcoming person like myself?" I said.

"After my meeting with Ms. Fiore, I got the feeling she wasn't going to allow you to talk to me," he said.

"She's been giving me more and more responsibility lately," I said. "Last week she even gave me back my car privileges."

I unlocked the door and showed him in.

"So we're cool?" he said.

"Too soon," I said

I offered him coffee. He said he tried not to caffeinate in the afternoon. I told him he was the type of Goody Two-shoes who ruined things for the rest of us.

"You know why I'm here, obviously," he said.

"I know what Rita told me," I said. "But why don't you give me your version."

"Well," he said, "I guess you could call me a bit of a disruptor. That's as good a place to start as any."

I took a closer look at him across my desk. He and Daniel Lopez could have been brothers. Or at least relatives. He was wearing skinny jeans, black leather sneakers with white soles, a T-shirt with NOAH KAHAN on the front, over an image of a guy swinging a baseball bat.

"I assume I should know who Noah Kahan is," I said, pointing at the shirt.

"Singer," he said. "I actually made a trip up to Boston last summer to see him in concert at Fenway Park." Baez looked down at the image on his shirt, then back at me. "You haven't heard of him?"

"Clearly I have not."

"'Stick Season'?" he said. "His big hit song?"

"Whatever you say."

I got up and Keurig-ed myself a cup of coffee. Screw it, I thought, I wasn't going to be caffeine-deprived with a second straight podcaster, whatever time of day it was, and even if he was being a show-off.

When I sat back down I said, "Before you start, let me just point out that I know Daniel's story, told to me by Daniel himself when he was seated in that very same chair. And I was with Vic Hale earlier today doing some disrupting of my own."

"So you're saying we can skip through any further small talk," he said.

"With alacrity," I said.

"Alacrity," he said. "Wow."

I toasted him with my mug. "I know even bigger words than that," I said. "Want to hear some?"

"I did some asking around when I decided to come over here," he said. "And what I heard is that you're somewhat of a hard-o."

"Only somewhat?" I said. "What kind of a reporter are you, kid?"

"Enough of one to have figured out that Vic Hale is Daniel's father before Daniel got around to telling me," Baez said.

"Hale says it's not true."

"And I call bullshit on him," he said. "Or at least to that."

"Rita thought you knew a lot more than you shared with her on this matter," I said.

"I do," he said. He shrugged and grinned. "Now what?"

I sipped some of my coffee. It had quickly gone cold because I'd forgotten to use my temperature-controlled mug. Maybe the universe was telling me I shouldn't be drinking coffee after lunch. On days when I actually got to have lunch.

"You mind if I vape?" Baez asked.

"Yes."

It stopped him.

"Really?"

"Really."

"Yup," he said. "Hard-o."

"Now you're finally getting somewhere."

"I'm sure Ms. Fiore told you that I'm both an investigative journalist and a podcaster," he said. "It's what I do. But who I am, Mr. Spenser, is a soldier on the front lines of the war being waged in this country against people who came to it the way my parents did from Cuba. And the way Daniel's late mother did. All the people who have been demonized by the likes of Vic Hale because they did come here looking for a better life and are currently being hunted down and then thrown out of this country."

"Homeless and tempest tossed," I said.

He smiled now. "Looking for that lamp beside the golden door," he said. "Except people like Vic Hale don't just want that door closed, they want it locked and bolted. Dead-bolted, if necessary. And they want to take the lamp beside the golden door and hit you over your head with it."

I waited, really out of respect for his passion, the sheer force of it. Baez was clearly a true believer, on fire with his beliefs. He didn't need me or anybody else to validate them, of course, confirm he was on the right side of this, and history. He was too busy fighting his war.

"Vic Hale is the enemy," Ricardo Baez said. "And this is our chance to take him the absolute fuck down."

"Our chance?" I said. "Daniel didn't sound to me as if he's looking to pick a fight with anybody. For starters, he just wants to know his father, and have his father know him."

I could hear Baez's phone buzzing. He took it out of a front pocket of his tight jeans, though I wondered how he'd been able to fit it in there, checked it, put it away.

"You're right about that, no doubt," he said. "But it's my job to get Daniel to understand that this is bigger than him, and bigger than me. And perhaps share things I know with him before too very long."

"But not with me," I said.

"Nah," he said.

"Are you looking to help him write his story," I said, "or rewrite it in your voice?"

"One of my goals," he said, "is for people, when they do finally *hear* the whole story, to not know where Daniel ends and I begin."

He told me then about how Daniel Lopez first appeared on his radar when he saw Daniel give a speech on the central quad at the University of Miami a few months earlier. There was another student at the school, there on an expiring F-1 visa, who had been falsely arrested on what was known as a federal immigration hold, even before the real crackdown across the country was in full force.

"It was a pretty big deal in South Florida at the time, because the kid was such an outstanding student and so well-liked," Baez said. "It turned out to be a case of mistaken identity because, hey, so many of us look alike, right, when we're swarming into America to take all the good jobs? Anyway, there were rallies throughout the Latino communities. But Daniel's speech, which I just happened to catch in person, was far and away the most impressive, especially for a twenty-one-year-old. Completely blew me away."

I said, "How old are you, by the way?"

"Twenty-five," he said. "But as actors like to say, I can play older."

"They don't have mirrors at your house?" I said, grinning at him.

"Are you ever serious?" he said.

"You have no idea."

"You still mind if I vape?" he said.

"Yes," I said.

He said that once he got to know Daniel Lopez, it became apparent how much potential he had. And now it wasn't very difficult for Ricardo Baez, an activist himself, to look down the road and see someone like Daniel being the face of so many of the things that mattered to him, in the political arena, on the border, everywhere. So he wrote about him on the *Libertad* website and was just starting to put the podcast series up on its legs when Daniel's mother was murdered.

"At which point the story changed," I said.

"Got changed and got bigger," Baez said. "Another nightmare in what had started to become the American dream for people like us. And, frankly, little did we know at the time that things were about to get worse."

Daniel had already told Baez, in the interviewing process, about the father he'd never met, the one who had died before making it across the water. Or so he still thought, because that is what his mother had told him. Ricardo Baez was, by his own admission, a dog with a bone by then. He made a trip to Guatemala but could find few people who remembered Marisol Lopez or a husband, or the parents she had told Daniel she lost in the earthquake of 1976. Or Marisol's grandmother. Could find no other living relatives, period.

"So then I shifted my attention to Boston," Baez said. "This was after Marisol had died, because Daniel had told me that she had moved to Boston after she had made it safely—if illegally—into Texas. He just said she'd worked housekeeping jobs, didn't say for who. After that, it was the same for me as I'm sure it is for you when you're working a case. I started pulling on strings. And finally established that she had worked for Vic Hale. That sonofabitch."

"At which point you also must have figured out that the timeline of her being pregnant when she was making her way across the river actually didn't line up," I said.

He shook his head. "Not even close."

"Now here we are," I said. "And here you are wanting to light up Vic Hale."

"Like fireworks over your Charles River on the Fourth of July," he said.

Baez smiled again. But this was no actor's smile, no pose, no artifice. This was a shark smile. One that really did make him look much older than he said he was.

Much older.

"On our nation's birthday," Ricardo Baez said.

THIRTEEN

I assumed that we were done, at least for now, as if Baez had just delivered some kind of mic-drop exit line, when I heard his phone buzzing again. He took it out again, studied it, looked pleased as he put it away this time.

"*Muy bueno,*" he said.

"*Bueno* for whom?" I said.

"Another good lead," he said, "maybe even for the greater good."

He stood and said, "I need to be on the move."

I said, "I know you think this is your story. But it really is his, whether you're the one telling it or not. And you're smart enough to know that without Daniel, you're just a jockey without a horse, no matter how talented you are."

"Did you mean to say 'horse' or 'horse's ass,' Mr. Spenser?"

"Without sounding patronizing, I don't look at you that way," I said. "But this is a very powerful man you're up against, when and if you do go up against him. A powerful and potentially vindictive man with powerful people behind him. And from what I've been reading, somebody who has a lot more money at stake these days than what he sent Daniel and his mother."

"I'm not interested in money," he said.

"Apparently, no one is."

Baez said, "What's that supposed to mean?"

"Daniel says the same thing," I said. "But what happens if this all rolls out exactly the way you want it to? It turns out that Vic Hale really is Daniel's dad, and he can prove it, or somebody can, and then you do set out to take him down. If that does happen, don't you get a lot more famous in the process than you are now? I hate to use this expression, but wouldn't that be great for your brand?"

"This isn't about my brand," he said. "It's about Daniel's. And about the immigrant brand in this country, and the immigrant experience, which you have noticed is demonized almost on an hourly basis."

"Listen, I have no standing with you," I said. "I have no official standing with Daniel. And while you haven't asked for my advice, I'm going to give it to you anyway. You need to be careful how you proceed with this. I'm sure Rita told you the same thing."

"She did," he said. "And I will be careful, I promise."

He leaned down and leaned forward now, and put his hands on my desk. Not in an aggressive way. Almost to let me know that now we were done.

"You take down bad guys, right?" he asked.

"Every chance I get."

"Well, that's what I'm trying to do with Vic Hale," he said, "with or without your help."

"I could help you more if I knew more of what you know," I said. "Or think you know."

"When the time is right," he said.

I took my own phone out of the middle drawer of the desk, next to the Mookie Betts signed baseball Susan had somehow gotten for me a couple birthdays ago, right after he'd been traded to the

Dodgers, something that had sent me into a dark baseball place. I asked Baez for his number and he gave it to me and as soon as he did I called it.

Then I wrote out the number for the landline I still had at my apartment on one of my business cards, and the cell number, and even Susan's cell number, and handed the card across my desk.

"Business cards are old school," Baez said.

"Or just old," I said.

"I feel as if you're sending me off to camp," he said, "and not an interview."

I asked him where he was staying in Boston and he said The Lenox, at the corner of Boylston and Exeter.

"Speaking of old school," he said.

"We know how to get in touch with each other if we have to," I said. "You get into any kind of situation while you're doing your reporting, you can call me."

"A situation?" he said.

"One where you might require the services of a noted hard-o," I said.

"Don't worry about me," he said. "I'm known as one myself, even if I haven't been at it as long as you have."

When he got to the door, he turned around.

"Speaking of situations, the message I just got a few minutes ago indicates that the one on the ground may have changed," he said. "Isn't that what they say in a war?"

"When they're not saying war is hell," I said.

Little did either one of us know.

FOURTEEN

I hadn't told Susan or Hawk, but occasionally in the afternoon I would drive over to Harvard Stadium and run the stairs the way I used to, before my knees started to feel as if they had known much better days in the same way the stadium had.

Some days I could still make it all the way to the top, on the press box side, without stopping, the way I could do that back when I was running the steps with either Susan or Hawk.

I wasn't going to invite either one of them to join me until I was sure I could hold my own and not get trash-talked all the way out to Soldiers Field Road.

Today was one of the days when I had the whole place to myself, the sun high in the sky, the temperature in the high 60s, just a slight breeze at my back, even as I was running up what felt like my own personal Heartbreak Hill. My own wind was good today. It was the flesh that was somewhat weaker, or at least not as strong as it had once been.

When I was young?—Ah, woful When!, Coleridge had written in "Youth and Age." *Ah! for the change 'twixt Now and Then! . . .*

I had made it up and back down three times, having to stop only once. One-for-three. A .333 batting average. Progress. Now I was sitting on the lowest step, squarely at the fifty-yard line, wondering just where exactly I was between Now and Then, when Vic Hale's guy Bobby and the other guy, the one in the green Red Sox hat, suddenly came walking in my direction.

They took aisle seats on either side of me. I remained on my step. Out of breath, alert, completely unarmed.

"Want to race me up the steps?" I said. "Loser buys the beer. We could make a day of it."

"You don't strike me as a Harvard type," the one named Bobby said.

"Would it impress you to know that I'm sleeping with a Harvard Ph.D.?" I said. "By the way, Bobby? I'll save you checking your phone. It stands for doctor of philosophy."

A sad look played across Bobby's ham face then. I didn't think it was because I'd hurt his feelings. More as if I'd disappointed him. But then I often ran into that with my sense of whimsy.

"Did Vic send you?" I asked.

"We don't technically work for Vic," Bobby said. "We just work with him sometimes, don't we, Deke?"

It was the first time I'd heard the other man's name.

"More like we get outsourced to Vic on occasion," Deke said, in a voice so deep he sounded like Darth Vader.

"Who do you work for?" I said.

"Let's call him an interested party," Bobby said.

"All you need to know for now," Deke added.

I couldn't tell whether Deke was trying to look menacing, even in repose, or whether he came by it naturally, the way Hawk did. But there was a cool to him, the way he looked completely comfortable as he did in his own skin, something else that reminded me of Hawk.

"I have intuited that this isn't a chance meeting," I said.

"Our boss has asked us to deliver a firm, but respectful, message," Bobby said. "At least that's how he described it to us, almost in those exact words."

"And the message is?"

I looked at Bobby, then back at Deke. I noticed now that I could see only one of Deke's hands. The other one was hanging casually behind him. I didn't believe he had a gun back there, or would actually consider shooting me in broad daylight because of the few minutes I'd spent with Vic Hale. But I shifted enough on my step, acting as if I were stretching, to keep a better eye on him.

Bobby said, "The message is for you to not bother Vic. Like, say, ever again."

"Not to make too fine a point of things," I said. "But I wasn't aware that I *had* bothered him."

"He hides his feelings well, Vic does," Bobby said.

"Since when?" I said.

Bobby ignored me. Deke was looking out at the football field. Even when his eyes had been on me, he'd stared at me as indifferently as a snake would.

"I'm trying to make myself as clear as possible," Bobby said. "Our boss . . ."

". . . the aforementioned interested party," I said.

". . . would prefer that you no longer come around asking questions about Marisol Lopez, or her son," he continued. "And would prefer you pass that along to any reporters of your acquaintance who might be coming around with similar questions."

"And why is that?" I said.

"Being someone who obviously prides himself as being so fucking smart," Bobby said, "you are probably aware that a very big deal is about to go down with Vic and *his* bosses. And our boss is pretty insistent that there not be anything interfering with that."

"Like any more of your bullshit," Deke said.

"Ohhh," I said. "*That* kind of interference."

They didn't speak now. Neither did I. I put my head back and looked up into the blue sky and drank in some air and let it out. Still alert. But at least my breathing was back to normal.

"So have we made ourselves clear?" Bobby said.

"Yes," I said.

"So you just walk away from this now," he said.

"Oh, fuck, no," I said.

I heard Deke chuckle softly.

To Bobby he said, "Told you we were wasting our time before we got over here and wasted it for real."

"No?" Bobby asked me.

He sounded genuinely curious.

"Just to make *my*self clear," I said, "I will walk away from this when I'm good and ready. And if that causes a spot of bother for either Vic or your boss—or the two of you—then we'll all just have to work through our relationship issues when the time comes."

Bobby nodded. "Final answer, like they say on that show?" he said to me.

"And I didn't even have to phone a friend," I said.

With that, Deke's right hand flicked out from behind his back and he hit me hard with his crowbar, generating a lot of speed in a very short distance, a direct hit on the outside of my left knee, where I knew full well by now was where my lateral meniscus was located. It felt as if he had stuck a knife in there, the sudden stab of pain enough to momentarily knock the breath right back out of me, as if trying to knock it all the way through the goalposts.

"That the bad one?" Deke asked.

"Yeah," I said in a thick voice.

"Thought so," he said. "Saw you favoring it on the steps."

My breathing was just starting to get back to normal again when Bobby said, "Think about what we said when you've had more time to reflect," and then the two of them were down on the field and walking toward the end zone that had the Dillon Fieldhouse as its backdrop.

I thought I could hear Bobby whistling the Harvard fight song but couldn't be sure the farther he got from me and the closer the two of them got to pay dirt.

Ten thousand men of Harvard want victory today . . .

I was going to yell out "Next time" to Deke, but he had to know that there would be one, whether I gave him a heads-up on it or not.

All I knew for sure at the moment was that my left knee hurt so bad that I felt certain I was out of the Yale game.

FIFTEEN

I drove straight home, got an oversized ice bag out of the freezer, stretched my leg out on the coffee table, carefully placed the bag on my left knee, prepared to do some thinking while I iced, ever hopeful that the thinking wouldn't make my head hurt as bad as my knee did at the moment.

The two bruisers said that Vic Hale hadn't sent them. But that didn't mean that he hadn't. But if not, then who had? Todd Jakes, the producer, not only worked for and with Hale, he was the one who had set up my meeting at the Fens. By now Jakes had to know why I'd gone there and everything that had been said when Hale and I were there, by both of us. Was Jakes the type to send two guys like Bobby and Deke to brace me, just on the basis of that one conversation about a long-lost son?

Better question, Doctor:

Could someone as smart as Jakes had to be, someone who'd played such a big part in making Vic Hale a media sensation, do something as dumb as trying to run me off?

I planned to ask him about that.

Just not yet.

I continued to ice, and think, pleased that the thinking was proceeding in a relatively pain-free manner, at least for now.

If it wasn't Hale starting the action, and wasn't his producer, then it really was another interested party. By now I knew that Hale's parent podcast company was called Brass Ones Inc., for what seemed to be an obvious if ham-handed reason. I also knew it was owned by a former WWE executive named Woody Giles, who'd been involved on the broadcast side of pro wrestling, gotten rich off it, gotten out when WWE sold off 51 percent of the company to Endeavor, and was now in the podcast world, a world in which he had not only hitched his wagon to Vic Hale, but was about to rehitch it, for fun and profit, but mostly profit.

Susan had met Giles a few times at Boston charity events, and used the same word to describe him every time she did.

"Gross," she would say, and then frequently add that it must have been destiny that brought him and Vic Hale together.

The only other essential player in Hale's orbit was his lawyer, Bill Jones, someone who had found his way to respectability after having done more than a little legal work in the past for Tony Marcus, among other local luminaries over there on the dark side with Tony. I had actually lost track of Jones for several years until he had reappeared and reinvented himself as an "entertainment lawyer." As far as I could tell, Jones had been with Hale since his first big contract with WTKK.

They'd all been featured in a recent *Boston* magazine profile of Hale: Hale himself, Jakes, Giles, Jones. There was a cover photograph of the four of them underneath a headline that read HALE OF A TEAM. When I showed the cover to Hawk, he said it was like looking at the Four Horsemen of the Apocalypse, just without the damn horses.

Susan and also Hawk's date had been invited to the apartment for dinner tonight, having been promised a recent specialty of mine, Tuscan chicken pasta. So a little after five o'clock, I removed the ice from my knee, took a hot shower, shaved, applied just a discreet amount of cologne, put on a black pullover and jeans and a pair of old Rockport walking shoes from which I simply could not part. I opened a bottle of Quilt even though it was not quite the cocktail hour, gave myself a generous pour as a reward for what Deke had done to my knee, and began to lay out the fixings for the upcoming feast while I waited for my guests.

No one could ever say that Spenser didn't play hurt.

SIXTEEN

The woman Hawk had been seeing for the past several months, Emma Cole, owned the city's hottest new fitness club, located at Downtown Crossing, called Buff. From what Hawk had told me, it featured the most up-to-date classes and machines and bells and whistles, had a day spa attached to it, and catered to both men and women, though Hawk said most of the clientele was comprised of women.

I'd asked him why he never worked out there.

"Emma say she worried it would be too much like being in a candy store," he said.

"For you?" I asked.

"Only in the general sense of me being the candy," he said.

But he'd called on his way across town to tell me that Emma wouldn't be joining us for dinner, there had been a burst pipe in the basement of the club, and she might be there all night supervising the cleanup.

"Not much of a delegator, our Emma?" I said.

"Depend on the situation," Hawk said.

So it was just Hawk and Susan and Pearl the Wonder Dog in the kitchen while I prepared the food. Hawk had brought two bottles of Moët & Chandon Dom Pérignon, one for him and one for Susan and me to share if we were interested. But I elected to stay with my cabernet. Susan was drinking Sancerre, though drinking seemed to be a rather overblown description of what she was doing, as the girl of my dreams could make one glass of wine sometimes last longer than an extra-inning Sox game.

By now I had laid out everything I needed on the kitchen counter: pasta, chicken breasts, olive oil, garlic powder, a half-cup of white wine, Dijon mustard, sun-dried tomatoes, basil, spinach, heavy cream. I had two frying pans at the ready, the smaller one for the chicken breasts, the larger one for pasta that I had already boiled to near perfection. I'd already tossed a salad of romaine lettuce, cucumbers, parmesan crisps, cherry tomatoes. And radishes. I felt there had never been a salad anywhere, in all of dining history, not enhanced by radishes.

I asked Susan and Hawk if I'd ever mentioned my radish theory to them.

"*Yes!*" they both said at once.

When it was finally time to stir the pasta and cream and all the other ingredients into the simmering pan, I said, "Heaven will probably smell like this."

"Like garlic?" Hawk said.

"Says a man who drinks champagne out of a bottle," I said.

"Yum yum," he said, and drank.

As I stirred, I finally got around to telling them about my encounter with Bobby and Deke, culminating with the cheap shot I'd taken to the knee.

"Shouldn't be hard to find them," Hawk said, "if you want to, uh, reencounter with them with the sides more even."

"Us against them wouldn't be a fair fight," I said.

"Be fun to shove that crowbar up the brother's ass, though," Hawk said.

Susan giggled.

Hawk said, "You think Hale the one who sent them and they lying about that?"

"The thought has occurred," I said. "But I keep asking myself why escalate a thing that hadn't even become a thing off that one meeting."

I tasted a piece of rigatoni. Almost there.

"I mean, if Tommy Hale told Vic anything at all about me, he has to know that I'm not the type to let a visit from a couple head-bangers like that go," I said, "and just let bygones be bygones."

"Then who did send them?" Susan said.

"Been focusing on that all afternoon," I said, "along with the plight of this rumpled existence."

"Don't lose your focus now and think we need to know who said the rumpled thing," Susan said.

"You're sure?" I said.

"Yes," she said again, and then she took another small sip of her wine.

She was wearing a gray wrap dress and slingback shoes that looked to me like all the other slingback shoes in the closet she kept here, and the even bigger shoe closet on Linnaean Street. Her hair was pulled back tonight and gleaming even more than usual, allowing her to show off the diamond studs in her ears. I started to tell her she looked lovelier than springtime, but then realized she looked much better than that. As usual.

"I'm sorry," I said. "What was the question? Your beauty has once again distracted me."

"Blah, blah, blah," she said. "I had simply asked about Vic

Hale, and if he didn't send those two men to the stadium, then who did?"

I told her that the list of possible suspects was probably quite small, listing the members of Team Hale, all of whom were invested, to varying degrees, in the new podcast deal going through with flying colors.

"They all got skin in the game," Hawk said. "Only you don't. So you got to explain to me why you'd stay in for even one more day." He smiled. "Or knee, now that you down to only one worth a shit."

"Hawk's right," Susan said.

"Ain't no rumpled existence for me," he said.

"This just shows all signs of ending badly, from what you've told us," Susan continued. "For the young man and for this young reporter."

I covered the pan for about thirty more seconds, then removed it, turned off the flame, stirred one last time.

"But what if they both get what they want?" I said. "Daniel gets to know who his real father is, once and for all. And if the reporter can get him to go along, they both take down Vic Hale, and maybe in more than just a symbolic way."

"Or they end up all the way down the rabbit hole, and you get dragged down there with them," Hawk said. "And maybe somebody ends up with more than a busted-up knee 'fore you're through."

"It's not as if I have to see this *all* the way through," I said. "Maybe just give it a little shove in the right direction, and then step aside."

"May I remind you this is Hawk and me you're talking to here?" Susan said.

I poured the pasta into a giant Campagna serving bowl that had been another gift from Susan.

"This kid, Daniel, got dealt bad cards, as well as he's turned out," I said. "Whether the money kept coming in all those years or not. Got lied to about who his real father was. Lost his mother the way he just lost her. More than anything, he's just looking for some kind of closure."

"Not to overstate the obvious," Susan said, "but Daniel Lopez is not your client. It sounds as if he's not really Rita's client, at least not yet. But now, in the space of a day, you have already been threatened and attacked."

"Isn't overstating the obvious part of your job description, by the way?" I said.

"Ha, ha," she said. "But seriously? If you go forward with this, whatever the hell this is, you are making a choice to involve yourself in the life, not to mention the business, of someone I consider to be dangerous just on his beliefs alone. Meaning Vic Hale. I know you think you can fix everything except my laptop. But for all of the reasons I have mentioned, and Hawk has mentioned, I really do believe nothing good can come of this, for the young man or for my cutie."

"Noted," I said, and began to fill their bowls with pasta.

"Noted and about to be ignored," she said.

"Never heard of nothing like *that* never happening before," Hawk said.

"I just feel like I can help here in a way nobody else can," I said.

Susan did what I'd always considered to be a pretty strong impression of Hawk, especially for a female Ph.D. from Harvard.

"Never heard of nothing like that never happening before," she said.

"And on that note," I said, "bon appétit."

When we were all seated at the table, Hawk said, "Gonna say this one more thing, then drop this for the rest of the night. You either all the way in or you're out."

"I'm getting there," I said.

"In or out?" he said.

"I'll know when I get there," I said.

I served strawberries that I'd purchased the day before from the Copley Square Farmers Market and freshly whipped cream for dessert. After that we all helped clear the table and load the dishwasher. I had one more glass of wine. Susan finally finished her first, against all odds of laws of probability.

Hawk had gotten a call from Emma and been told that the crisis at Buff had been contained, and was then off to meet her for drinks in the bar at The Newbury. And despite the Aleve I'd taken for the throbbing in my knee, I played hurt once again when Susan and I took Pearl for a walk in the Public Garden.

When we were back inside the apartment and Pearl had been relegated to the living room sofa with a bone as a consolation prize, Susan said, "Are you sure you're not too injured for intimacy?"

"Are you asking me if I'm ready to get it on?" I said.

"That's a less elegant way of putting it," she said. "But yes."

"My answer is yes," I said.

Then she smiled a smile full of wickedness and endless promise and said, "In that case, big boy, let's get it on."

"I could carry you into the bedroom if you want," I said.

"Maybe when you have your health," she said.

We were both sound asleep in the half-light before sunrise when I heard my phone from where I'd left it on the coffee table, playing "Dirty Water," the Red Sox anthem after a victory.

I quietly slid out of bed, Susan having not stirred, and walked into the living room, picked up the phone, and looked at the illuminated screen.

Belson

"Hey," I said, keeping my voice down.

"Got a body," Lieutenant Frank Belson said.

I waited.

"Think it's a young guy you might know," he said.

Frank Belson paused then and said, "Or knew, I guess is a better way of putting it."

SEVENTEEN

I had seen this movie too many times in my life and not just in Boston, always with the same blue flashing lights and crime scene tape and cops walking and crouching and talking and taking pictures and a body being bagged if it hadn't already been bagged by the time I arrived.

The initial response would have been two marked units and one supervisor, who then called a supervising detective, Frank Belson himself in this case. Upon his arrival at the scene, Belson would organize a uniformed neighborhood canvas, starting from where the body had been discovered and then expanding out to the immediate area in whatever neighborhood the body had been found. Most of the time at least three officers would be part of the canvassing, no matter what the hour of day or night. Another three, at least, would stay behind to do what was known as "holding the scene," doing their best to keep the gawkers with their cell phones from TikToking and Instagramming the show for endless and grisly entertainment on social media. Before long there would be at least one investigator from the District Attorney's Office showing up, generally in an unmarked car, and somebody representing the State Police, often bringing his or her own flashing lights.

One crime scene van. One from the Medical Examiner's Office. The body usually removed within fifteen minutes of the ME getting there.

It just hadn't gone exactly that way this morning, Belson having told me they were waiting for me to arrive and ID the body, since one of my cards had been in one of the deceased's pockets, why he'd called me in the first place.

I had told Belson that I thought I had an idea who it might be but didn't want to give him Ricardo Baez's name until I was sure it was him. What was the point of that?

It was all playing out, all over again, in the Savin Hill Beach section of Dorchester this time, a part of South Boston bordered by I-93 and Morrissey Boulevard and hard by the water of Dorchester Bay.

A big uniformed kid working the perimeter closest to where I had been allowed to park was about to stop me until we both heard Belson say, "Let him pass," and so the kid did.

"The lieutenant and I go way back," I said to the kid as I passed him.

Belson said to the kid, "Try not to let that get around, or I'll never fucking make captain."

I could see the other cops slowly moving around, inside and outside the tape. More familiar choreography. There were a handful of onlookers on the other side of the tape, locals either out for an early-morning walk on the trail near the water or just drawn here by the flashing lights, by the kind of real-life cop show that had finally come to their neighborhood.

The body was still on a stretcher behind the coroner's van, the bag unzippered. Belson walked me over to it now, telling me the cause of death was two bullets to the chest, point-blank.

I looked down, nodding to myself, worst fears realized as I'd known they would be. Ricardo Baez's eyes were closed. He could have been sleeping, except for all the blood covering the front of the Noah Kahan T-shirt he'd been wearing in my office.

I could feel Belson looking at me looking at Baez.

"So it's who you thought it was," he said.

"Yeah," I said. "Ricardo Baez is his name. Twenty-five. Reporter from Miami. And a podcaster."

"Isn't everybody these days?" Belson said.

I let that one go.

"Why'd he have your card?" Belson said. "I assume he didn't just find it out here like a sand dollar."

"He talked to me about a story he was working on," I said. "My office."

"When?" Belson asked.

"Yesterday."

"What kind of story?"

"It's complicated," I said.

"And we're off," Belson said.

He made a motion that they could close up the bag.

"No wallet on him," he said. "No phone. Just your card. If it was a robbery, whoever did this didn't think the card was anything of value."

I watched them load the body of Ricardo Baez into the van, watched them shut the doors, the door slam sounding as loud as another gunshot out here, saw the van slowly head for Morrissey Boulevard, spraying dirt.

"You got any idea why he might've ended up here in the middle of the night?" Belson said. "Was he staying around here?"

I shook my head. "The Lenox," I said.

"But you know why he was in Boston," Belson said.

"He was working on an immigration story," I said. "Like I said, it's complicated."

"Lucky for you I'm such a good listener," Belson said. "And, as you might imagine, I got nothing but time."

Belson was wearing his usual raincoat. He had either a day's growth of beard going or an hour's worth, it had always been almost impossible to tell with him. But there was more gray to it now, I could see now that the sky had gotten brighter, which figured just because I felt as if I had known Frank Belson for about a hundred years. At least he no longer walked around with a cigar in his hand, lit or unlit, having admitted to me a couple crime scenes ago that he was now chewing CBD gum instead, quickly adding that it wasn't what he called "that gummy shit." I'd pointed out that they were called edibles, and he'd said, "Eat me."

He was chomping away now.

"The story was related to the murder of a woman in Miami not long ago," I said. "A woman who came here about twenty years ago from Guatemala and used to work here. Got herself shot to death near an ATM. Still unsolved. Been a string of murders like it down there."

It wasn't technically a lie, I knew, but nowhere near the truth. But I wasn't ready to tell him about Daniel Lopez, and I certainly wasn't ready to bring Vic Hale's name into this, certainly not yet.

"So he had some kind of lead that brought him to our fair city?" Belson said.

"I asked him that," I said. "He's the one who told me it was complicated."

"And you didn't press him."

"His story, Frank," I said. "Not mine."

"Oh, for fuck's sake," Belson said. "Why don't we just skip ahead through your usual bullshit and you tell me now what you're not telling me because you're always not telling me something, at least until you need something from me, in which case I can often not shut you up."

"You make our relationship sound so transactional when you put it that way," I said.

"If he was your client, you would've told me," Belson said. "And even if he was and you *didn't* tell me, he's still dead at the present time."

"I had one conversation with the kid, Frank," I said. "It's not as if he opened up his notebook for me."

"Why did he come to you in the first place?"

I said, "He's friends with a client of Rita's."

Another partial truth, as a way of getting me to where I wanted to be right now, which meant my car. I would eventually tell Belson more, he was right about that. But not until I knew more, and not until I had spoken with Rita, and Daniel Lopez, in no particular order.

"When did it happen?" I said, if not trying to change the subject, then at least redirect it.

"ME thinks sometime around midnight," Belson said. "There's a couple cameras on the trail, just not on this side. We'll find out if anybody heard anything, unless it was a targeted hit, in which case the shooter probably used a suppressor."

He put his cop eyes on me again, giving me the same feeling the look always did, as if there was a laser dot on my forehead from a scope rifle.

"I take it you don't think this was a robbery that turned to shit," Belson said, "even with no wallet and no phone on him."

"We both know that if he wanted to take a late-night stroll, the

Public Garden and the Common were not much more than five minutes away from his hotel," I said. "The only thing that makes sense to me, having *gotten* a sense that the kid was a bulldog, is that he was here meeting with a source."

"Who picked the spot," Belson said, "the kid being an out-of-towner."

"Yeah," I said.

Belson asked for the name of the friend I'd mentioned, Rita's client. I told him it would be better if Rita told him that, if she chose to tell him at all.

"Seriously?" Belson said.

"I don't mean to be hurtful," I said. "But given a choice, I'd rather piss off you than Rita Fiore."

I told him the name of Baez's website then, telling him that was the only contact information I had for him in South Florida. I started to walk away, already knowing the first stop I was going to make in a couple hours after getting back to my apartment, but knowing that I had to call Rita, whether she was awake yet or not.

"Spenser?"

It was Belson, calling after me.

I stopped and turned back to him.

"Try not to act like a dick for once," he said.

"That's private dick to you," I said, and kept walking to where I'd parked on Denny Street.

EIGHTEEN

I called Rita from the car. She told me Belson had already called, probably before I broke his perimeter, wanting to know exactly why and how Ricardo Baez's life, when he still had one, had intersected with her own.

Rita said, "I told Frank, as respectfully as possible considering he'd prevented you from awakening me, that telling him that would violate attorney-client privilege."

"I'll bet that put some pep in his step," I said.

"Not so much," Rita said. "Then he wanted to know if you'd been bullshitting him, and if Baez is the one who had been my client. I told him no. He asked me again for my client's name, and the conversation pretty much devolved from there to some ugly name-calling."

"From him?"

"Kind of went both ways," she said.

There was a silence now between us that seemed to cover the distance from where I was on the expressway to her place on Joy Street.

"What the hell is going on here?" she asked finally.

"We will, the two of us, eventually find that out, simply because we always do," I said. "For now, what we know is that Baez was here in Boston, and why he was here. We know why Daniel Lopez is here, still. We know that after I discussed Daniel with Vic Hale, who may or may not be his father, two men who had acted as Vic's body men at the Fens followed me to Harvard Stadium and strongly urged me to leave this whole thing alone before one of them elected to smash my knee with a crowbar, causing me both pain and even greater embarrassment in the process."

"You could have told me about the crowbar thing as soon as it happened," Rita said.

"I was icing at the time."

"Oh."

"Furthermore," I said, "Ricardo Baez told me right before he left my office that there had been some kind of interesting development in the case, but didn't share what it might be, after having admitted there was much he was not sharing."

"And now he's dead," she said.

"Very much so," I said. "So Daniel came to Boston about Vic Hale and Ricardo Baez came with him, with malice aforethought for Vic, as you legal eagles say."

There was another silence. Inbound traffic was beginning to increase, so I got off the highway and commenced taking city streets back to Marlborough, taking pride in the fact that I didn't require WAZE to do it.

I was the one who ended the silence this time.

"Do we know if Baez had a wife or girlfriend or family?" I said.

"I'll ask Daniel," she said. "I'm going to be the one to have to tell him about Baez, soon as we end this call."

"He was the real thing," I said. "Baez."

"You know I didn't mean I hated him in particular when I said I hated the media," she said.

"I do know that," I said.

"We both just saw him and now he's dead," she continued. Paused and added, "Do you think Daniel might be in danger?"

"Almost without question if he stays here," I said. "And probably even if he doesn't."

"I will officially make him my client," Rita said, "though I've been thinking of him that way from the start. That means he gets the same privilege from you that he gets from me going forward."

"I'm not working for you," I said.

"You are now, big boy," Rita said.

NINETEEN

I had been waiting in the parking lot outside the headquarters of All Hale Productions on Market Street since eight o'clock, already feeling as if I had been up all night, which I effectively had.

At a few minutes before nine, I saw Todd Jakes pull up in a Tesla at the parking space I'd already seen was reserved for him. I got out of my car and quickly covered the distance between us despite the barking from my knee.

It startled him, seeing me standing right there and having left him barely enough room to step away from the car, but he did his best to hide it.

"Spenser," he said.

He had what looked like an expensive leather bag slung over his shoulder.

"We need to talk," I said.

"Bad time," he said. "I'm only here for a few minutes, then I have to head out to Vic's place for show prep, and then the show itself."

I heard the Tesla emit a soft beep that indicated it had locked itself, the way it could probably do everything else except pay his cable bill.

He reached into the pocket of his jeans and came out with his phone.

"We can set up an appointment for after the show," he said. "Maybe back here late this afternoon."

He started to casually move past me, to his right, and away from the Tesla. I blocked his way.

"You don't seem to understand," I said. "This *is* the appointment."

He tried to go left then, like a running back trying to find an opening after a hole had closed. But I blocked him again. Even on a sore knee, I still had a few lateral moves left. I just didn't back up as easily as I once had. But he didn't know that.

"Hey, man," Jakes said.

We were close enough that I could see the first hint of sweat forming on his forehead.

"Somebody sent a couple of Vic's guys after me after I spoke with the boss," I said softly. "Since then, a young reporter from Miami who was friendly with Marisol Lopez's son has been found dead in Dorchester. And even though I'm not a betting man, I'm betting that if that reporter reached out to me, he reached out to you."

His eyes were darting around now. I had read once about how if they moved in one direction, it meant a person was telling a lie, or about to. I just couldn't remember which side in the moment.

"We can talk later, I promise," he said. "But for now you really have to let me get to work." He looked past me, as if hopeful that the cavalry might be pulling off Market Street and into the lot to come rescue him. "And I'll be sure to mention all of this to Vic when I get with him."

"No," I said.

I had now gotten even closer to him, making me think of the old

Marx Brothers line, the one from Groucho about how if I were any closer to Todd Jakes in this moment I'd be behind him.

"Unlock the car," I said.

"Why would I do that?" he said.

"We're going to take a drive," I said.

"I told you I have a show to get ready for," he said.

"Same," I said.

I smiled broadly at him.

"By the way?" I said. "I've always wanted to take a ride in one of these babies."

TWENTY

I remembered having read once that castles were defined as private fortified residences.

Vic Hale's home was that. And all that.

There was a gate and guard shack at the entrance to the property, with high, spiked walls stretching out in both directions, almost as far as the eye could see. As soon as we arrived, a guard came out of the shack, walked slowly toward the Tesla, motioning for Jakes to lower the window on his side, something that happened with barely a whisper.

When the guard leaned down he saw me in the passenger seat. I winked and gave him an enthusiastic thumbs-up sign.

"Who are you?" the guard asked.

"Ted Lasso," I said. I gave him another thumbs-up. "Believe," I added.

I glanced at Jakes and saw him briefly close his eyes.

"His name is Spenser," Jakes said, starting to act as if he was the one who had been up all night. "Vic is expecting us, I called ahead."

"He didn't tell me," the guard said.

He was big and thick and red-haired, and his face had quickly gotten almost as red as the hair, as if even this short a conversation had elevated his heart rate.

"Well, now I'm telling you, Wally," Jakes said. "Now, please open the gate."

There was just enough snap in Jakes's voice. Wally stepped away from the car and pointed his phone at the gate. When it was open, Jakes noiselessly put the car in gear and we drove through it.

As we made our way up a long, winding drive, Jakes said, "What's your plan after Vic tells you that neither one of us had anything to do with anybody paying you that visit, and nothing to do with a reporter being killed, and that all you've done is waste my time and his?"

"I'll cross that bridge when we come to it," I said, the main house just starting to come into view. "There is going to be a toll bridge, right?"

The studio from which Vic Hale's podcast was beamed out to both the civilized and uncivilized world was in a gatehouse at the far end of the property, near where a back lawn that looked manicured enough to be a grass tennis court at Wimbeldon finally ran up against a heavily wooded area. There were two satellite dishes on the roof.

When we were inside, Jakes pointed out where the control room was, a glass wall separating it and the people inside it from Hale's desk. Jakes informed me that he sat in the control room during the show, coming out to speak with Hale only during the breaks, and not always then. He said his assistant was in there with him, and an engineer. Outside, there were two cameras pointing at Hale's desk, as the podcast also aired on YouTube TV.

The backdrop behind Hale featured a replica of the original American flag, thirteen stars in the upper-left corner, white against blue, representing the original thirteen states. Situated around it were framed photographs of Hale with various politicians and athletes and celebrities.

I made a sweeping gesture with my hand that took in the pictures and said to Jakes, "Doesn't look like much of a rainbow coalition."

"What can I tell you, Spenser?" Jakes said. "Vic knows how to play to his base."

He showed me to the green room then, reserved for the occasional in-studio guest, and told me I could wait there while he went and collected the host.

"Please make it clear to Vic that it wasn't my choice to bring you here," Jakes said.

"Done," I said.

"You might not believe this," I said, "but I would have gotten here with or without you. You being my ride just streamlined the process."

"He's still not going to be happy," Jakes said.

"There's probably something he can take for that," I said.

Vic Hale came walking into the green room ten minutes later, wearing a gray Dropkick Murphys sweatshirt cut off high up near his shoulders, showing off the arms and upper body of a weightlifter, and carrying himself as if proud of that.

Perhaps a Proud Boy in every sense.

With Hale was a tall, slender, and buzz-cutted white guy in a fatigue-green T-shirt that showed off tattoos running up and down lean, sculpted arms.

"This is Lee Chase," Hale said. "He's my assistant, but I guess some people might call him more of a body man."

"How come he wasn't looking out for your body when we met that day in the park?" I said.

"Well, to be perfectly honest with you, Spenser, that would fall into the category of none of your fucking business."

I turned to Chase. "I'm wondering, Lee," I said, "what does *body man* actually mean other than looking tough?"

"You want to find out how tough?" he said in a low, raspy voice.

"Maybe when we both have more time," I said.

"Lee's the only person who's been with me as long as Bill Jones and Todd have," Hale said. "He likes to say that he'd be willing to take a bullet for me."

"Or perhaps put a couple in somebody?" I said.

"What's that supposed to mean?" Chase said.

"Just me being fanciful," I said.

"Anway, I'm hoping it never comes to any shooting, either way," Hale said.

"Who would?" I said.

Chase looked me up and down then, like I was a horse he was thinking of buying, then walked out of the room without saying another word.

"Just so you know," Hale said when he was gone, "I got nothing to do with what you came here to talk to me about."

"And good morning to you, too, Vic."

"Yeah, yeah, yeah," he said. "I didn't send Bobby and Deke to pay you that visit Todd just told me about."

"Then who did?"

"I'm not the ace detective," he said, "you are."

"Not really feeling like much of one right this second," I said.

"And I don't know anything about some dead reporter, either," Hale said. "Not that you asked."

"Well, somebody in your orbit does," I said. "Or did. The reporter was up here asking around about Marisol Lopez and her son and you. And knew an awful lot about all of you that I'm pretty sure he didn't merely find out from Google."

Hale hadn't moved much past the doorway, standing there like a bull deciding whether or not to charge, arms crossed in front of him. Jakes was behind him, looking as if he'd just swallowed a hamster.

If Bobby and Deke were somewhere in the vicinity, they had not yet made their presence known. It didn't mean they weren't around. Nor did it mean Lee Chase, the body man, wasn't close by.

"Vic already knows that Baez had reached out to me, I told him as soon as he did," Jakes said. "But I told Vic what I told Baez, that neither Vic nor I had anything to discuss with him."

"Well, I guess I wasted a trip out here!" I said brightly, clapping my hands together.

"Good," Hale said. "Now, beat it."

He turned toward the door and Jakes made room for him.

"Not done yet," I said.

Hale wheeled around and was once again facing me.

"Ex*cuse* me?" he said.

"I'm not actually ready to leave," I said. "I was just being fanciful again."

"What the *fuck* are you talking about?" he said.

"Two headbangers who work for you show up and tell me to leave this case alone," I said. "Not long after that, a reporter working the same case gets shot dead at Savin Hill Beach, two in the chest, goodbye. Stop me if I'm going too fast for you."

"And you stop me if I'm going too fast for you, hotshot," Hale said. "Marisol's boy isn't mine. I told you that already, and I just told you I know nothing about some dead kid reporter."

I smiled. "Who said the reporter was a kid?" I asked.

"Figure of speech," he said. "Here's another one: Fuck you."

"Or not," I said.

"We'll see about that."

"We'll also see how things roll out when the cops are made aware that the great Vic Hale is the nexus in a murder investigation," I said. "And when they are, I'll bet they won't have to scale the palace walls to get to you."

"Cops love me," he said.

"Well, maybe, until they think you might be a material witness in a homicide investigation."

"You wish," he said.

"Let's move on," I said. "Who put Bobby and Deke on me?"

"Ask them," he said.

"Bobby told me they had been sent by an interested party," I said.

Hale pulled his phone out of the pouch in front of the sweatshirt.

"I got no more time for this shit," he said. "You got more questions, talk to my lawyer, provided he wants to waste *his* time talking to you."

"See, there," I said. "You're ready to talk to the cops already. Or not."

He left without saying another word. So did Jakes.

Bobby and Deke appeared in the doorway then.

Good times.

TWENTY-ONE

Neither appeared to be holding a weapon, but that hadn't mattered when they'd shown up at one of the playing fields of John Harvard. Perhaps they thought that just being here, and having me outnumbered yet again, was weaponization enough.

I looked behind me to see if Lee Chase was with them, but he was not, perhaps off doing other body-man things. Or perhaps he just assumed that Bobby and Deke didn't need backup escorting me off the property.

"Leave the hard way or the easy way?" Bobby said.

"There must be one other option," I said.

They each took a step into the green room. Bobby made a motion meant to start ushering me out of here.

"Move it," Bobby said. "Boss has a show to do."

"Does this mean I don't get to stay and learn?" I said.

"Now," Bobby said. "You can call an Uber from the gate. Or walk back to Boston, for all we fucking care."

I walked through them and out the door. They didn't speak. I didn't speak. We went past the studio and out of the gatehouse and started to make our way across what was truly a spectacular backyard.

Halfway to the main house, I stopped and pivoted and kicked

Bobby in the groin with my right leg, my good one these days. Or close enough. Before Deke could react, I planted and turned and hit him with a left hook to the middle of his face that I was almost certain, from the feel of the punch and the cracking sound it made, had broken his nose.

The punch surprised him enough that it put him on his back the way Frazier had done to Ali in their first fight at Madison Square Garden in the old days. By now I had my .38 out of the side pocket of my leather jacket, one for which the guard hadn't checked, nor had Todd Jakes. I stepped back a few paces so as to point it casually at both of them, all of us knowing it was for show more than anything else. But the feel of my favorite handgun was comforting to me, now that I saw the crowbar that Deke must have had inside his windbreaker in his right hand as he slowly came to a sitting position. He was using his left hand to stop the bleeding from his nose, if in vain.

I reached down and took the crowbar away from him, keeping Bobby in my range of vision, though he didn't seem like much of a threat at the moment, as he waited for the pain to go away and continued to sound like an injured bird.

"I try not to be as much of a grudge-holder as I once was," I said. "But I decided to make an exception for the two of you."

I tapped Deke's broken nose with the crowbar and then he was on his back again, both hands pressed to his face.

I threw the crowbar in the general direction of the woods, then backed away from them until I got to the main house, finally headed for the guard shack.

If Bobby and Deke were still willing to try me at this point, even in their current conditions, at least I was well armed this time, and feeling almost as bold as Sir Lancelot having stormed the castle, if with a much thicker neck.

TWENTY-TWO

I didn't call Vic Hale's lawyer directly, but did the next best thing, knowing full well that Bill Jones had once worked for Tony Marcus and likely still did. I reached out to Tony once back in my office, telling him I needed to call in the favor he owed me.

"Don't owe you shit," Tony Marcus said. "After the way I helped you out, out the goodness of my heart, after Rita got shot, if anybody owes anybody anything, it's you owes me."

"We need to stop keeping score this way," I said. "It makes our relationship seem so crass."

"Tell me what you want," he said. "I got a real business to run, unlike you."

"I would like you to set up a meeting with Bill Jones," I said.

"Set it up yourself," Tony said. "What am I, your personal assistant?"

"Just set up the meeting," I said, "and then my charm will take it from there."

"Shee-*it*," he said. "Your charm couldn't get you from my door to my damn desk."

"Nevertheless," I said pleasantly.

"What's in it for me?" he said.

"Favor to be named later," I said.

He said he'd call me back. With Tony Marcus that could mean fifteen minutes, or the fifteenth of Never. It turned out to be the former this time.

"Meet Bill and me in an hour," he said. "Courtyard Tea Room at the Library. Let's go scare us some white folks."

"I assume you're not including me in a race-based statement like that," I said.

"You'll probably scare them least as much as a couple of brothers," he said. "They'll probably be wondering when the Tea Room hired a fucking bouncer."

I discovered while waiting to go meet Tony that there still had not yet been a formal announcement of Ricardo Baez's death on the *Libertad* website. The story about an unidentified male body being found earlier today at Savin Hill Beach was a small, three-paragraph item on *The Globe*'s website. I checked out Baez's public posts on Instagram, found nothing remarkable or out of the ordinary there. It was the same on Twitter, which I refused to call X, simply on principle, or use much any longer. No posts there for the past three days, same as Instagram. I tried, and failed, to find any presence for him at TikTok.

So I sat at my desk and listened to some of his original podcast with Daniel Lopez, along with clips from a few others. And learned, not really to my surprise, that the young man had been a pro. He was a revolutionary, too, the kind who could see only one side of an issue, in this case immigration, legal or otherwise, his own rhetoric having become more heated as things had gotten so much worse for his people over the last year. It hardly made *him* appear remarkable or out of the ordinary, not in this world, where so much of the population, on social media especially, lined up pretty much the same way, no matter which side of a particular issue they were on:

I'm right, you're an idiot.

His message, just from the snippets of podcasts to which I listened, and from his commentary, was both proud and consistent, which meant consistently fierce.

"We will," he said and wrote, "return this country to a time and place when immigrants could live their lives without having to apologize for it, and not spend their time waiting for the knock on the door in the middle of the night."

I finally closed my laptop before it was time to walk over to the Boston Public Library on Boylston, right across from where they blew up the finish line at the Boston Marathon that time, and sat at my desk for what felt like a long time in the sad, heavy silence of my office, somehow still full of what had been the passionate presence of Ricardo Baez.

Out loud I said, "Now I've got a client."

TWENTY-THREE

The elegant and spacious room was all soft colors in the soft afternoon light, mostly beige and white, from the walls to the tablecloths.

"A beautiful thing, two brothers in here, even if Bill here got that lighter-type mocha shade going for him," Tony Marcus said. "We look as out of place as Jackie Robinson must've looked to white folk when he first got to the big leagues."

"It's often said that the contrast of black and white in art can be both serious and playful at the same time," I said.

Tony turned to Bill Jones, seated to his left. "Get used to it," he said. "Sometimes he only stops talking his shit long enough to catch his breath."

"Oh, I'm well aware," Jones said. "Amazing our paths haven't crossed over the years."

"Your loss," I said.

Tony snorted.

Jones's skin color reminded me of Derek Jeter's, as if one of his parents had been white, too. He was much more compact, and slender as a stir stick. He wore a light gray suit whose jacket fit him in a way my jackets never fit me, starting with the blazer I had worn to the Courtyard Tea Room. White shirt. Mint-green tie, the knot thick but not too thick. Pocket square a shade of green just slightly darker than the tie. Understated diamond cuff links, but diamonds without question. You hung around Susan Silverman as long as I had, you knew the real things when you saw them.

Tony had put on more weight since I'd seen him last. It made him look soft, even though I knew he was the opposite of that. He wore a royal-blue suit today, white shirt, red power tie. He'd had the grace to leave his own two body men, Ty-Bop and Junior, outside, presumably so no one would call the cops.

"Nice outfit," I said to Tony. "You running for office?"

"No point when you already king," he said.

If we hadn't reached maximum occupancy for high tea yet, we were certainly getting there. The crowd in the room generally looked older than the Longwood Cricket Club.

"I really have heard a lot about you, Mr. Spenser," Jones said.

"From Tony?" I said. "Or a credible source?"

"Mostly what I told him is that you're not nearly as tough as you think you are," Tony said.

"Nothing is impossible if to do that thing you're able," I said.

"Rest my case on the talking shit," Tony said to Bill Jones.

We had been offered our choice from a vintage book that looked as if it had been pulled from a library shelf. Loose-leaf tea, mostly, with options that included black, oolong, green, herbal. I went with the Blue Flower Earl Grey blend, just because it was the only brand I recognized, and thinking it would be gauche to ask one of the waiters to run across to the Dunkin' on Boylston and pick up a large to-go cup, milk and two sugars. Jones ordered what I ordered.

Tony said he'd go with oolong.

He pronounced it "ooooo long," stretching out the first part.

"Rhymes with *too long*," Tony said. "Obvious reasons."

I turned to Bill Jones. "As subtle as ever."

Jones said, "You should have known him before he started smoothing out the rough edges."

"I thought it was prison did that," I said.

"Fuck you," Tony said.

"If you say that too loudly here," I said, "you'll end up back in the joint."

When our tea had been delivered, Bill Jones said, "So how exactly can I help you?" He smiled. "Or not."

I took him through everything that had happened since Rita had brought Daniel Lopez to my office, all the way through my visit to Vic Hale's studio.

"I'm aware of most of this," he said. His voice was deep and soothing, like he's the one who would have made a good on-air host. "But at the same time unaware of why you think I can possibly help you."

He smiled again. It was as soothing as his voice. As if he were trying to be helpful, even though we both knew he wasn't.

"Man makes a solid point," Tony Marcus said.

I turned to face Jones more fully.

"I am aware that the money currently on the table for Vic Hale is what is described these days as being generational money," I said. "I am likewise aware that the people who stand to profit the most are Vic himself, his lawyer-slash-agent, and the owner of the podcast company, who has already gotten rich off Vic and obviously feels he is about to get a lot richer." I shrugged. "Just making conversation here, of course."

"I'm sorry," Jones said. "Was there a question in there?"

"Here's one, just to break the ice," I said. "Could a sharp guy like you actually have been enough of a slow thinker, just in a bad moment, to send a couple bangers after someone like me?"

Slow thinker made his eyes widen, if only slightly.

Then he nodded, the smile having disappeared.

"You mean the slow thinker about to make so much money on this deal he could buy a small-timer like you and then sell him for parts?" he said. "Just making conversation myself, of course."

"Of course," I said.

He sipped some of his tea.

"I'm telling you straight up that I didn't send anybody after you," Jones said. "But had it been me? You need to know that you would have walked away with more than a tap on the knee. Provided you could have walked away at all."

"See why we boys?" Tony Marcus said.

"I didn't send them," Jones said. "Might have been my style at another time in my life, and my career, but no longer."

"Whole truth and almost nothing but," Tony said.

"Additionally," Jones said, "I know nothing at all about the unfortunate death of this reporter, something I hadn't even heard about until you broke the news to Todd Jakes and Vic this morning."

He took his cloth napkin from his lap, touched the corners of his mouth with it, put it back, as if showing off some Tea Room moves for the rest of the clientele.

"Noted," I said.

"Note this as well," Jones continued. "You have at least given me the opportunity to deliver the same message that Bobby and Deke did, if clumsily. Leave this alone going forward, and leave my client alone."

He let that settle. Tony let it settle. So did I. There was the hush of conversation all around us, and soft chamber music still playing over the sound system. *Here I am,* I thought, *in the middle of this gilded-age room, with a couple thugs,* no matter how well appointed they were.

"No," I said finally.

Jones's eyes widened again, almost as imperceptibly as before.

"No?" he said, turning it into a question.

"Despite our elegant surroundings," I continued, "and despite the way I admonished Tony for his language before, what I really meant to say was 'Fuck, no.'"

"Listen to what the man just told you, Spenser," Tony said.

It came out "Spens-ah," as it so often did with him.

"You ain't the shark here, even though you think you are," Tony Marcus said. "Despite your build, you just a small fish who could get ate you don't watch yourself."

"Is that you giving me free advice, or your lawyer?" I said.

"No such thing as a free tea," Bill Jones said.

"Ain't that the truth," I said, "and almost nothing but."

I stood.

Jones looked up at me. He hadn't raised his voice yet, and didn't now.

"You don't want to be on the wrong side of this," he said.

"Not like I haven't been there before," I said.

I walked out of the room, wondering if the other patrons did think the Tea Room had hired a bouncer.

TWENTY-FOUR

Rita said that for the time being, she wanted us to keep our circle as tight as possible before we decided how to proceed. So she asked for me to meet her and Daniel Lopez at her place on Joy Street. I told her I was bringing Hawk with me, just because there was no circle that included me that shouldn't include him, whether he liked it or not.

"Goody," Rita said. "Will there be cake, too?"

Hawk had told me he could walk to Rita's, as his new friend Emma lived just a few blocks away, over on Acorn.

"Wow, Beacon Hill for Miss Emma," I'd said to him. "The fitness thing is obviously working for her."

"You mean at her club, or with her and me?" Hawk said.

"Feel the burn," I said.

"Nobody says that no more, Father Time," he said.

An hour later we were all seated around Rita's living room. Even though it was late afternoon, I asked if I could maybe have a cup of coffee, even having just come from the Courtyard Tea Room and high tea with Tony Marcus and Bill Jones.

"You know where everything is," she said, gesturing impatiently toward her kitchen. "What am I, the maid?"

I saw Hawk smile. "I love you," he said to her.

"Talk, talk, talk," she said. "Just like the big lug."

"Was she this snippy after she got shot? I can't recall," I said to Hawk.

"More," he said. "Soon as the anesthesia wore off."

Daniel Lopez was the one who looked as if he hadn't slept, as if he'd just gotten off a red-eye, unshaven and distracted despite the subject matter at hand and almost in a mild state of shock. Or perhaps not so mild. Every few minutes, as if talking to himself more than to Rita or Hawk or me, he would say, "I still can't believe this happened."

To me directly he finally said, "You really believe Ricardo is dead because of me?"

"You and Vic Hale," I said.

"And your mother and the whole damn thing," Rita said.

"It's the only possible connection to make here," I said.

I studied the young man more closely. Henry Cimoli had always told me, and Hawk, that most boxers could hit, just some better and harder and smarter than others; they wouldn't step into a ring if they couldn't. But he said you found out a lot more about a fighter after he'd *been* hit. Daniel Lopez, thinking he was about to start a whole new life for himself at Harvard Law, had been hit when his mother died in a random and violent way. Now a different version of that had happened to a friend, a thousand miles from his home. I did imagine him as a fighter suddenly, even as he sat across from me in one of Rita's antique chairs, trying to get himself to one knee, but not close to being all the way up.

"Could he have been working on something else that might have put a target on his back?" Daniel said. He closed his eyes. "Or on his chest?"

"It seems unlikely," I said. "The way it seems unlikely that this was the kind of robbery that ended your mother's life."

"Yeah," Daniel said. "I hear you. Ricardo used to joke that his only current client was me." Closed his eyes again, longer this time. "I know he thought of me as a friend. I was obviously a subject for him. But that's what he liked to call me. His client."

"Defending your life," I said. "And your mother's even after she was gone."

Not for the first time today did I get the feeling that Daniel Lopez, as strong as he so clearly wanted to appear in front of us, as tough, might be about to cry. I wondered if perhaps he'd thought himself to be cried out after the death of his mother. Or maybe he had mourned the loss of the only family he'd ever had another way.

"I got sick after Rita called to tell me about Ricardo," he said. "Like, literally."

"We're all sick about this," Rita said. "It's why, going forward, we need to come up with a plan now that the stakes have changed."

"We need to get justice for Ricardo is what we need!" Daniel Lopez snapped, the words hissing out of him like steam.

We all let that settle before Hawk was the one who spoke next.

"People always talk like that, after somebody dies who shouldn't've," he said. "Except even if you do get it sometimes, justice, I'm talking about, the person you wanted it for still dead."

Daniel turned to him. "So then what are we talking about here, revenge?" he asked.

"Uh-huh," Hawk said. "Served cold."

"Cold service," I said.

"Uh-huh," Hawk said again.

I had been waiting to tell them about my visit to Vic Hale's studio, but did now, and about my conversation with Tony and Bill Jones at the Public Library.

"So you're saying that somebody on their side might have killed Ricardo or had him killed because of some *podcast* deal?" Daniel said. He made the sign of the cross. "*Santa Madre de Dios.* Holy Mother of God. So both *my* mother and my friend might have been killed over money?"

"Just a lot more money on the table now than what your mom took out of that ATM that day," I said.

"Makes the world go 'round, money like we're talking about here," Hawk said. "Till it don't."

Rita said, "Okay, how long before Frank Belson figures out why Ricardo was up here and what he was working on, and gets up in everybody's grills, as you boys like to say?"

I said to Daniel, "How many people at *Libertad* knew that Ricardo was in Boston, and why he was?"

"Maybe not anyone, actually," he said. "I asked him one time who his editor was and he said, 'Me.'"

"Rita and I will be able to hold off the cops," I said, "but only until we can't."

"Speak for yourself," Rita said, giving a quick toss of her hair. Sometimes I wondered if she even knew she was doing it.

She was dressed in tight black exercise clothes, because either she'd just worked out or she was just showing off. Being a guy, and even knowing I could once again be called out as Father Time for objectifying a woman as beautiful as Rita, it had already occurred to me that her exercise clothes fit in a way that made my heart feel as if it had wings.

Only as a friend, of course.

"Belson will come after me hard, and maybe tag team with Martin Quirk if he thinks I'm stonewalling him," I said to Rita.

"Which you already are," she said.

"Who's Martin Quirk?" Daniel asked.

"Think of him as the Rita of cops," I said. "Or what a cop would be like if he had the strength of ten, as I do."

"Haw," Hawk said.

"But until such time," I said, "we need to find a way to keep Daniel safe."

"You really think that's necessary?" he asked.

"You know everything that Ricardo knew," I said. "And probably more. And what he knew almost certainly got him killed. And is still a potential and massive threat to Vic Hale."

"I got a place we can stash him," Hawk said. He grinned at me. "One I ain't even told you about."

"And you think you know somebody," I said.

"I can put him there when I can't watch him," Hawk added, "and know that when I'm *not* watching him, he be safe."

"That's very generous of you, Hawk," Rita said. "And yet another reason why I love *you*."

"'Course you do," he said.

Then he was addressing all of us. "One way or another, that kid is dead because of Vic Hale," he said. "Him or somebody in his own damn circle."

Hawk turned to Daniel. "And whether it turns out that he's your blood or not," he said, "you need to know something."

"What?" Daniel said.

"I hate that motherfucker," Hawk said.

TWENTY-FIVE

There were so many photographs of jacked-up and bronzed-up and probably juiced-up pro wrestlers on the walls of Woody Giles's office that I worried that one of them might jump down and try to body-slam me to the canvas.

"Like the décor?" Giles said after I had taken a seat across from a desk as big as a wrestling ring, watching me as my eyes surveyed the pictures.

"I'm sure they all came by those physiques with a good diet and exercise program," I said. "And getting the proper amount of rest."

"Hey, who gives a shit!" Giles said in a booming voice. "They're not trying to get into the Baseball Hall of Fame, are they?"

There was a loud, in-your-face quality to him, like he was in training to be the next Vince McMahon, king of the wrestling promoters, as if McMahon were some kind of training film for the character that Giles himself fancied himself playing. Brushed-back steel-gray hair, too much tan of his own, too many muscles of his own trying to bust out of a lemon-colored sports jacket, all that in-your-face volume. He was wearing one of those oversized and diamond-studded rings, the kind you got for winning the Super Bowl, on his right hand, brighter than the North Star.

"So how can you help me?" Giles said.

"I'm sorry," I said. "Isn't it supposed to be the other way around?"

"Not in this office it's not," he said. "And not at these prices. Why do you think I call this company Brass Ones?"

"It's like somebody said once, I forget who," I said. "We hold these truths to be self-evident."

"You sound like Vic," he said. "What's coming next, the fucking Pledge of Allegiance?"

"Yeah, that's Vic and me," I said. "Our country, love it or leave it. Just don't try to get into it, asshole."

Giles smiled. "But what do you *really* think of our boy?"

"Not gonna lie," I said. "Up until lately, I haven't much thought of him."

"I know your girlfriend, by the way," Giles said.

"I prefer to think of Dr. Silverman as the girl of my dreams," I said.

He barked out a laugh. "Not just you, buddy."

I smiled now. "Not your buddy," I said.

"Let me repeat then: How can you help me?"

"Somebody sent a couple of your goons to brace me the other day," I said. "Would that be a good place to start?"

"I don't think they'd appreciate being called goons," he said. "And from what I hear, you braced them back pretty good, first chance you got."

"One does what one can," I said.

"Just so you know, they want to have another go at you, first chance they get," Giles said. "Climb back into the ring, so to speak."

"Please tell them that nothing good could come of that. Or, better yet, I can have a friend of mine pass along that advice if you tell me where to find them and save me the trouble."

"You referring to Hawk?" Giles asked.

"I am."

"I always thought he would have been great for WWE," Giles said, sounding almost wistful.

"So did you send Bobby and Deke to pay me a visit?" I said.

"Hale, yeah," he said.

Giles kept going from there, as if he'd been waiting for a chance to get himself even more revved up than he normally was, and way over the speed limit. Even still seated behind his big-guy desk, meaty hands folded in front of him, light reflecting off the big ring, it was as if he had the floor now, and the microphone, getting ready to introduce Whatever Night of the Week It Was Raw. I was already fighting the temptation to tell him that I was right here, and could hear him.

"Consider that visit they paid you to be what we like to call in the business a soft rollout," he said.

"Tell the soft part to my knee," I said.

"Deke said it wasn't much more than a love tap."

"Somewhat like the love tap from me that broke his nose," I said.

"Listen, they were just there to deliver a message, clumsy or not," Giles said. "And fact is, they did."

"Did you really think that was going to be enough to make me walk away?" I said. "Even your wrestling scripts aren't that dumb, which, even you'd have admit, is saying a mouthful."

He shrugged. "The script was for us to eventually have a frank and earnest conversation like the one we're having right now," Woody Giles said.

"I'll be Frank," I said with a shrug. "You be Earnest."

"I heard you had a smart mouth on you."

"You could have just called me and saved us both a lot of trouble," I said.

"Whatever," he said. "One way or another, the real message you needed to get, from me, is that I'm not jacking around here. Or looking to get jacked around. So I'm the one telling you, straight up, as Vic likes to say, that you need to stay the hell out of my way on a deal with Vic that could be part of an even bigger deal just up the road."

"A reporter is dead," I said. "Much bigger deal."

"None of us on our side had anything to do with that," Giles said. "You got my word."

He saw me grinning at him.

"What?" he asked.

"It just occurred to me that you were being serious."

He leaned forward just slightly and squinted at me then, as if trying to bring me back into focus after he'd lost me for a second. Put one of the meaty hands to his chin and rubbed it, the ring sparkling all over again, and almost more brilliantly than before, as he did. Maybe he was just squinting at the reflection from it.

"These deals are to die for," he said. "But not to kill over."

"I'm curious about something else now," I said. "What's this bigger deal to which you just referred?"

"Let's just say that once I keep Vic in the fold, I might have a guy waiting just offstage who can do for Brass Ones what Endeavor did for WWE back in the day, when they bought a little more than half of the pie and made a lot of people rich, including yours truly." He smiled again. "And I can't tell you how much I love pie," he said.

I looked past him and over one of his shoulders, to a picture of Giles standing between Vince McMahon and another geeked-up wrestler I had no chance at identifying. Over his other shoulder was an oversized blowup of the *Boston* magazine cover featuring him and Hale and Todd Jakes and Bill Jones.

All Hale.

"A young reporter is dead, Woody," I said.

He said, "Not *my* story, just because there is no story involving Vic or me or any of our people."

I leaned forward slightly now, put my elbows on my knees, and looked at him as if he were suddenly the most interesting man in the world.

"What happens to your deal, or deals, if it comes out that the son of a migrant mother has Vic Hale for a father?" I said.

He was still trying to look tough in the moment. Just not nearly as tough as he had been.

"It won't," Giles said finally. "Because he's not Vic's son. So *end* of story."

"Or not," I said.

"Go ahead and take your best shot," he said. "And tell the kid to take his best shot. But if he does and misses, all he's really doing is opening himself up to a world of hurt. You know what they say about coming to kill the king."

"Now you're sending a message to him?" I said.

"Listen," Giles said. "I obviously come out of what people still call pro rassling. And in that world, the story is always the same. Good guys and bad guys. Heroes and villains. I know you've decided we're the villains here. But we're not. Maybe the kid wants Vic to be his father so much that he's convinced himself that he is. But I'm telling you for the last time, he's not the father." He paused and said, "You're in way over your head with this."

"Boy," I said, "if I had a nickel."

We both stood, almost in the same moment, and almost as if on cue.

"We're done here," he said.

"Not even close," I said.

He nodded, more to himself than to me. "You know when The Rock was still a wrestler," Giles said, "he had a lot of catch phrases, most of which he now owns the rights to, the smart SOB."

"Good to know."

"One of those catch phrases is something you and your young friend ought to keep in mind," he said. "'Know your role and shut your mouth.'"

"You first," I said, and left him standing there, surrounded by all his old rassling friends.

TWENTY-SIX

I had first met Andrew Crain when he was still the sixth-richest man in America, having gotten there by inventing a synthetic form of lithium as effective as the real thing, a product of his imagination that had reimagined the world of batteries forever. Bill Gates with alkali metal.

His wife at the time, Laura, a friend of Susan's, had hired me because she thought her husband was in trouble, but had no idea what kind, just that he was spinning out of control, and acting like his own worst enemy. Laura Crain was later murdered, and I eventually discovered that her husband's partner and best friend was Crain's worst enemy imaginable. In the process of unraveling all that, I had likewise discovered a dark secret from Crain's own past, one on which I ultimately let him slide, despite the fact that doing so challenged my own code, such as it is, and my very own belief system about good guys and bad guys and heroes and villains.

Crain had managed to survive all of that and so had I, even after getting myself shot. He had remarried by now, a woman named Claire Megill, who had once been his executive assistant and whose own life had been profoundly altered because of Crain's secret past, one she didn't learn the circumstances of until I did.

Now Crain was no longer the sixth-richest man in America, mostly because he'd spent a lot of time since I'd last seen him giving a lot of his fortune away, spending it on good causes around the world, most of which involved oppressed and abused women, at least partly because Claire Megill had been an abused woman, and more than once.

She and Crain were living in the same Brookline mansion where he'd been living when I'd first come into his life and he, because of his late wife, had come into mine. I knew from some of the stories about the two of them that they had turned his own gatehouse into the offices for his nonprofit, called Best Selves, financed by Andrew and largely run by Claire, which surprised me not even a little bit, as I was now convinced she could run everything except a small country. And perhaps even one of those.

I had made the relatively short drive there from Woody Giles's office in Brighton after Claire had told me now was a good time, and to come along.

"And, frankly," she said, "where you're concerned there is no bad time, not for my husband and certainly not for me."

When she asked if the matter I wished to discuss was urgent, she then didn't even give me the chance to answer, I could just hear her laughing to herself.

"I don't even know why I said that," she said. "You seem to operate in a perpetual state of urgency."

"I've been clean for a while, if that counts for anything," I said.

She laughed again. "We all knew it was never going to last."

Crain looked much as I remembered him, like the nerd who'd not only struck it rich, but who had gotten the girl. Twice. His hair might have been more fashionably cut and he might have been wearing more stylish eyeglasses than before. But he wore the same kind of long-sleeved polo shirt he'd been wearing the first night Susan and I had dined with him at Davio's on Arlington Street, and khakis and scuffed boat shoes. Still looked to be in very good shape, for a science guy.

The only thing I could see that had changed with Claire, somehow making her even lovelier, was how happy she appeared, now that after having loved Andrew Crain as she had, he finally loved her back.

We sat in the same living room where I had once prevented Crain from shooting Claire's former boyfriend.

They told me they had recently returned from another trip to Africa, where Claire said a third of the women had experienced some kind of physical or sexual violence.

"Just trying to make the world a little better, and a little safer, especially for women," Crain said.

"Not just a little," I said.

I watched as he took his wife's hand where they were sitting on their couch.

"One woman at a time," he said, and smiled at her.

"So what can we do for you?" Claire said. "Because if we can, you know we will, after everything you did for the two of us."

There was no reason not to tell them all of it at this point, and so I did tell them all of it. My first meeting with Rita and Daniel Lopez. My first meeting with Vic Hale. Then Ricardo Baez. My two encounters with Hale's producer. And my two with Bobby and Deke. Finally, my interaction with Woody Giles.

"You've been busy," Andrew Crain said.

"Man needs a hobby," I said.

"You still inhabit a dangerous world," Claire said. She smiled. "Urgently."

"Tell that to all those women in Africa," I said.

"So what can *we* do?" Crain said.

"At the end of my conversation with Giles," I said, "he mentioned that his current negotiation with Vic Hale might be folded into an even larger one at some point."

"I've encountered Giles a few times," Crain said. "Both Claire and I have. And it was clear as day that he and Vic Hale deserve each other, all the way down there at the bottom of the barrel."

I grinned. "A barrel getting more crowded by the day," I said.

"We're gonna need a bigger barrel," Claire said, smiling at me again.

"Anyway," I said, "I would never make the assumption that all rich guys know what's going on with other rich guys. But I'm of the growing feeling that whatever is going on with Giles and Hale and that partnership might have gotten this reporter killed. And further believe that the life of Daniel Lopez might also be in danger, whether it turns out he's Hale's son or not." I took in some air and let it out. "Basically, it would be useful for me to know what this bigger play might be for Giles, and who the additional player might be," I said.

"I'll make some calls, absolutely," Crain said. "As I said, we both owe you."

"You don't owe me a thing," I said. "I was the one trying to make your world a better place."

"You saved us, is what you did," Claire said.

"You saved each other," I said.

I told them that by now, no one had to show me out. Crain said he would get in touch with me if, and when, he knew something. I thanked him in advance and left.

I was in my apartment later, getting ready to head over to Cambridge for dinner with Susan and a sleepover, when Crain called, much sooner than I'd expected him to.

"I just found out something quite interesting from a Wall Street friend," he said, "though I'm not sure you're going to be pleased with the news."

I waited.

Crain said, "My Wall Street friend said that although everything sounds as if it's proceeding in almost complete secrecy, the lid as tight as it could possibly ever be, that the additional player in the game involving Vic Hale's future employment is a man named Mauricio Estrella."

I whistled softly then to myself, though it sounded much, much louder in the empty apartment.

"You know he's the man who owns Ricardo Baez's website, right?" I said.

"*Libertad*," Andrew Crain said.

"Oh, ho," I said.

TWENTY-SEVEN

Susan and I were eating at Pammy's, a relatively new trattoria between Harvard and Central Squares that had managed to achieve a sweet, neighborhood feel to go along with great food. I knew that one of the reasons it had a neighborhood feel was because the couple who owned it, Chris and Pam were their names, lived right up the street.

"So Daniel Lopez is safe?" Susan said.

"If Hawk says he is, then he is," I said.

"And just where is he safe, exactly?"

"Being an experienced sleuth, I posed the same question," I said. "And Hawk said that he was safe where he's safe."

"Well, then," Susan said, "asked and answered and let's eat."

My main course was gnocchi with lobster in a San Marzano sauce. Susan was having wild mushroom lasagna, most of which would eventually be mine, I was once again playing the long game with one of her entrées. I was drinking red wine, a Barbera. Susan, having thrown caution completely to the wind, had gone with a pink zinfandel.

As we ate—well, as I ate while she occasionally forked a tiny piece of her lasagna—I had been telling her what Andrew Crain had told me about Mauricio Estrella, and what I'd learned about Estrella and his background with the research I'd managed before making the drive across the river.

"Wouldn't this be a rather outrageous example of sleeping with the enemy if it's true?" Susan said.

"Not sleeping with the enemy," I said. "More humping it like a dog in heat."

"I'm glad the baby isn't around to hear a comment like that," she said.

"Just keeping it real, sister," I said.

"Ewwww," she said.

She was wearing a burgundy turtleneck and a pair of the looser jeans for women that had somehow caught the fashion curve without me having gotten a vote. She also wore a pair of Golden Goose sneakers, which I knew were stupidly expensive, even though they looked as if they'd come out of a remainder bin when she'd purchased them.

"Not to restate the obvious," Susan continued, "but this would mean that the wealthy and powerful Latino man who employed Ricardo Baez to fight the good fight on immigration might be about to partner with a sleazoid like Woody Giles and a much bigger sleazoid like Vic Hale?"

"Sleazoid?" I said. "Is that an expression used in cognitive behavioral therapy?"

"It is," she said. "You just have to read all the way until the end of the book to get to that chapter."

"By the way?" I said. "It's not a proven or even established fact that this deal is going to happen. Andrew says it's still the equivalent of the Wall Street dark web. And he told me no one is quite sure what Estrella's potential involvement might look like."

She sipped some of her pink drink.

"But this Estrella might be another big guy looking to double-dip, so to speak?" Susan said.

"Wouldn't be the first," I said.

She absently switched her plate with mine. Hers was still more than half full of lasagna. Mine looked as if it had just come out of the dishwasher. But she was fully engaged now on the subject of Mauricio Estrella, I could see it in her frown and eyes and, as often happened, could almost hear her thinking over the other voices in the room at Pammy's.

In all ways, the doctor was officially in.

"Let's play this out," she said.

"I was hoping we might," I said. "Or *you* might, to be more precise."

"Even the parts of this that would seem to make no sense?"

"Isn't that your specialty, trying to coax sanity out of madness?"

"One of many," she said, and then hit me with a smile.

"Wow, wow, wow," I said.

"What?"

"Just trying to regroup after a smile like that," I said.

"I've got better."

"Save one for later," I said. "And please proceed."

"Let's assume, for the sake of this conversation, that Mr. Estrella could be about to buy an interest, even a controlling one, in Vic Hale's parent company," she said. "Wouldn't it diminish the very brand he's absorbing—or even destroy that brand—if it comes out that Hale is the long-lost father of someone whose mother was a migrant?"

"It almost certainly would," I said.

"But his star reporter was up here on what we both think was a brave attempt to bring that very fact into the light," she said.

"You go, girl," I said, and drank some of my own wine.

"But on the other hand," she continued, "if all of that did come out before the deal got done, and Vic Hale's career somehow survived, the purchase price would likely go down, right?"

"Unless Vic got run out of business for being a bigger phony than some of those TV evangelists who used to get caught with their pants around their ankles at the motel," I said.

She smiled at me again. But she was right. I knew she had better. "At least you didn't talk about humping," Susan said.

She put a hand in the middle of the table and I covered it with my own. We were both quiet for the moment, as if all the ambient noise around us had suddenly dropped away.

Finally she said, "I'm glad you didn't walk away from this even though Hawk wanted you to."

"Never really an option," I said. "But you already knew that."

"So what's the next move?" Susan asked.

"I need to speak with Mauricio Estrella," I said.

"Are you planning to go to Miami?" she asked.

"As luck would have it," I said. "He's here."

TWENTY-EIGHT

I had broken down and hired an intern a few months ago, primarily to help me with the Internet, which could still make me feel almost as inadequate as when I would try to keep my passwords straight. Same church, different pew.

"You know what they say," I'd said to Susan at the time. "You can't say *Internet* without *intern*."

"No one says that," she'd said.

To be more accurate, Hawk had hired him for me, but not until the kid in question had tried to boost his Jaguar.

The young man's name was Cassius. He didn't tell either one of us his last name until he'd finally given it up one day in my office, when it was just Hawk and him and me, and we'd bullied him into a confession at long last.

"Moore," he'd said, then grinned. "Or less."

"How did someone as smart as you end up being a thief?" I said.

"I looked at Hawk's car more as a onetime investment opportunity," the kid said.

"And lived to tell about it," Hawk said.

Cassius said he was eighteen. Hawk said he'd never set eyes on the kid before he'd turned out to have big brass ones and was behind the wheel of the Jag in Louisburg Square until Hawk arrived on the scene and pulled him out.

Cassius was tall, handsome enough to be a male model, not bald the way Hawk was, choosing to rock a soft, modified Afro instead. When I'd pointed out to Hawk that Cassius was both younger *and* better-looking, he'd said, "Only brother prettier than me was the original Cassius. *Clay*."

But there had been something about Cassius Moore, despite the circumstances of their first meeting, some spark, that had made Hawk want to take him in and life-coach him. Because this was Hawk, there was never any thought of turning him in. They talked through the night and a kid that Hawk originally thought was both a dumbass and a wiseass turned out to be street-smart as a whip, much like Hawk had been at his age.

There was something else that created a connection for the two of them, from the beginning: Cassius was as guarded about his childhood—Cassius liked to say he came from the *Wire* section of Baltimore—as Hawk had always been, even with me. The most we'd gotten out of Cassius, even now, was that he'd never known his father, his mother had died when he was three, his grandmother had raised him until she died when he was thirteen, and he'd been on his own after that. The only job he'd held down for very long was at the Apple store in Towson, Maryland, after manufacturing a résumé. He'd spent only six months there, but turned it into a graduate course in all things computers. He was there when he wasn't inside a library.

So much of the rest of his growing-up years he kept to himself. I told Hawk we could find out more about Cassius Moore—if that's what his name really was—if we wanted to.

"Not if he don't want us to," Hawk said. "He be telling us the rest when he ready."

"You ever going to be ready to tell me all the parts of your own life story I still don't know?" I asked Hawk.

"Getting there," he said.

"Slowly," I said. "Very, very slowly."

"Need-to-know basis," Hawk said.

"Well, I do need to know," I said.

"Other than the shit you don't know and might never, I be pretty much an open book," he said.

"You ever steal a car?" I asked.

He looked at me, almost incredulously.

"*A* car?" Hawk said.

There was one other thing Hawk had in common with Cassius Moore, apart from their good looks and having been products of the street:

They were both smarter than AI.

Once Cassius had survived what Hawk called their come-to-Black-Jesus meeting behind the wheel of the Jag, he had decided to put the kid up in what he still insisted on calling an undisclosed location. And I started putting Cassius to work a few days a week. The rest of the time Hawk had arranged with a dean at Northeastern whom he had once dated for Cassius to start auditing classes there.

It hadn't taken long for me to become abundantly aware that Cassius, however old he really was and whatever his name really was and wherever he'd actually come from, could do everything with a laptop except get it to conduct the Boston Pops.

His only deal with Hawk was that he not break any laws, especially the ones that applied to hacking. Or boosting cars.

My deal with the kid was even more basic than that:

Find out fast what it would take me all day to find out, if then, and not give me a tutorial afterward about exactly how he'd found it out.

"If you do, I will be forced to pull my gun before telling you to get off my lawn," I said.

He'd shaken his head sadly.

"Just because you're being facetious," he said, "doesn't make the reference any less dated."

He also spoke English better than either Hawk or I did, at least when Hawk occasionally felt the urge for the King's English.

Cassius was behind my desk when I arrived at my office the next morning. As we were in the process of giving him a brand-new life, I could see no good reason in not giving him a key.

Next to his laptop, which he'd set up next to mine, was an unopened box of Dunkin' Donuts, looking to me as if it belonged under a Christmas tree with a bow around it.

"You've already got the gig," I said, pointing to the donuts. "You don't have to come bearing gifts."

"Just reading the room," he said. "*This* room."

"A dozen donuts is actually too big to be a gift, but too small to be a bribe," I said.

He slid the box across the desk and I was about to open it when he said, "Six Boston Kremes."

"Well," I said, "maybe not all *that* small to be a bribe."

Cassius seemed quite comfortable with me sitting in one of the client chairs, making no apparent move, not even a muscle twitch, to get out of my chair.

He was just back from being in Baltimore for a few days, taking care of what he'd called "personal business." I hadn't pressed him on what the business might be. Nor had Hawk. He'd texted me last night to tell me he was back, and I'd asked him to meet me here in the morning. I hadn't mentioned donuts. They were optional. But, as always, I was ever hopeful.

"I don't want you to mistake my generosity with donuts as sycophancy," he said.

"How come you never talk like Hawk even though we both know Hawk isn't really talking like Hawk?" I said.

I hadn't taken my first Boston Kreme out of the box yet. Before I did, I got up and Keurig-ed myself a cup of coffee, rejecting the coffee warmer-upper for the moment. Then I grabbed a small plate, came back to the desk, carefully selected my donut, sat back down in my client chair, and took my first bite, just not of the creamy part in the middle. I was building up to that.

"In answer to your question," he said, "my grandma was a rapper. In her case, that meant I'd get my knuckles rapped for bad grammar."

He got himself a plate and then picked out a donut of his own and took a big bite.

"Sometimes the cream is better when they've just come out of the oven," he said. "It is today."

"Spoken like an expert," I said.

He put his hands together and bowed. "Thank you, sensei," Cassius said. "So what do you need?"

When we'd spoken on the phone last night, I'd briefly caught him up on everything that had happened while he'd been away, doing whatever he'd done in Baltimore. It hadn't taken very long into our relationship to conclude that Hawk might be even more of an open book than this kid, who'd essentially become his ward, though none of us would ever actually describe the relationship that way.

Now I filled Cassius in on the rest of it, finally getting around to the possibility of a shared business interest between Woody Giles and Mauricio Estrella, or perhaps some side hustle for one or both of them.

When I started to explain more fully who Estrella was, beyond him owning *Libertad*, Cassius held up a hand to stop me.

"Would you like to know where Mr. Estrella went to high school in Guatemala City?" he said.

"Show-off," I said.

"But as you like to say, I come by it naturally."

"Basically, just see what you can find about this deal, if it really is a deal and might be about to go down," I said. "And any connection that might exist between Giles and Estrella because of it, or even apart from it. And any possible hidden agenda on either side."

He smiled. "So you want me to do me," he said.

"Word up," I said.

"Don't make me come over there," he said.

He closed his laptop, stuck it in his case, stuck the case in his backpack, and got up out of my chair.

"You can work here if you want," I said.

"I need to get back to my undisclosed location," he said.

"You know," I said, "you and Hawk aren't nearly as funny with that as you both seem to think you are."

"If you're even making that observation," he said, "that means that we are."

"Don't make me tell Susan," I said.

"If you must know, I'm having lunch with my new roommate," he said.

"You have a roommate?"

He smiled. "Daniel Lopez," he said.

"Wait," I said. "The safe house is *your* house?"

"It is, as it happens," he said. "And I'd be happy to tell you where it is, I really would, but Hawk won't let me."

"Sycophant," I said.

He grinned and shrugged. "Who are you more afraid of, Hawk or me?" I said.

"Hawk."

"You're fired."

"Hawk won't let you," he said.

Then he said: "Anything else before I go?"

"Estrella's office in Miami told me he's in Boston," I said. "I'd like to know where he's staying."

"A couple hundred yards from here," he said. "The Mansion suite at The Newbury."

"Okay," I said. "You're not fired."

From the doorway, he said, "He's registered under R. Menchú, not that you asked."

"Who's R. Menchu?"

"Rigoberta Menchú. The Guatemalan activist, a woman, who won the Nobel Peace Prize about thirty years ago."

"Show-off," I said again, but he'd already closed the door.

TWENTY-NINE

I walked across Berkeley and took a right, passing the side entrance to The Newbury, where Cassius said Mauricio Estrella, who might or might not be folding Vic Hale's podcast deal into a much larger one and perhaps selling out his own dead star podcaster in the process, was currently a guest.

For now, though, I kept going, crossing Arlington and entering the Public Garden before I got to Beacon, on my way to where I knew Frank Belson was waiting.

"Meet me at George Washington," Belson said on the phone a few minutes after Cassius had left my office.

"I could bring donuts," I said.

"Five minutes, hotshot," he said.

"It may take longer, Frank, as I have a bad knee," I said.

"Six, then," he said.

As I entered the park I saw that Belson had not come alone, and that Martin Quirk was with him.

Being a career tough guy, I resisted the impulse to make a run for it.

Martin Quirk was a legendary Boston cop, a commander now in the BPD, someone to whom the rank-and-file thought the commissioner reported and not the other way around. Quirk should have been retired by now. He had actually tried to retire a couple times, but kept coming back. I'd asked him once why retirement never seemed to take with him and Quirk had said, "Fuck fishing, does that answer your question?"

He wore a tweed sport jacket even on a summer day, a blue shirt, a blood-red tie that I'd once called a power color until he threatened to arrest me if I ever did it again. Dark gray dress pants, cordovan loafers that gleamed the way they always did with Martin Quirk.

"I feel as if I've been called to the principal's office," I said when I got to the statue. Then I looked up and pointed at Washington and said, "Just please don't either one of you embarrass me in front of the father of our country."

"He probably runs into a lot of mothers like you, just sitting there on his horse," Belson said.

"Least I didn't have to bring my dad with me," I said.

"Let's take a walk," Quirk said.

The three of us walked toward the Swan Boat lagoon, which to my mind wasn't just the centerpiece of the Public Garden, but sometimes felt like as much the centerpiece of downtown Boston as the old State House, with a lot more green around it.

"You know these boats were created by this guy, Robert Paget," I said. "Back at the end of the nineteenth century. He loved Wagner, and particularly loved that opera where the hero crosses a river in a boat drawn by swans."

"This may come as a shock to you," Quirk said, "but I'm in no mood for your usual line of crap today."

"I'm not in the mood for it any day," Belson said. "Just throwing that out there."

Quirk said, "Tell me what this dead reporter has to do with Vic Hale."

"Well," I said, "it appears the two of you have done some reporting of your own."

"Fancy that," Quirk said. "Now, talk to us before Frank achieves one of his lifelong dreams and clips you for obstructing a homicide investigation and locks you up in a place where even Rita Fiore can't find you."

"What I believe Commander Quirk is saying is that before you say something else you think is smart, don't," Belson added.

"How much do you know?" I said.

"Doesn't work that way," Quirk said. "You're here to tell us what *you* know. Because I presently have the PC all the way up my ass now that the mayor is up *his* ass because the reporter's boss is up here from Florida and threatening to call a press conference."

"And if you're wondering if we know about the other kid, that Daniel Lopez, we do," Belson said. "Not that we're able to locate him, which is another reason why the three of us are taking this leisurely stroll in the park."

"I can't locate him, either," I said.

"What did I just say about your usual load of crap?" Quirk said.

"All I know is that he's with Hawk," I said.

"Where?" Belson said.

"Hawk won't tell me," I said.

"Why, for fuck's sake?" Quirk said.

"Because he's Hawk?" I said.

We had angled left away from the Swan Boats and made the turn that took us past the Make Way for Ducklings statues. I decided it wasn't the right moment to tell them that the statues had been inspired by Robert McCloskey's book of the same name. Cassius Moore wasn't the only one who could read a damn room.

Maybe another time.

"Are you guys sure you want to risk getting sideways with Vic Hale?" I said. "He's not right about very much, as far as I can tell, but it did sound right when he told me how much cops love him, at a time when not everybody does."

"Now look at who's acting like an ace reporter," Quirk said. "Or maybe just Captain Obvious."

I took them through it then, leaving out the parts I knew they'd leave out if they were telling it to me. If they knew about Hale and Daniel Lopez, they were going to find out what I had and what they didn't, eventually. So I further told them about my two meetings with Vic Hale, and the ones I'd had with his not-so-merry men. How Hale had sworn up and down that he was not the father of his old housekeeper's son. How Daniel Lopez believed he was Hale's son and wasn't looking for money, just acknowledgment. And how Ricardo Baez had arrived in Boston on a far different mission, wanting to expose Hale as a public hypocrite because of the relationship he'd once had with Marisol.

I told them what I knew, or thought I knew, about Woody Giles and Mauricio Estrella, who had been Ricardo Baez's boss, and who might have his own agenda the way Baez had.

"And you say you got threatened before the reporter got aced," Belson said.

"I did," I said. "Though it probably won't shock either one of you that the threat didn't take."

"But the reporter was a threat," Quirk said.

"And if he was, Daniel Lopez is," I said.

"Doesn't mean that Hale or one of his guys had it done," Quirk said.

"Many things can be true at once," I said.

"No shit?" Quirk said. "I never heard that."

We had made our way back to George Washington by then.

"You're being even more truculent than usual today," I said to Quirk.

"Get bent," he said.

Quirk almost smiled then, but managed to bring himself back from the edge. "I always liked that expression, don't ask me why."

"Listen," I said. "Vic Hale gets hurt, and hurt badly, if Daniel Lopez can prove that Hale is his father. He loses value, and standing, with his audience if it's true, perhaps permanently. And if it *is* true and the kid *can* prove it, Hale suddenly isn't worth as much to his company, if he's still worth anything at all. Like somebody once said: A nick here, a nick there, and before you know it you're bleeding to death. But having said all that, it doesn't make sense that he'd have a reporter killed over something he says isn't even a thing."

"This kid, Baez, seems like he was a lot," Quirk said.

"He was," I said.

"Then we need to make this right for him," Quirk said.

Now I smiled. "We almost always do," I said. "It's why the three of us make such a good team."

"Not a team," Quirk said.

Belson said, "We are going to need to talk to Daniel Lopez."

"I will make it happen," I said. "We're not trying to bust balls here, we're just trying to keep him safe."

Quirk checked his watch, then looked at me. "Anything else you'd care to share?"

"Not without my attorney present," I said.

"Says the mother of our country," Belson said.

I walked with them to Quirk's car, which had suddenly appeared even though I hadn't seen either one of them pull out a phone while we walked. The driver got out and opened the back door on the park side of the car and they got in. I waited for the traffic to clear on Arlington before I started to cross.

"Spenser!"

I turned. Quirk had rolled down the window and leaned out.

"You gonna find out for sure if Hale is the father?" he said.

"First chance I get," I said.

Then I pointed one last time at George Washington on the other side of his car.

"I cannot tell a lie," I said.

THIRTY

Susan was having dinner with one of her old professors at Harvard, so the dining experience for Hawk and Daniel Lopez and me was at the Boston Burger Company on Boylston. I had invited Cassius, too, but he said he wanted to work.

"Still showing off," I said.

"You know what I like?" he said. "Having a J-O-B."

We had a table in the middle of the big, noisy room, underneath the bright BOSTON sign, one that provided a good view of the flat-screen TV hanging from it, one on which the Sox were playing at home against the Twins. And winning. We had been in first place since the first week of the season, but I knew it wouldn't last. Despite all the World Series my Sox had won over the last twenty years or so, old habits died hard. Especially mine.

"Good to have that BOSTON sign right over our heads," Hawk said, "so we don't get confused and think we in Cedar Rapids."

He looked around. "Tell me again why we're here," Hawk said.

"For the burgers," I said. "I assumed that the name of the place would give you a heads-up."

"People always tell you that you got to go here or go there, just got to, or you'll miss out on the best burger you'll ever have," he said. "Then you get there and find out that it's just another fucking cheeseburger."

"Are you going to be like this all evening?" I said to him.

He smiled. "Talk to me after my fucking cheeseburger," he said.

Daniel Lopez's face seemed to brighten, if only slightly, for the first time since he'd sat down.

"Has anyone ever mentioned that the two of you bicker like an old married couple?" he said.

"Often," Hawk said.

"If it means anything," I said, "we're not particularly proud of it."

"I'd dump his ass if it wasn't for the damn prenup," Hawk said.

The two of them ordered regulation cheeseburgers. I went with the Big Papi, in honor of David Ortiz. Smoked bacon, griddled hot dog, fried egg, guacamole, onions, lettuce, and what the menu described as "Papi sauce."

"All the basic food groups," I said when I read them the ingredients off the menu.

"'Cept blood thinners," Hawk said.

While we waited for food the waitress delivered three Green Head IPAs in frosted mugs. When we'd each taken a sip, Hawk said to Daniel, "You gonna ask him or you gonna leave it to me to tell him?"

"Hardly anything good ever comes after you put it like that," I said. "It's like when somebody says 'all due respect.'"

Daniel took in a lot of air, then let it out.

"I need to talk to Vic Hale myself, and more than ever," he said to me. "And I'd like for you to set it up."

Hawk turned to me and raised one eyebrow in a way I thought was both cool and artful, a look that had never been in my tool kit.

"I understand where you're coming from, I do," I said to Daniel. "But we're not doing this, kid. At least not yet."

"I'm not a kid," he said.

"Sorry," I said.

"It's my life," he said.

"And we want to keep it that way," I said.

The waitress arrived then with our burgers, so we briefly put the conversation on hold. I watched Daniel while he cut into his cheeseburger. He didn't look as tired tonight, or as shaken, as he had when I'd seen him after Ricardo's death. Mostly he just looked stubborn, even concentrating on his dinner at the moment.

He ate some of his burger, drank more beer, then said, "I don't need the two of you fighting my battles for me."

"Yeah," Hawk said quietly. "Yeah, you do. Whether you be thinking you do or not."

We all ate in silence for a few minutes. I was thinking that a burger combined with a hot dog was like combining baseball with sex, not that I thought it in my best interest to ever share that observation with Susan Silverman.

I drank some of my beer.

"We still need to keep you out of this for now," I said to Daniel. "I can tell you that Rita wouldn't want you anywhere near Hale or his people until we've got a much better handle on things than we do."

"So I report to the two of you and you report to her?" Daniel said. "Just trying to understand the chain of command."

Hawk turned to him. "You and Ricardo ended up in the middle of something and maybe he never thought it could get him dead, but it did, and now here we are. And if anybody else in this thing gonna end up dead, it ain't gonna be you, on account of that sure as shit ain't gonna happen on our watch."

Daniel drank more of his beer. He had been asked to show an ID when we'd ordered our drinks. It occurred to me as he showed his driver's license to a waitress who didn't look much older than he did how much had happened in this young man's life over the past few months, even though he was barely old enough to have a legal drink in the state of Massachusetts.

"I still don't see as how I need your permission, or Rita's, to have a face-to-face with the man who might turn out to be my father," he said. "How does that work?"

"Here's the problem," I said. "It's the same with a bad idea as it is with a good one. Once it gets inside your head, it can be impossible to get it out. But you confronting Hale at this point is a bad idea, even though you clearly think it isn't."

"Listen to the old man," Hawk said to Daniel. "When he right, he right. Happens sometimes twice the same day, like a stopped clock."

"Stopped clock," I said. "And you call me old."

"This all started because I came up here to Boston," Daniel said. "If anybody's going to see this through, it should be me."

"When the time comes," Hawk said.

"And when exactly will that be?"

"When we know, you know," Hawk said.

Daniel looked at Hawk, then at me.

"I'm in Boston looking for someone who might be my last living parent," he said. "But that doesn't mean I need the two of you to act as if you're my parents."

He turned back to Hawk then and said, "Not to play what-about, but aren't you busy enough doing that with Cassius? Parenting, I mean?"

Hawk stared at Daniel Lopez now, for what felt like a long, baleful time. I'd seen him train a look like that on other people before and was always surprised when he did that it didn't turn them into pillars of salt.

"Got enough bandwidth to do it for two," Hawk said finally.

"Okay," Daniel said. "*Okay*. But I'm not going to wait forever."

"Nor are we," I said.

Eventually I called for the check. The young waitress, pretty and tall and blond and young, brought it over. I was the one taking it from her, but she was looking at Hawk, smiling at him and saying, "I hope everything was to your satisfaction."

"Food was real good," Hawk said.

"Only the food?" she said.

I handed her my credit card and she reluctantly walked away.

"Speaking of kids," I said to Hawk, "in case you were getting any ideas."

"What do you mean, 'getting'?" Hawk said.

He had parked the Jaguar right in front, ignoring the hydrant there. It had reached the point where I wondered if he even saw them.

"So what's your next move?" Daniel asked me when we were all out on Boylston Street

"In the morning, I plan to annoy someone," I said.

"His best thing," Hawk said to Daniel.

"I even give references," I said.

THIRTY-ONE

The background Cassius provided on Mauricio Estrella highlighted the massive heart attack Estrella had suffered several years ago, and how much he had walked on a daily basis ever since.

"Wherever he is, Miami or back in Guatemala City or being a master of the universe somewhere else in the universe," Cassius said, "he walks three miles every morning, at a bare minimum. Said in this one interview that he considered walking to be his real heart medicine."

Cassius gave me a look that guys his age frequently gave to guys my age.

"Something you could consider," he said.

"Something you might want to consider?" I said. "How much you said you liked this J-O-B."

He grinned, nodded, continued. "And he likes to walk early. His morning constitutional is generally around seven, home or away."

Cassius had been with me in the office since six, like a kid turning in a term paper on the life and times of Mauricio Estrella, so much of it about the huge export business he'd built in Guatemala, dominated by coffee.

"Guatemala is one of the largest producers of coffee in the world," Cassius said.

"Who doesn't know that?" I said.

"You?" he said.

"Is the business legit?" I asked.

"Well," he said, "as legit as the coffee business can be in that country."

"Do tell."

"From everything I've read," Cassius continued, "when Estrella was moving up in the rankings, it was still like the Wild West down there. More then than now, I gather."

"So you're suggesting that some of his practices might have been more below board than above?"

Cassius said, "There's an old rap song, 'Survival of the Fittest.' Mobb Deep sang it originally, then they remixed it later on."

"Who doesn't know that?" I said.

He grinned again. "Probably on your playlist right after Ella Fitzgerald," he said. "Anyway, there's a lyric in the song about how there ain't no such thing as halfway crooks."

"You're saying that Estrella was some kind of criminal?"

"Not saying that with any sort of real proof, or any charges ever filed against him," he said. "Just something I've intuited from my research. When Estrella *was* coming up in the coffee business, it's a fact that only the fittest did survive. And not only did this guy survive, he flourished, while a lot of his main competitors just gradually fell away."

"Literally?"

"He didn't kill any of them, at least not that I could determine," Cassius said. He smiled. "But let's just say he managed to live quite nicely once they were out of the frame."

"And then arrived in the land of opportunity and commenced building a different kind of empire," I said. "One that might soon include Vic Hale, at least according to Andrew Crain."

Cassius said, "Gracious such a thing, as my grandmother used to say."

"But in the process, wouldn't that mean screwing his own brand by going against everything *Libertad* stands for?" I said.

"Here's something else I've intuited by researching this man hard," he said. "Old Guatemalan proverb: He is not someone to be fucked with."

"With whom to be fucked," I said.

"I know," he said. "I was just being colloquial."

"For which country?" I said.

"You have officially been warned on this one," Cassius said. "Though I'm assuming that will not deter you."

"It hardly ever has," I said, and then headed over to The Newbury, feeling heart strong and ready for my own morning constitutional.

Well, this one morning, anyway.

THIRTY-TWO

There were three of them coming out the side door of The Newbury, onto Newbury Street, Estrella and what were clearly two bodyguards. I was on the opposite side of the block, just down from the corner of Arlington and Newbury, near where the Burberry store was located until a few years ago.

Estrella was a small, trim man in an expensive-looking jogging suit, black, matching his running shoes. He wore a black Florida Marlins baseball cap. The bodyguards wore roomy-looking windbreakers, easier to hide the guns I assumed both of them were carrying. Unless they were stupid or arrogant or both, I assumed they had approved license-to-carry permits for Massachusetts.

I thought they all might head left out of the hotel and head for the Public Garden. But they turned right instead and headed down Newbury, the two bodyguards a few yards behind the boss.

I stayed a half-block behind all of them on the opposite side of the street, trying to blend in with the people already on their way to work.

On occasions when I would attend an afternoon game at Fenway, still a joy of my life, I liked walking down Newbury, staying on it after crossing Mass Ave until it took me over the Brookline Avenue Bridge and finally to Jersey, the street of dreams.

They might very well be taking the same route. Estrella was wearing the Marlins cap. Maybe it meant he was enough of a baseball fan to want to see Fenway, even from the outside. And I happened to know from experience that the distance would be about right for him, a mile and a half over to the ballpark or thereabouts, and a mile and a half back without detours.

Or maybe, if he went all the way down to Mass Ave, he could take a left there, head over to Huntington, and walk all the way down to the Fens, where I had been with Vic Hale and *his* two bodyguards.

Everybody had bodyguards except me.

I didn't count Hawk.

If I described him as a bodyguard, I was certain he'd pull his own gun, registered or unregistered, on me.

Estrella was walking at a brisk pace. I continued to hang back on my side of Newbury, deciding when and where to pick my spot, approach him in a nonthreatening way, at least nonthreatening for someone of my size and weight and with this much neck. There was no need for him to know, at least not this morning, and no reason to give him a heads-up that the one with whom not to fuck was me.

If anything, Estrella seemed to pick up the pace the farther down Newbury he got. It was a good thing, at least for me, the bodyguards being forced to keep up with him and not look back to see if, in the immortal words of Satchel Paige, something might be gaining on them.

Or, in this case, someone.

It was old Satch's advice for staying young at heart. It was just one more piece of what both Susan and Hawk called useless information from me. But another area where I refused to be deterred, mostly because it helped keep me young.

We were about a block away from Mass Ave when Estrella stopped, reached into his pocket for his phone, checked it, then leaned against the wall of the brownstone that housed the Starbucks on his side of Newbury. I could only assume that call was important enough for him to stop, if only briefly.

I made my move then, smiling my way across the street as I got closer to him.

"Excuse me, I don't usually do this," I said. "But aren't you Mauricio Estrella?"

When he realized I was addressing him, he looked at me in my black T-shirt and jeans and ancient Boston Braves cap as if I might be about to panhandle for coffee money.

Estrella gave an almost imperceptible nod to the bodyguards, who quickly positioned themselves between the boss and me, as if it were all part of a well-practiced drill.

I immediately raised my hands in mock surrender and said, "I don't mean to bother you, but I just wanted to thank you for what you and your people are doing with *Libertad*. Because, let's face it, we need that voice now more than ever."

Estrella said, "I have to call you back," then put away his phone.

To me he said, "Thank you for those very kind words."

"I was wondering if I could have one more word with you, actually," I said.

The taller and bulkier of the two bodyguards said, "You already had your word. Now, beat it."

"Well," I said, "you're clearly not cut out for Massachusetts Welcomes, are you?"

"The fuck are you talking about?" the bodyguard said.

"I'm sorry," Estrella said. "I've interrupted my walk long enough, and need to be going."

He nodded at the bodyguards again and took a few steps toward Mass Ave before I said, "But I bring you greetings from Vic Hale. And Woody Giles. And Bill Jones."

Estrella stopped then and did a slow, almost theatrical turn, finally facing me as if I were the camera.

"I thought I could join you on the rest of your walk and we could even discuss mergers and acquisitions and other fun stuff like that," I said.

I wasn't sure how he'd play it, or whether I was about to be rousted if the bodyguards were foolish enough to try me.

But now he crooked a finger at me, waving me forward, as if about to add me to his team.

"Come," he said.

I did as called.

Massachusetts Welcomes had nothing on me.

THIRTY-THREE

We headed back up Newbury Street after I had introduced myself.

"Just one name?" Estrella said.

"I'm a minimalist," I said.

"And a rather impertinent one," he said.

"I'm trying to quit," I said.

"It would have been just as easy for José and Hector to drag you into the nearest alley and teach you some manners," he said.

I smiled at him again. "Or not," I said.

"Just because you throw these names at me does not mean you know as much about my business as you think you do," he said. "Or anything about my business at all, for that matter."

"And yet here the two of us are, plowing headlong into the morning," I said.

"Perhaps I am just amused by you," I said. "And your odd way of speaking."

"Want to hear a joke?" I said.

"Do you think this conversation will continue if you continue to go out of your way to irritate me?" he asked.

I thought I might have seen a slight smile, unless there was too much sun in my eyes.

"Or you can continue to irritate me and wonder why you weren't looking behind you right before José and Hector put you on the sidewalk," he said. "That is another way of looking at things, of course."

"I just want information from you," I said.

"As do I from you," Estrella said. "But only to a point."

Now that we were side by side, I could see he wasn't much bigger than a jockey. But I could also see there was some rope to the man, the two bruisers behind us notwithstanding. Maybe I was even starting to have an insight, if a tiny one, into a man who had built one kind of empire in his native country and was now in the process of building a bigger and even more formidable one in the world of the media. Perhaps big enough to include Vic Hale.

"You have as long as it takes us to make it back to my hotel to say what you want to say," he said. "That's if you can keep up with my pace."

I grinned. "I could keep up with your pace if I was giving Hector a piggyback ride," I said. "But I digress."

"Un-digress," he said, "and quickly."

"Are you in Boston because of the death of Ricardo Baez?" I said. "Let's start there."

"You know of Ricardo?" he said.

"I knew *him*," I said. "I was actually helping him with a story on which he was working in Boston. Are you familiar with that story?"

"No," he said.

I gave a quick look down, trying to read his face and get a sense of whether or not he was telling the truth. But there was no change of expression. He was, without question, a tough out. Takes one to know one.

"I thought of Ricardo as my rogue cop," Estrella continued. "But in the best possible way, breaking stories and generating more traffic to our site than all of my other reporters and podcasters combined." He gave a shake of his head. "What happened to him, it is an unimaginable tragedy."

We were across from Stephanie's on Newbury, one of my favorite lunch spots.

"He was up here working with Daniel Lopez," I said. "You're obviously aware of how much he and Ricardo had been working together."

Estrella nodded. "I was briefly with Ricardo in our offices a couple weeks ago," he said, "and told him that young Daniel was a star in the making. Ricardo said he was perhaps about to become a much bigger star, but I did not press him on why." He blew out some air. "And now this tragedy," he continued. "I have assured Ricardo's parents that I will spare no expense in bringing his killer to justice."

"I believe the work he was doing with Daniel may have been a contributing factor in his death."

He slowed down just slightly as he looked up at me. "In what way?"

"Still trying to determine that," I said.

"With your detecting."

"We never close," I said.

"Still impertinent," he said.

"If only there were a way for me to monetize it," I said.

We were at Dartmouth, which meant I was almost out of time. And runway.

"But what does Ricardo's death have to do with Vic Hale?" he said.

"I'm trying to determine that as well," I said. "But what I have determined, from a quite credible source, is that you might be in negotiations to buy a show—or at least purchase shares in one—that represents everything *Libertad* despises. And that your own star podcaster despised. And I'm trying to understand why."

"Who is your source on such a ridiculous story?" he said.

"You know I'm not going to tell you that," I said. "But I know people who know people. Is it true?"

We stopped then to wait for traffic to pass on Berkeley. Almost to the end of the runway.

Now Estrella turned to face me.

"No," he said.

"My source indicated otherwise."

"Find a better one," he said. "And now, good day, Mr. Spenser. I can't say it was a pleasure meeting you, even if this has been an occasionally interesting conversation."

When we got to the other side of Berkeley, I stepped in front of him.

"These people of whom we have spoken might have had something to do with Ricardo's death," I said.

"I assume you have proof of this?" he said.

"Not yet," I said.

José and Hector now moved closer to me.

"I wouldn't," I said to them.

"Or what?" either Hector or José said.

"Or I will hurt you," I said.

To Estrella I said, "But if they did have something to do with his death, I can promise you I will find out, the way I will find out if you have been lying to me."

"Is that so?" he said.

"Kind of," I said.

"But at what cost?" he said softly.

He surprised me then by reaching out his hand. I shook it one more time. Then he smiled fully.

"For the time being, you would be well advised to get the fuck out of my way,"

I stepped aside. He and the bodyguards walked the rest of the short distance back to The Newbury. It occurred to me as I watched that the little guy wasn't nearly as fast as he seemed to think he was.

THIRTY-FOUR

When I returned to the office, Cassius and I shifted our attention away from Estrella and his potentially dirty deal and to Marisol Lopez's DNA test at the hospital in Milton that was long since closed, but still a touchstone of my investigation, such as it was.

Cassius had his primary laptop fired up, along with the backup he kept in my office. He had them side by side on his side of my desk, and occasionally one-finger-typed on both of them at once, almost like synchronized web surfing.

"If a hospital closes down," he said, "the personnel records and medical files generally become the property of the state medical board, or the relevant local health department."

"Can they be retrieved in a timely manner?" I said.

"The retrieving part is where it gets murky," he said. "These files can't be destroyed without going through proper legal channels. But technically, we're also talking about medical records that would by law belong to Daniel's mother. Which obviously does us no good whatsoever."

"But what about Daniel being the child in question?" I said. "He must have some kind of legal standing there."

"He would probably have to file a public records request, unless HIPAA hadn't already kicked his ass," Cassius said. "But there's no way of telling how long that process might take."

He was wearing a T-shirt that had an image of Malcolm Gladwell on the front, and skinny black jeans, and continued to shift his attention from one MacBook Pro to the other. His focus in moments like these was as intense as Susan Silverman's, which meant he could probably charge both laptops off himself if he could just find the right power cord.

"Forget the medical stuff for a minute," I said. "What about the personnel files from the hospital at that time? Is there some way for us to find out the doctor whom she might have seen there, or nurse or nurse practitioner or the lab person who might have conducted the test?"

He shook his head sadly, a look on his face that said I had once again let him down. I was convinced he'd learned it from Hawk.

I tried to distract him by walking over to the refrigerator and taking out a Boston Kreme I had saved. Then I sprinkled a little water on top and underneath it on a paper plate, put it in the microwave for a few seconds, and it was suddenly as fresh as when it had come out of the box. Trick of the trade.

"You're asking me to find out staffing at a hospital that closed down around the time I was born?" he asked. "Just trying to process the request here."

"Growing up in Wyoming," I said, "my father and my uncles used to tell me that the easy jobs generally don't pay very well."

"Neither does this one," Cassius said. "Just saying."

"Okay," I said, "let's go at this from a different direction. Might there be a way to at least find out if the place got the test result in-house or farmed them to an outside lab? It doesn't say on the form

Daniel showed us. It's actually impossible to even read the patient ID number."

I handed over my phone and managed to find the screenshot of the DNA results.

"Damn," Cassius said, "you're right."

"Try not to sound quite so surprised," I said.

He handed me back my phone and went back to tap-tap-tapping away. The only difference between the two MacBooks is that one had a bigger screen, I could never keep straight how many inches.

"Where do you want to go today?" I said.

"You just told me where you want me to go," he said.

"No, that was the catchphrase from an old Microsoft TV commercial," I said. "From back in the nineties."

"Pretty recent for you," he said.

The only sounds in the office now were the hum of Cassius's laptops and his fingers on the keys. I finally got around to reading *The Globe*. I fixed myself another cup of coffee. Occasionally I would hear him sigh, and look over to see him frowning, and then his fingers would be flying again, on one laptop or another or both.

He looked up finally and said, "Our best hope, as best I can determine, is somehow finding the personnel records from Stuart Medical, and pray that the place was fully digitized before it closed down. Then we can try to find out who was in charge of their prenatal testing, and say another prayer that the testing actually *was* done in-house."

"This might be an unknowable thing, but I'd really like to know why Marisol picked that particular place," I said. "It's not as if Milton is the next town over from Newton, which is where Hale was living even before he moved into Buckingham Palace, I checked."

Cassius looked up again. "Do we even know who requested the test?"

"Daniel has always been of the assumption that it had to be his mother," I said. "It certainly wasn't Hale. Unless he initiated another test somewhere else, and whose results he's also been denying ever since because he didn't agree with them."

"I know we've gone over this," Cassius said wearily. "But couldn't this all be solved by getting both Hale and Daniel to submit to a DNA test now?"

"What are you, some kind of Pollyanna?" I said.

"Who?" he said.

I made more coffee. I finished *The Globe.*

A few minutes later, Cassius looked up again.

"Can you give me a little more time?" he asked.

"Am I bothering you?"

"Little bit."

"You want me to leave, is that what you're saying?" I said.

"Maybe not in so many words," he said.

"It *is* my office," I said.

"Maybe you could go for a walk," he said.

"Already did that with Estrella."

"There must be someone else you can annoy," Cassius said.

I pondered that for a moment and then told him that as luck would have it, there was.

"How did you know?" I asked him as I got up from behind the desk.

"Law of averages," he said.

THIRTY-FIVE

Despite vast means, and despite presiding over a vast criminal operation that the Boston cops and the Feds had failed to dismantle despite their best efforts from what felt like the Boston Massacre until today, Tony Marcus still maintained his primary office at his South End restaurant, Buddy's Fox.

I had called Tony after being kicked out of my own office, knowing he usually rolled into Buddy's around noon, which it now was.

"Can't come to the phone right now, motherfucker," he said as soon as he answered. "But if you leave your number after the beep, I won't get back to you."

"You've always said that you were never too busy for me," I said.

"You day-drinking again?" he asked, before asking why I was bothering him.

"Vic Hale," I said.

"What now?" he said.

"At the risk of trying your patience," I said, "I've got a few more questions."

"Ain't no patience left for you to try," he said, but told me to come ahead.

The lunch crowd was just starting to form in the front part of the restaurant. I actually noticed a few white faces today, but just assumed these were people who had gotten lost. The rest of the clientele studied me as I walked toward the back room, as if I were wearing an evening gown and pearls.

In the past year, Tony had somehow managed to get a permit from the city to build out from the back of the place, into what had once been his own parking lot. I hadn't been here since the makeover but could see right away that not only had the previous cave décor brightened considerably, but the office was twice as big now, and perhaps even more than that.

Junior and Ty-Bop, still his two sidemen, had been posted at the door. Ty-Bop, a street kid from Blue Hill Avenue who'd moved up through the ranks because of his skills as a shooter, looked as he always had, skinny as a line you'd draw with a pen, with a teenager's face and eyes as old as the Harbor, wearing a Larry Bird No. 33 Celtics jersey, perhaps as a DEI statement. Junior was as big as ever, to the point where I wondered, as always, how he managed to get through the front door without greasing both frames. He wore a sweatshirt and a porkpie hat too small for his head, really the only thing in miniature about him.

I was going to tell him that Rocky Balboa wanted his hat back, but didn't want him to think my cultural references were as dated as everybody else seemed to.

"You're looking trimmer than the last time I saw you, Junior," I'd said as he showed me in. "The Ozempic thing working for you?"

"Fuck off," he said.

"As you wish," I said.

Tony was behind a desk even more spacious than his previous

desk, with a cup of tea in front of him, along with four iPhones and two landlines, as if they were all getting ready to choose up sides for a pickup game.

"Which one is the Bat Phone?" I asked as I sat down.

He gave me a familiar prison-yard stare. Since I'd played a large part in sending him to prison once, I chose not to share that reference with him, as timeless as I knew that one was.

"I'm just curious," he said. "All the times you've ever been here transacting with me, you notice there ain't ever been one fucking time when I acted as if I appreciated your sense of humor?"

"I've tried not to dwell on it," I said.

"Susan think you're funny?" he asked.

"A scream," I said.

"She the one humoring you," he said. "Now, get to it, I've got real transacting to do."

I said, "How significant is your stake in whatever kind of deal is about to go down with Hale and Brass Ones?"

He sipped some tea. His nails gleamed.

"Put it this way," he said. "It ain't *in*significant."

"I'm just trying to get a better sense of how motivated you are to see the deal come to fruition."

He smiled and nodded.

"Fruition," he said. "You can't just talk about the deal going down like normal people would?"

"Me talk pretty sometimes," I said.

"Why do you care if this is one more thing I got a piece of?" he asked.

"I know how invested Hale must be, and Woody Giles, and your man Bill Jones," I said. "I'm just trying to get a better sense of exactly how invested my friend Tony is."

He smiled again, only now it was his eyes that looked as old as the water a few blocks away.

"Not your friend," he said. "Not ever been. Not ever gonna be. You know when I'm gonna forget you helped put me away? When you dead."

"Or you are."

"After you, motherfucker," he said.

"You know," I said, "sometimes I stop by just to feel the love."

"That all you come here for?" he said.

"Mauricio Estrella," I said.

I saw his eyes change, as if suddenly adjusting to the light in his own office.

"What about him?" he said.

"You know him?"

"I know a lot of people," Tony said. "What about him?"

"Is he looking to get a piece of Vic Hale, too, despite Hale's politics?" I said.

And now Tony Marcus laughed, a full and foreign sound, as if at long last he did think I was funny.

"What the fuck do politics have to do with it when there's this kind of money on the goddamn table?" he said.

"One of Estrella's reporters died over this," I said, "maybe just for asking questions about the deal."

He reached into his desk drawer then and came out with one of his thin cigars, went through the process of lighting it and blowing a couple perfect smoke rings toward the ceiling of his new office, looking as pleased watching them float above him as he was making me wait.

Finally he said, "What makes you think he wasn't asking them questions about his own boss?"

THIRTY-SIX

That evening Hawk and Daniel joined Susan and me for dinner at Alibi on Charles Street, which had been the Charles Street Jail in a previous incarnation.

What was now the ground-floor bar had even once been the jail's drunk tank. The jail's original bluestone floors had been retained, along with brick cell walls. The doors and windows still featured prison-type bars. Homey.

Some of the walls were lined with old mug shots mixed in with celebrity photos. The whole place was now part of the Liberty Hotel.

"Think I mighta seen Sacco and Vanzetti I was walking in," Hawk said. "Weren't you one of their first calls after they got locked up here?"

"Ageism is a form of discrimination," I said.

"'Bout damn time," Hawk said.

Daniel looked at Susan.

"Are they always like this?" he asked.

"Even when I threaten to keep them after class," she said.

We were having drinks in the lounge before heading into the main dining room.

"I'm already announcing that I'm having spaghetti with cracklings and hot pepper," I said.

"Oh, goody," Susan said to Hawk. "I win the pool."

Susan, having decided to live a little tonight, was having an espresso martini. She had tasted one on a recent girls' night out, declared it yummy as chocolate milk, and had now ordered one of her own. I was drinking a regulation dirty martini with the Sicilian olives they stocked here. Hawk was drinking champagne, and Daniel a Harpoon Ale.

I had waited until the drinks had arrived at the table to tell them about my meetings today with Estrella and Tony Marcus. Daniel seemed far more interested in the walk-and-talk I'd had with Estrella.

"But he didn't admit that he might be trying to buy Mr. Hale's company, or at least buy into the deal, right?" he asked.

"But he also didn't deny it," I said, "which leads me to believe he could even be trying to buy the whole thing. It's like an old line I heard about George Steinbrenner when he was still running the Yankees and had a bunch of limited partners. One of them said that there was nothing more limited than being one of those with old George."

"Let the big dog eat," Hawk said.

"I don't want to sound less evolved than we all know I am," I said.

"Since when?" Hawk said.

"You didn't let me finish," I said.

"Ah know," he said.

"But I was thinking in terms of a much smaller dog," I continued, "and that in terms of Estrella's heritage . . ."

"Please stop talking now," Susan said.

"Okay," I said, "but only because you said 'please.'"

Hawk smiled. "He don't want you to treat him like a naughty boy," he said to Susan.

"Well, not yet," she said, somehow managing to wink at both of us.

We all drank our drinks. I liked this bar, and not just because of the look and feel and history of the place, along with the fun the owners had clearly brought to it.

"This makes no sense with Mr. Estrella," Daniel said finally. "Even before I knew Ricardo, I knew what a force for good *Libertad* was. They've been on the right side of the debate about immigration and who real Americans are, almost for as long as Vic Hale has been on the dark side."

"And now has more company than ever over there," Susan said.

Daniel leaned back in his chair, closed his eyes, opened them.

"Ricardo was the one leading the fight, at least as much as he could, against everything Vic Hale stands for," he said. "I'm not saying his voice would ever have been nearly as powerful as that, of course. But people were paying more and more attention to it, and to him. So why would his boss suddenly decide to switch sides?"

I reminded him what Tony Marcus had said about money.

"It was right before he told me to get out of his office before Junior threw me out," I said.

Hawk smiled again and drank champagne out of a flute tonight, having decided it would be unseemly at Alibi to drink out of the bottle.

"That's just Tony playing the hits," Hawk said.

"And he really suggested that Ricardo's boss might have had something to do with his death?" Daniel said.

"It has been my experience, over many years, that Mr. Marcus can be an extremely unreliable narrator," I said.

"Who *are* these men?" Daniel said, almost mournfully.

"It sounds as if they all deserve each other," Susan said.

"This is just one more reason why I need to talk to Vic Hale myself," Daniel said. "Hopefully before my law school classes begin."

"Listen," I said. "Vic Hale can absolutely be a world-class prick, and the face of everything Ricardo hated, and that you've come to hate as well. But it can also be true that he had nothing to do with his death."

"But he might have," Daniel said.

"Yup," I said. "One more thing for me to find out if I can. But I need to do that without putting your life in danger, even if I'm not progressing as quickly with this case as you'd like. Or I'd like, for that matter."

Susan turned to Daniel then. "If at the end of this you are unable to determine whether he's your father or not, will you be able to live with the not knowing?"

His voice suddenly sounded raw. *"I don't know,"* he said.

"May I ask something else?" she said.

"Of course," Daniel said.

"What do you see happening if he does in fact turn out to be your father?" she said. "You probably have thought about little else since you first discovered your mother's hidden belongings."

"I know this sounds naïve," he said. "But it's not just about that. There's a part of me thinking that if he really sees me, and really hears me, he might start to look at the world differently, no matter what the personal cost to him, and to his brand. Whether I'm his biological son or not."

Susan smiled brilliantly, raised her martini glass, and motioned for him to raise his beer.

"I'll drink to that," she said, and the two of them did while Hawk and I watched them have a moment.

I studied Daniel's face, still lit by her smile, and knew all over again why people were so comfortable telling her their secrets and dreams and fears and perhaps even their Social Security numbers.

She gestured with her glass at Hawk and me.

"These two men are the best I know," she said to Daniel. "They will settle these matters, the one between you and Vic Hale and the matter of your friend's murder, as only they can."

She paused and said, "You just have to continue to trust them."

"I do," Daniel said. "It's just that I feel as if I can be doing more to help."

There was nothing for me to do in the moment except finish my own martini, which I did.

"I really do need to meet with Vic Hale," Daniel said.

"And I understand why you want to, because I would, too," I said. "And even knowing you don't want to keep hearing this, but we're still not there."

Then I asked him to come by either the office or my apartment tomorrow, there were some things about his mother I wanted to discuss with him. He asked what and I said it was a longer conversation that could wait until tomorrow. For now, I was focusing on my spaghetti and cracklings.

"Forgot the hot peppers," Hawk said.

"Did not," I said.

I saw Daniel Lopez looking at me, just a slight smile playing across his lips.

"Rita Fiore said you can do anything," he said.

"Well, almost anything," Susan said.

"I believe she was referring to my professional skills," I said.

"As was I," Susan said.

THIRTY-SEVEN

Hawk had parked his Jaguar directly in front of Alibi. When we were all outside, he reached over and plucked the ticket that was underneath one of his wipers.

"Damn litterbugs," he said, and crumpled up the ticket and stuck it in the side pocket of a leather jacket that looked softer than a baby blanket.

Susan and I walked back to my apartment from Charles Street holding hands.

"That young man is in a lot of pain," she said, "though I'm not sure even he's aware just how much."

"I was thinking tonight that he'd be better off getting officially shrunk by you in your office, and not just from across a table in a restaurant," I said.

"What really concerns me," she said, "is that at the end of this case, there might be more pain awaiting him."

"Can't be worse than what he's experienced already with his mother and his friend," I said.

"The cumulative effect can be just as intense," she said, "and often just as debilitating."

We took a right on Beacon. It was a beautiful evening. I looked at Susan and in that moment felt a familiar happiness rise up out of the deepest part of myself.

"Penny for your thoughts," she said, turning to me.

"I thought we were getting rid of pennies," I said.

"I'm willing to go higher if I have to," she said.

"As the poet said, 'Speak to us of Beauty.'"

"Who dat?" she said.

"Gibran," I said.

"He lived in Boston, you know," she said.

"I do know that."

"Of course you do," she said.

We walked for a bit in silence then, across from the great evening quiet of the Public Garden, under a lovely quarter-moon.

Finally Susan said, "Sometimes I can hear you thinking." She smiled. "Even when you're not thinking about me."

"There are things I need to know before moving forward, and not just randomly," I said, "and not just about the pending deal of the century."

"Because you essentially feel as if you're working more than one case here," she said.

"I got Daniel and I got Vic Hale," I said. "I got Ricardo's murder. I got the aforementioned deal of the century. And I've got a DNA test conducted at a hospital that closed down when the second Bush was still president."

Susan said, "All of which may be connected."

"Or *some* of which may be connected," I said.

"Yikes," she said.

"And then throw in the event that started everything," I said. "Or restarted it."

"The murder of Daniel's mother," she said.

"Which also might be connected to the rest of it, and not just because it's what brought Daniel to Boston," I said. "And is probably connected to the rest of it, the more I think about it."

"You don't think it was random?" Susan said.

"You know my theory about coincidence," I said.

She smiled again. "By now even people you haven't yet met know that, snookums," she said.

We crossed Arlington.

"I need to know more about that DNA test," I said. "Did Marisol initiate it on her own? Did she have help?"

"And why did she pick a hospital in Milton if they were living in Newton at the time?" Susan said.

"I have asked that question myself, Doctor," I said.

I asked if she wanted to walk a little more.

"Aren't you concerned that the mood for sex might pass if we do?" she said.

I squeezed her hand and told her that if she was willing to risk it, so was I.

We made our way down the greenery that was the Commonwealth Avenue Mall until we came to a bench and sat down.

"Admit it," I said, "you missed the old neighborhood as much as I did."

"C'est impossible," she said.

"French?" I said.

"It is the language of love, after all," she said.

"I love you," I said.

"And I you, sailor," she said.

And kissed me, enthusiastically, like we were a couple high school kids making out, as if turning the middle of Back Bay into the backseat of a car.

The traffic in front of us was heading in the direction of Kenmore Square.

"So you think it *all* might be connected, then," Susan said.

"Yup," I said.

"Have you even suggested to Daniel that the same person who killed Ricardo might have killed his mother?"

"What I want to talk to him about tomorrow, among other things," I said. "But he's too smart for the thought not to have occurred to him."

I leaned back and looked up into the night sky. Somewhere from the east I heard a siren, and I could see the lights of a small jet banking over the Charles. And then I heard a night bird sing.

"Play this out," Susan said. "If she died because someone was worried about the secret of Daniel being Vic Hale's son coming into the light, why now, after more than twenty years?"

"TBD," I said.

"Did you actually just say that?"

"I know," I said. "LOL."

"So Daniel could be in real danger, and not just here," she said.

"Why do you think I've got him staying with Hawk?" I said. "And he will continue to stay with him until I've got a better handle on all of this. Or any kind of handle, for that matter."

She turned and looked up at me, her eyes bright. They got that way a lot, but more so when she was engaged fully in the subject being discussed, almost any subject, really, with the exception of sports.

"No matter how you look at this," she said, "everything runs through Vic Hale."

"No other way *to* look at it, brown eyes," I said.

"Does it worry you that in the end you may somehow end up

helping Vic Hale more than you help Daniel, if you somehow prove that Hale isn't the father?" she said.

"Facts are stubborn things, Suze," I said, "even when they're not the ones you seek."

"Have you seen any signs of humanity from the man?" she asked. "Even when he's been discussing the feelings he once had for Marisol?"

"Rarely," I said.

"Maybe the mask really has become the man," she said.

"Even if it has," I said, "he's still Tommy Hale's kid, I keep reminding myself of that."

"And you still owe Tommy Hale even though he's long since dead," she said.

"Gone from sight but forever held," I said. "Or something like that."

I put my arm around her and pulled her close and kissed her again, even more enthusiastically than before.

When we pulled back I said, "Is there any way of trading sex for you walking Pearl when we get back to the apartment?"

She smiled, even more brilliantly than before, which was saying plenty.

"Don't general managers in sports get fired for making trades like that?" she asked.

It was as I had long suspected, then.

She knew a lot more about sports than she let on.

THIRTY-EIGHT

Hale's producer, Todd Jakes, was waiting for me outside my office when I arrived in the morning, if not ambushing me the way I had ambushed him in his parking lot that day, at least surprising me. It was a little after eight, but I'd told Cassius to show up at nine today, knowing the kid was as punctual as the bells at the Old North Church on Sunday.

Jakes had his leather bag over his shoulder and was dressed as he had been before in my presence, and perhaps for every workday forever: V-neck sweater, white T-shirt showing just above the *V*, light-colored denim jeans tapered ever so slightly and fashionably at the bottom, white tennis shoes.

"I don't recall having ordered breakfast from Uber Eats," I said.

"Call it a spur-of-the-moment type thing," he said.

"Does your boss know you're here?" I said.

"He does not," Jakes said, "but thanks for asking."

When we were inside, I offered him coffee. He declined, saying he'd been at the Starbucks on the corner for the past hour, still trying to decide whether or not meeting me was a good idea.

I did make myself a cup of coffee, stirred in cream and sugar, sat down behind my desk, said, "So what's on the mind of Vic Hale's brain?"

"Clever," he said.

"I have my moments," I said. "You should see me at parties."

"Before I say what I came to say," Jakes said, "I have to trust you on this meeting never having happened."

"Depends on why it actually is happening," I said.

He tossed his bag on the floor, took out his phone, quickly checked it, put it back in his pocket.

"My backup phone," he said. "The one Vic can't track. I left that one in my office before I came over here."

"He does that?" I said. "Tracks you?"

"He likes to know where I am," Jakes said.

"What if he tries to reach you on the phone you left behind?" I said.

"I tell him I was out for a run," he said.

"You a runner?" I asked.

"When I need to be," he said and shrugged.

"So why *are* you here?" I said.

"To warn you," he said.

He said he would have that coffee now, black would be fine. I made him a cup and handed it to him and sat back down.

"Vic might not fire me if he knew I was here, but he would definitely not be a happy camper," he said. "Same with Woody Giles. Both of them are grading high on paranoia these days as they get closer to closing the deal."

I nodded. "There's a line from *Glengarry Glen Ross*, I forget which character said it," I said. "First prize is a Cadillac El Dorado. Second prize is a set of steak knives. Third prize is you're fired."

"You got it," he said. His hand was shaking a little as he brought the cup to his mouth. "Listen," he said. "I want this deal to go down as much as any of them, even though my cut, though quite substantial, will be small change compared to theirs." He nodded. "The boss has taken very good care of me for a very long time, and is about to take even better care."

Jakes shook his head suddenly, as if there were bees around it. "But I didn't sign on for anybody to get killed over it."

"Do you have evidence that Ricardo Baez was killed because he threatened the deal?" I said. "And not just in an existential way."

"Nothing else makes any sense to me whatsoever," he said, "even though if he somehow did manage to connect with Vic, he didn't go through me to do it."

"And everybody goes through you to get to Vic," I said.

He shrugged. "I'm just trying to connect dots here, basically," he said.

"Join the club," I said.

Then he looked around the office. "You got anything stronger than coffee?" he asked.

"Even at this hour?" I said.

"You know what they say," he said. "It's five o'clock somewhere."

I reached into the bottom drawer of my desk, came out with the bottle of Jameson I kept there even when it was five o'clock only in Pakistan. He handed me his mug, I poured some whiskey into it and handed it back, and watched him take a good swallow.

"Cheers," I said.

"Or not," he said sourly.

He sank back into my client's chair now, kneading the fashionable stubble on his chin.

"I know who Vic is," he said. "I frankly know who he is better than he does. Lately he's even been talking about signing this new contract, playing it out, and then walking away. And guess what? If he does, I'll be right out the door behind him, and into the rest of my life."

"So you're sick of politics that you told me are not your own?" I said.

"I'm just sick of being in the barrel, and every day being a fight to the finish until we get ready to do it all over again," he said. "End of the day, though? My only affiliation is to Vic, not to his politics. But what I'm seeing and hearing lately as everybody involved in this thing tries to shove Vic over the line like that tush push they use in football scares the shit out of me. And maybe ought to scare you." He drank some more of his own Irish whiskey. "Because from where I sit," he added, "your friend Tony Marcus isn't the only gangster at the table."

"You know of Tony Marcus's relationship to all this?" I said.

"Vic knows, too," Jakes said. "But chooses to look the other way."

"I assume the other gangster to whom you're referring is Mauricio Estrella," I said.

"You know about him?" Jakes said, looking surprised.

"I'm a trained investigator," I said.

"And it's not just Estrella to keep an eye on," Jakes said. "Woody Giles might be more gangster than any of them. Only with him it isn't rassling now. It's fucking real."

We both let that settle.

"You said you were here to warn me," I said. "Has there been some indication from one of the principals, or maybe all of them, that they might make a run at me next?"

"I know you can take care of yourself," he said. "I've done my own investigating about you, so I know you'll never be the one to walk away from a fight any more than Vic's old man did."

I waited.

"I'm frankly more concerned about Daniel Lopez," he said, "simply because the threat to Vic and to the deal obviously originated with him, even before what happened to Ricardo Baez happened."

"But you say you have no proof that knowledge of Daniel's, ah, circumstances is what got Baez killed?" I said.

"I don't," he said. "You have to trust me that if I did have any knowledge like that, I would have come to you. Or gone straight to the police, even if I would have been setting my career on fire by doing that."

"So what are you really telling me here?" I said.

"That the one who needs to walk away is Daniel, whether he's Vic's son or not," Jakes said. "Before he's the one who's next."

THIRTY-NINE

He started to get up out of the chair, as if that had been some kind of mic-drop comment, but I motioned for him to stay where he was.

"Happy hour isn't quite over," I said.

"I said what I came to say, and I need to get back to my office and then over to Vic's, he's expecting me," he said, "if he isn't already trying to reach me."

"Like the loyal employee that you are," I said.

"Is that supposed to be snark?" he said.

I shook my head sadly. "If you even have to ask," I said.

Then I said: "You are clearly under the assumption that I'm to take it on faith that your motives are pure here, for Daniel and for me, and perhaps even for yourself."

He'd picked up the leather bag, but dropped it again.

"Fuck, no, they're not," he said. "I do want this deal to go through, because it *is* life-changing money for me, the payday I've been waiting for my whole life. To-die-for money, as Vic likes to say. But I don't want anybody else to actually die over it, if that's really what happened here."

"Least you're being honest," I said. "Or as honest as someone in your world can be."

"Don't try to sugarcoat it," he said.

"Actually," I said, "that *was* sugarcoating it."

He looked down at his empty mug, rather forlornly, I thought, and despite the hour.

"Whether you want to believe me or not," Jakes said, "I came here today from a good place, because from everything I know, Daniel Lopez is coming to all of this from a good place. He just wants to know. It was different with me, so you know. I was adopted and never wanted to know my birth parents."

"Mind if I ask why?"

"I liked the ones I had," he said, "not the ones who gave me up."

Nothing to say to that, so I didn't.

"I just don't want anybody else to get hurt," he said, "and that includes me."

"And for the last time," I said, "you've got nothing concrete or credible that ties Vic or Giles or Estrella or anybody else to Baez getting shot to death."

"I swear I don't," he said. "But if somebody in it ordered it done . . ."

The rest of it just hung in the air like dust particles in the shafts of morning sunlight coming through my blinds.

"They'd be willing to do it again," I said.

"You said it, not me," Todd Jakes said. "Now are we done?"

"Almost," I said. "What do you know about Marisol's DNA test?"

"Just that there is one, according to Vic," he said. "The one you showed him. And that he refuses to believe it, as stubbornly as ever, and for a very long time. But then Vic wants the world to be what he wants the world to be, and if not, well, fuck you."

"You have any idea why she would have gone to a hospital in Milton instead of finding one closer to Newton?"

"Not a clue," he said.

"You obviously know about the money he kept sending," I said, "to a woman he steadfastly maintains is not the mother of his son."

"We still being honest?" he said.

"Well, I am," I said.

"The way Vic's career was starting to take off Marisol needed to go away, and I wasn't bashful about telling him that," he said. "Was it hush money? Yeah, as a practical matter it was. About the kid? In the end, Vic didn't want to know what he didn't want to know, except for this: how much any of this or all of this coming into the light could hurt him."

"Was the money his idea?"

"He always said it was his father's," Jakes said. "But I sure didn't discourage him."

"But now all this time later," I said, "we're all the way back to the beginning."

"Ain't it grand?" Jakes said.

I stood then.

"I'll be in touch," I said.

"I sincerely hope not," he said.

He stood, slung his bag over his shoulder, thanked me for the drink, and headed for the door.

"Todd?" I said.

He stopped, hand on the knob, and turned back to me.

"You better not have been lying to me," I said. "Just because I've got some gangster in me, too."

"That's what they're saying," he said, "all over town," and left.

FORTY

Rita and Daniel and I had a quick lunch at Rita's house. I picked up sandwiches for us at Cobblestones on Charles Street. While we ate, I told them about Todd Jakes' visit, and what he said about Daniel being in danger.

"So what does that mean in the grand scheme of things?" Rita asked.

"Not very much," I said.

"We didn't need him to tell us Daniel might be in danger. It's why he's staying with Hawk and Cassius. And when he's not with them, he's with me."

"Almost like being in church," she said.

"Just with more bad words."

When we were finished eating, she said she was taking an Uber back to her office. As there was still time before Hawk was driving over from working out at the Harbor Health Club to pick up Daniel, I asked Daniel if he was up for getting some air, and a brief tour of Beacon Hill.

"You'll like it," I said. "Sort of like taking a trip back in time."

"Right now," he said, "I'd settle for any other time except this. It wasn't too very long ago that my whole life was about getting ready for Harvard Law."

"It still can be," I said.

"You mean if I make it," he said.

At first, we wandered aimlessly and mostly in silence, up and down quaint, tree-lined streets, some of them with cobblestone walks, past the Vilna Shul, slowly making our way in the general direction of what I'd always felt was the capital of Beacon Hill, which meant Louisburg Square.

It was like a long circle route that took us to Mount Vernon and down to Beacon Street, past the African Meeting House on Smith Court. Eventually, I knew, we would make our way back to Joy Street, and to Rita's house.

"You've been asked to process a lot and deal with a lot," I said. "And having said that, I know that you still can't see a resolution in sight."

"Sometimes I can't decide whether I'm pushing a rock up a hill," he said, "or carrying a backpack full of them."

"Would it make you feel any better if I told you I feel the same way?" I said.

"Not so much," he said, but I could see him smiling.

I said, "You don't need me to tell you that your mother's death might not have been the random act it first appeared."

"Not until Ricardo died the same way, anyway," he said. "At which point I would have had to be an idiot not to see a pattern, or at least a connection. I *do* plan on being a lawyer, remember."

"It just wasn't quite the connection you came to Boston seeking," I said.

"Oh, fuck, no!" he said, with enough force that both of us had no choice but to laugh.

We walked a bit more. He asked about the cobblestone streets and I told him this was the only place to find them in Boston, most notably on the street we'd just been on, Acorn.

"Let me ask you something I probably should have asked before this," I said then. "Can you think of anything out of the ordinary that happened to your mother, or with her, in the time right before her death?"

"Don't think I haven't asked myself the exact same question," he said, "even though that period of time, right before she died and especially right after, is mostly a jumble for me now."

"See if you can cut through," I said, "and remember something or anything that might be helpful, or might actually provide a connection for us." I paused and added, "Give us a way to make something happen on our own."

I looked at my watch. Still time before Hawk said he'd be at Rita's. And I was in no hurry. I liked this young man, and enjoyed his company, even in circumstances like these. He reminded me, and more than somewhat, of Paul Giacomin, someone whose own childhood had mostly been a hot, dysfunctional mess, but who had not only survived it but come out on the other side, and into adulthood, as one of the best people I knew, of any age. And in the process had become as close to a son as I was likely to ever have, at least until Cassius Moore came into my life.

I joked about that with Hawk one time, saying, "Cassius has two daddies." And Hawk said, "There's really something off about you, I ever mention that?"

"Constantly," I said.

We had meandered to West Cedar and Myrtle and were halfway up Myrtle to Joy when Daniel stopped.

"Hold on," he said.

"Holding on," I said.

He was jabbing his index finger into the air in front of him, as if pushing hard on a button.

"It was a couple days before . . ." he said. He paused. "Before it happened," he said, his voice softening.

We were facing each other suddenly and, in that moment, I understood completely what Susan said when she said she could hear me thinking. Because I could see it and hear it happening right in front of me with Daniel.

"I was in a complete lockdown mode because of finals," he said. "But I called to check in the night before my last two tests. And I could tell she was being kind of quiet. When I asked if something was bothering her, she said she was fine, nothing for me to worry about, she'd just gotten a visit from an old friend, she'd tell me all about it when she saw me, no big deal, and for me to get back to studying, or else. Just being Mom. She always said that she never wanted her problems to be mine."

I watched as he took in a lot of air then, took a long time before letting it out.

"Only I never saw her again," he said.

"Did she happen to mention the friend's name?" I said.

"Maybe she did, but *if* she did, I can't recall it, right now, anyway," he said. "Maybe it will be one of those things where if I let this go for now and stop thinking about it, it will pop into my head later."

We were walking again then, a block away from Rita's front door.

Then Daniel stopped again.

"Hold on," he said.

"Still holding on," I said.

"I think she described her as her *nurse* friend," he said.

FORTY-ONE

Cassius was once again on my side of my desk when I got back to the office. I took one of the client chairs and told him about the last part of my conversation with Daniel, about his mother having been visited by a nurse friend.

"Doesn't mean it was a nurse involved with her test," he said.

"Doesn't mean it wasn't, either," I said.

"Sure, be that way," Cassius said.

He pushed back in my chair, which looked as comfy as ever, smiled, and said, "Want to hear about my day, dear?"

"Has it been productive?" I said.

"Yes and no," he said, and then informed me that there were still two hospitals in Milton, Beth Israel Deaconess, the big one, and a smaller one called Milton Memorial. Further said that after Stuart, the one at which Marisol Lopez had been tested, had closed, its medical records and personnel records had been transferred to Memorial.

"That's good for us, right?" I said.

He smiled. "Yes and no," he said.

"Be that way," I said.

Cassius said, "The good news is that Milton Memorial got them when Stuart closed in 2005, even though Stuart hadn't gone fully digital at that time. The bad news, unfortunately, is that they only kept the records for ten years."

"Alas," I said, "and alack."

"Are you aware that *alack* comes from Old French and not Middle English?" he said.

"Smart alack," I said.

"There is *some* good news, however," Cassius said. "Stuart, even being an even smaller operation than Milton Memorial is now, had its own reference lab before the place got shuttered."

"So her test was conducted in-house?" I said.

"In all likelihood," he said.

"I assume there's no way of accessing all of Marisol's medical records."

He shook his head. "It would involve me accessing HIMS," he said.

"Wait, isn't that the erection medicine I see constantly being advertised on TV?" I said.

He sighed. "Health Information Management System," he said. "But even if I could access that with both skill and guile, I'd then run up against HIPAA, even though Marisol is deceased."

"So you're telling me the dead hospital is a dead end," I said.

"Not necessarily," he said. "I have a request in to United Healthcare Workers East, the union, to see if they might be able to find personnel records from Stuart all this time later. But I'm told that could take more time than we'd prefer."

"But if they can find those records, then maybe there is a way to get some names and start contacting these people and see if one of them was involved in Marisol's test," I said. "If anybody can remember one paternity test from twenty years ago."

"Tell me again why this is so important," Cassius said.

"Because if the test was legit, then we already have the answer we need about Hale and Daniel," I said. "And if for some reason it's not, then Daniel has been wasting his time unless we can get Vic Hale to agree to a new test."

"It would help if he could give us a name on the nurse," Cassius said.

"Pretty to think so," I said.

"*The Sun Also Rises*," he said.

"Show-off," I said, and then told him I wanted my chair back.

FORTY-TWO

Cassius finally left to spend time with Daniel back at the safe house, saying that Hawk had told him he had some personal business to which he had to attend.

He put quotes around "business."

"I think his friend Emma may have the afternoon off," he said.

"Man's got needs," I said.

"He said he might be a while," Cassius said.

"That's just him being a show-off," I said.

I was alone in the office then, with no real plan for the rest of the afternoon, beginning with what I hoped wouldn't be too long a wait to see what reaction there might be, if any, from Vic Hale and his merry men once they knew Frank Belson was poking around and asking questions about them.

I really did continue to feel as if I was trying to juggle multiple cases at once, if clumsily and no matter how convinced I was that they were all connected, all running through the deal that was about to go down like rivers running through it, without me knowing how soon: Marisol's death. Ricardo's death. Daniel's paternity.

And then, just to add to the fun, there was Mauricio Estrella's role in all this, and whether he was more interested in just one immigrant—himself—than he was in the plight of all the ones for whom he had been so publicly advocating for so very long.

I thought about lying down on the couch and putting Diana Krall on my sound system, closing my eyes and trying to figure out what I was missing here. First I tried to find my way out of the same deep, dark forest from which I'd escaped plenty of times before.

Instead, with eyes wide open, I flipped up the screen of my own laptop and found the link for Vic Hale's podcast, the one that was about to put all that money on the table for him and everybody else.

He'd said it himself at the Fens that day, probably not really hearing what he was saying, though I had the feeling that happened to him on a daily basis.

"Money to die for," he'd called it.

FORTY-THREE

I stretched out on my couch then and began to listen to Hale's podcast, certainly for the longest stretch I'd ever listened to it, hands clasped behind my head, cuing it up from the beginning.

And the way it began was the way I assumed most of them did, or perhaps all of them:

"Welcome to the real border, and the only border guard people who love our country need. This is the *Vic Hale Podcast*, all you patriots, as I continue to be not just the first line of defense, but the best line of defense, asking you once again to line up bravely behind me."

From there, he talked about how it had taken the federal government twenty years to follow his lead on the border and immigration, and finally come to its senses.

"You know the expression *lead, follow, or get out of the way*?" Hale said. "Well, you all know it's a little different here. Here it's *I lead, you follow, and people who didn't belong in this country in the first place get the hell out of* our *way*."

He chuckled.

"Or get the *Hale* out, am I right?" he said, clearly pleased with himself. "Well, of course I'm right, if I wasn't, then what are we all doing here?"

I was fully into the thunderdome with him by now and, even though I hadn't touched the volume, felt Hale's voice getting louder and louder the more he got rolling.

He talked about border crossings being down, just not down nearly far enough. He talked about the roundups going on all across the country, and the world of the American heroes of ICE and Customs and Border Protection and how because of their work more and more jobs were going to real Americans, at long last.

Hale spoke of all the anti-immigrant bills becoming state law, and how that was all just part of a new American Revolution, a different kind of Boston Tea Party.

"You all know I'm a child of Boston and that this podcast is broadcast from Boston," he said. "Only those of us fighting for our country two hundred and fifty years after the original Tea Party aren't disguised as Mohawks now, we're just waving a flag that didn't even come into existence until a few years after we dumped that damn tea into the Harbor."

He finally took a commercial break, and my office was once again quiet, almost mercifully so, my eyes still closed. It had been so loud across the show's opening segment that I hadn't heard Hawk come in.

Quietly Hawk said, "Give the people what they want."

I turned to see him leaning against the door, arms crossed in front of him.

"I thought you had a date," he said.

"Pleasure delayed," he said, "ain't pleasure denied."

"You hear enough?" I said.

"Lotta people think like him," Hawk said. "Awful lot. He just be the most awful out of them."

Then he nodded at my desk. "Yeah," he said, "you can turn that shit off now."

I got up off the couch and walked over and shut my laptop. As soon as I did, Hawk immediately took the couch.

"People listening to the man need to know what we know 'bout him," Hawk said.

"Ah, but where to begin?"

"With what a fucking hypocrite he is," he said.

"And whether Daniel is his biological son or not," I said.

"*Not* be a shame," Hawk said. "Just because it be so much better for our purposes if the boy is."

"Uh-huh," I said. "And just for the purposes of this conversation, remind me what our purposes are."

Hawk said, "Maybe it's time for the world to know just how full of shit Paul Revere is, 'fore he laughs his way all the way to pulling a damn Mega Millions ticket."

"Which means sooner rather than later," I said.

"'Fore Daniel's head explode," he said.

"But what if it turns out that Daniel isn't his son?" I said.

"Then let the motherfucker go around denying it," Hawk said.

He smiled then.

"Hale, yeah," he said.

FORTY-FOUR

Susan had a breakfast event the next day for the Jimmy Fund at the Fairmont Copley Plaza, just a few blocks from my apartment, and that meant another sleepover for her and for Pearl at my place, the second this week. More often than not, the normal routine for us was me spending a majority of our time together in Cambridge rather than on Marlborough Street. But then I would have been willing to swim across the Charles to have a sleepover with Susan Silverman.

"So are you going to arrange a meeting between Daniel and Vic Hale?" she said.

"I called Todd Jakes and ran it by him," I said. "And he basically said to leave him out of it, he wasn't going to bring it to Hale without his next job lined up."

"You couldn't appeal to his better angels?" Susan said.

"He's trying awfully hard to convince me he has some, but I believe the jury is still out on that," I said.

We had ordered pizza from The Upper Crust. Mushrooms and green peppers for me and a white pizza, plain, for her, which always made me want to ask her what was even the point. I was drinking a Samuel Adams Summer Ale out of the bottle. She was drinking Kris pinot grigio.

"It doesn't bother you that Kris has a twist-off cap?" I asked.

"You can take the girl out of Swampscott," she said. "You fill in the rest."

She cut off a small piece of her pizza. I had long since lost the battle on her eating pizza with a knife and fork. Pearl was underneath the coffee table, once again playing the long game. For Susan's pizza. My pie was mine, all mine.

"So how did you leave it with Jakes?" she said.

I said, "I simply told him when the time came and I couldn't hold off Daniel any longer, he was going to help make it happen, or else."

"So you threatened him."

"You always tell me to play to my strengths," I said. "By the way? Frank Belson had already reached out to Jakes by the time we spoke."

"That must have made him pleased as punch," she said.

"He blamed me," I said.

"What did you say to that?"

"That one of the great cops in the history of the Boston PD was more than capable of putting things together on his own," I said.

"So basically you lied," Susan said.

She studied her pizza, frowning slightly, but made no move on it.

"Also playing to my strengths," I said.

She finally cut off an even smaller piece of white pizza than before. My own pie was halfway gone.

"I actually think you are right to start forcing the action," she said.

"Wait," I said. "Aren't you always telling me that slow and steady wins the race?"

"Most of the time, yes," she said. "But I started to look at things differently after I talked this out with Hawk."

I smiled at her. "So you and Hawk were eliminating the middleman?" I said. "The middleman being me?"

"As a matter of fact, we were," she said. "And we both came to the conclusion that if these contracts get signed, then the unintended consequence of *not* bringing things to a head will be that Vic Hale will have been the one helped in the end, and not the person you set out to help, meaning Daniel. Which would be, to use a clinical term, really messed up."

"Hawk said pretty much the same thing to me," I said.

She smiled again. "I know," she said. "I ask good questions. Sometimes you'd almost think I was like a shrink or something."

I leaned over and kissed her.

"You taste like peppers," she said.

"You almost taste like pizza," I said.

I went to the kitchen and came back with another beer. At this point in the proceedings, Susan had finished only half of her first glass of wine. In my mind, I had turned it into a competition, whether she'd finish the wine first or what was still the only slice of pizza on her plate.

"Vic Hale simply cannot end up getting what he wants," she said.

"I just want what I want," I said. "And what I want is to know who Daniel's father is, or isn't. And I want to know who killed Ricardo Baez."

"And what if it turns out, and beyond a reasonable doubt, that

Hale is Daniel's father?" she said. "You just step aside and let God sort things out?"

"Well," I said, "Him or me."

We were cleaning up the kitchen together and preparing to walk Pearl the Wonder Dog in the park when Cassius Moore called.

"I got names," he said.

FORTY-FIVE

I brought breakfast for Cassius and me in the morning, picking up fresh corn muffins at the Levain Bakery on Newbury.

Cassius was already at the office, ready to work.

"There's over a hundred names on the list, even though Stuart Medical was a relatively small operation compared to bigger hospitals," he said. "Like I said, it would have been easier if the place was digitized, but not all of them were back then, as difficult as that is to believe, it wasn't all that long ago. And even though it's not a complete list, it might be as close as we're going to get. We would have been in a bad spot if the hospital had been bigger, but it wasn't, not even two hundred beds."

"Doctors and nurses and lab techs included?" I said.

"Yes," he said.

"How did you manage to put it together?" I said.

"Do you really want to know how the sausage gets made?" he said. "Because you're the one always telling me not to give you too much information about how I obtain the information."

"Just give me the CliffsNotes," I said.

"The what?" he said.

"Another blast from the past," I said. "Give me chapter, maybe without the verse."

"Public records, the hospital union, social media, which I know is one of your favorites," he said. "There were more avenues than that, but those were the most useful."

He showed me the printout of the staffing at Stuart Medical in the year before the prenatal test of Marisol Lopez was conducted, and the year after, from the CEO all the way down to candy stripers, he said.

"Are candy stripers even still a thing?" I said.

"You bet!" Cassius said. "I mean, as long as you know where to look."

"And you do?"

"You bet!" he said.

One of the problems from the list, he said, at least with the people he couldn't locate on social media, was that so many of the contact phone numbers and email addresses that he was able to obtain were obsolete, along with most of the addresses.

"I've still got the same email address and landline number I had from those years," I said.

"Don't take this the wrong way," Cassius said, "but that's not something I'd categorize as a spoiler alert."

He took a corn muffin out of the bag and said, "Still warm."

"You have no idea how fast I'm walking these days, even on these knees," I said.

"Look at you," he said. "Just like a big boy."

"So how do we do this?" I asked him.

"You want me to take you through it?" Cassius said.

"Until I start to feel lightheaded and the urge to lie down," I said.

"There's all sorts of ways that make it easier than it used to be," he said. "There's companies like DISA Global, which basically can find social media snapshots from way back, for a fee, of course, and that includes ones that people have tried to delete for various reasons. There's other companies, too, and they can help even if somebody has changed their name in the succeeding years or, in extreme circumstances, wants to disappear. Then I can go through Instagram and Facebook and places like Pinterest on my own. Then there's marital records, divorce records, arrests, all that fun stuff, a whole laundry list. If we want to really go crazy, I can start calling around to other local hospitals and look for matches there."

He looked up at me. "Still with me?" he said.

"Fading fast," I said.

"My best bet might be to just use AI, or ChatGPT," Cassius said, "and simply type in that I'm trying to locate such-and-such person who might have worked at Stuart Medical, Milton, in the period at which we're looking. Or pose a similar question like that. If I don't find what I want doing it that way, there are property records that might involve some of these names, or the DMV, or online obituaries. Or even calling the Milton police and running names by them and asking if some of these people might still be residents of Milton."

"Or perhaps, and before you have to go that deep down the field, we get lucky and make actual human contact with a doctor or nurse or administrator who remembers a pretty young pregnant woman who showed up for a DNA test over twenty years ago," I said.

"Sounds like a piece of cake," Cassius said.

FORTY-SIX

In a much simpler world, when I had gone back in time to locate the college history of a deceased former Taft University student named Emily Gordon, I had started my quest for any intel I could get on her with a list of three thousand students who had entered Taft along with her, back in her freshman year.

Eventually I had winnowed that list down to three hundred young women who might have known her or been friendly with her, and simply started making phone calls until I found some who could help me. It was the beginning of cracking a case that involved a gangster, long since deceased himself, named Sonny Karnofsky, whose own daughter was a Taft student at that same time, and who turned out to be the central figure in the backstory built around the murder of Emily Gordon.

I gave Cassius the CliffsNotes on that.

"It really turned out to be a story about a daughter whose mother wasn't someone she thought she was," I said. "I just didn't have DNA testing to determine that."

"Boy," Cassius Moore said, "those must have been the days."

In the end, I decided I was the one who should start making most of these phone calls while he continued to try to put more current contact information with the names, using whatever tools necessary. I told him that I was mostly interested in nurses and people from the lab, pointing out that there was no way of knowing from his list what the specific duties of the nurses on it had been.

It was grunt work all the way, for both of us, through the morning and into the afternoon, including some awkward conversations when I did run into a relative of someone on the list who had died. It didn't take long for me to feel like one of those people making spam and scam calls for a living.

By midafternoon I had achieved human contact with only a dozen people on Cassius's list, none of them nurses. When I did get a man or woman on the line, I would politely explain that I was looking for a doctor or nurse who had treated a pregnant friend of mine at the time.

If they asked why, I said that I would love to share that information, but would be violating attorney-client privilege if I did.

"So you're a lawyer?" one of the hospital's board members asked.

"Harvard Law!" I said enthusiastically.

But then was told that the man to whom I was speaking had had little contact with either doctors or nurses, he was more concerned in those days with the money that had stopped coming in, and the bigger hospitals that finally put his out of business.

Sometimes I would be sent straight to someone's voicemail and simply leave a message. As of yet, no one had responded. But I pressed on, stopping only long enough for us to eat sandwiches delivered from the Parish Café and Bar.

It was late in the afternoon when Cassius said, "I'm starting to get the idea that this wasn't exactly the breakthrough we originally thought it might be."

"Slow and steady wins the race," I said.

"Do you really believe that?"

"It makes more sense when Susan says it," I said.

"Most things do," he said.

A lot of the numbers had been disconnected. When they were, and there was also an email address attached to the same name, I would send a vaguely worded email about trying to locate nurses who'd worked at Stuart in those years.

I was ready to call it a day at a little after five o'clock, having consumed enough coffee to make me feel more restless than a willow in a windstorm, when Nancy Bayless, RN, actually returned a call I had made to her hours earlier.

I thanked her for calling back and sketched out what I needed, and when I finished fumbling, she said, "You need a phlebotomist."

I said, "Don't I know it, sister," and was pleased to hear her laugh at that.

"Some of our nurses specialized in that," she said, "even when they were only part-timers."

Then she said, "Do you actually have a copy of the test to which you're referencing? There would be an ID number on it somewhere."

"Impossible to read," I said.

She sighed.

"Patient's name?" she asked.

I told her. She said she was writing it down. I gave her the name of the father, and spelled out "Halgvist."

There was a pause then at her end until she said, "What's this about really, Mr. Spenser?"

"It's about a young man trying to determine who his father is, now that his mother has passed away," I said. "And me doing my best to help him."

"But you already have the test," she said.

"There is some doubt about its validity," I said.

"You're suggesting that the result was somehow manipulated at our hospital?" Nancy Bayless said. "Should I be insulted at the implication?"

"Not at all," I said. "It's not the young man doing that. It's the father who's questioning the result."

"All this time later?" she asked.

"It's complicated," I said. "But can you help me determine who collected Marisol Lopez's buccal swab, and who might have conducted the actual test at Stuart?"

There was another pause.

"It will take a little detective work of my own," she said. "But yes, I believe I can help you out."

"You were a head nurse, correct?" I said.

"Still think of myself that way," she said, "even though I retired a long time ago. And even though some call us unit managers these days, whatever the hell that means."

She said she needed to get off the phone now and start making some calls of her own, and would try to call me tomorrow.

"Should I take two aspirin until then?" I said.

"Only as needed," she said.

FORTY-SEVEN

I finally sent Cassius home, as he'd informed me that Hawk was taking him and Daniel out to dinner. Susan was having a girls' night with some fellow shrinks.

"And we both know how crazy that can get," I said, "once you get a couple drinks in you and start talking dissocial disorders."

"You of course know that we shrinks like to say that jealousy is rooted in fears and disorders a person might not even realize they have," she said on the phone.

"I'd frankly like to get a second opinion on that, Doctor," I said.

"Try not to miss me too much," she said.

I needed a break, and a drink, not necessarily in that order, just because slow and steady was officially wearing me out. And my most acute fear continued to be that both Hawk and Susan were right, that if something didn't break for me, and fast, Vic Hale was going to laugh all the way to the bank, whether Daniel was his kid or not.

Another fear, one I had shared only with Susan, was that even if the world found out that Vic Hale had fathered a child with an illegal immigrant, his audience might forgive him anyway, that this might be just another instance when they'd simply wait for him to tell them what to think.

But the world would find out only if Daniel Lopez wanted it that way, because in the end, whether or not to out Vic Hale as his father—if he could in fact prove conclusively that Vic Hale was his father—was Daniel's decision, and his alone. To here, all he'd said was that he wanted to meet with Hale, something that I knew wasn't going to happen until Hale allowed it to happen, no matter how hard I pushed.

Maybe Hale still didn't think Daniel posed a threat to him, absent a twenty-year-old DNA test, one he continued to maintain was as illegitimate as Daniel Lopez was.

But if the threat of public exposure wasn't real to Hale, or someone associated with Hale, then why was Ricardo Baez dead?

I decided there was one surefire way to clear my head, at least for a little while, and get the drink I needed.

I would head down to Fenway Park and have dinner for one at the Bleacher Bar, located—appropriately enough—under the centerfield bleachers.

When I told Susan my plan she said, "I thought you mentioned that your team was out of town."

"They're your team, too," I said.

"Keep telling yourself that," she said.

"Love me, love my team," I said.

"Blah, blah, blah," she said. "You're really going down to have dinner with a view of an empty ballpark?"

"Hot diggity dog," I said.

"Tell me this isn't just about you going down there to have a hot dog," she said. "Or three."

"It's called a Bleacher Dog on the menu," I said, "in case you were wondering."

"Knock yourself out," Susan said.

FORTY-EIGHT

I eventually ordered two Bleacher Dogs and washed them down with two Allagash White ales, with a side of cheese fries, while staring contentedly at the field in front of me, the grass looking impossibly green even under the ballpark lights, the seats empty, the place silent and solemn and quite beautiful.

The Sox–Orioles game was on all the sets in the Bleacher Bar. Our side ended up winning in the ninth, 4–3. Jarren Duran, our streak-of-light left fielder, singled and stole second, as he almost always did once reaching base, and then scored what turned out to be the winning run on a single by Alex Bregman.

A very good night at the ballpark, all in all, even with my team four hundred or so miles away. Before paying the check, I celebrated the victory and the night with a Brownie Sundae for dessert.

A win was a win.

And Lord knew I could use one.

I had parked my year-old Jeep Cherokee next to the gas station on Boylston I used when I was too lazy to walk to Fenway. But tonight it cost nothing. Another win. I was practically on a roll.

On the drive home to Marlborough, I thought about how the whole experience of being down at the ballpark tonight had felt to me like comfort food, and not just because of the hot dogs. It was the quiet of the whole place, the view, the feeling that baseball, even though absent, was still all around me, and made me remember a line I'd read once in *The Globe* from Bob Ryan, when he'd described baseball as the greatest game ever conceived by mortal mind.

Tonight had been about that for me, while I waited to see what information Nurse Nancy Bayless might provide me with tomorrow, if she indeed called me back tomorrow.

But that was for tomorrow.

For now, the Sox had made me feel as if I were on the board, even if the feeling was fleeting.

To access the small, private lot behind my building, the space there being something for which I paid more than I'd paid in monthly rent for my first apartment in Boston about a hundred years ago, I had to enter off Beacon Street.

Almost by reflex, I was preparing to collect Pearl for her last walk of the evening, before remembering she was in Cambridge along with Susan tonight.

I was out of the car for only a few seconds and starting the walk toward my building when someone opened fire.

FORTY-NINE

Whoever it was had to be using some kind of machine pistol, firing from the Beacon Street side, the sound clearly that of an automatic weapon as I took cover behind the front wheels, something I'd been taught as a rookie cop, the bullets already skipping past me, at least the ones that weren't pissing through the Cherokee. Another old cop expression, one doing me absolutely no good at the moment as the bullets kept coming, into the back tires and through the back windows.

A Sig, most likely. Or Glock. Or Smith & Wesson. Didn't matter. The gun that was shooting up my car was magazine-fed and self-loading. And relentless. A gun for mass shooters, except this shooter seemed interested only in me. And my car, the shots continuing to come nonstop, which, after all, was the point of weapons like these.

I stayed where I was, waiting to see if the shooter—there seemed to be only one—might now come closer. He did not. By now I had my own Smith & Wesson .38 in my hand, even knowing it was about as useful to me with what I was up against as a peashooter.

I could see lights going on behind me in my building. No sirens yet. But then, I didn't expect the shooter would still be here when I did hear sirens.

It would have ended by then, however it was going to end.

I leaned out just enough from the right-front headlight to get off some quick shots in succession, at least giving them something to think about if they did try to come for me.

But a part of me, a big part, knew this:

If the shooter had really wanted me dead, I would have gotten dead as soon as I was out of the car.

These were warning shots.

Lots of them.

And just as quickly as I had started taking fire, and knowing full well he could keep me pinned down for as long as he wanted to until we could both hear the cavalry about to arrive, the shooting stopped.

The night was quiet again, until this:

"Next time it's you, Spenser," a male voice I didn't recognize called out.

No discernible accent.

Didn't mean it wasn't Estrella's men, didn't mean it was. Or maybe Woody Giles had sent more of his own men, and told them to dial things up this time.

"First you," the voice called out. "Then the kid. Unless you walk away now."

"I think I'd like to shop around for a better offer, thank you," I called back.

There was another flurry of bullets now, passing through where the back window had been, shattering the ones on the side now because of the angle I'd parked at, skimming off the side doors.

Then the night was once again quiet, and I heard footsteps heading away from me, and I knew he was gone and that it was over.

I got up and walked through the broken glass and around what was left of the Cherokee and waited for the cops to arrive.

FIFTY

It was a little after three in the morning. Martin Quirk and I sat at my kitchen table with glasses in front of each of us, a bottle of Midleton Very Rare between us.

Frank Belson had left by then. The responding officers had taken my statement in the parking lot. The ones from Forensics had finished sweeping the lot, collecting cartridge casings in the hope that they might somehow be able to trace the markings. More cops had shown up to canvas the building, but no one had seen anything once the shooting stopped, they just knew what they'd heard.

Quirk was talking about the casings they had picked up, and how the collection of them was by the book and thorough and a complete waste of time in this case.

"By now the guns are probably at the bottom of the river," he said, "or have already been taken apart like fucking LEGOs."

He told me to take him through it again. I did, telling him how fast it had all happened once I was out of the car.

"If they wanted you taken out, you would've been taken out," Quirk said.

"See, there," I said, "that's how you made commander."

He fondly looked at the glass in his hand.

"So here we are again," he said. "Couple of tough guys talking about bad guys in the middle of the night."

"They got you out of bed for this?" I said.

"For some reason, Frank Belson seems to think I have the same soft spot in my heart for you that he does," he said.

"Frank has a heart?"

We drank. Quirk's only concession to the hour, at least sartorially, was the absence of a necktie. He was a big man, nearly my size, with big hands that made his glass look as small as a thimble.

"Frank gave me all the background after you so generously gave it to him," he said.

"I told him pretty much all that I've got," I said.

"First time for everything," Quirk said. "Like when the Sox came back on the Yankees that time."

We then silently toasted that.

"Now that I know what you know," Quirk said, "I want you to tell me what you think."

I poured myself more Midleton, then started to hand Quirk the bottle. He shook his head.

"I think Marisol Lopez decided to go back at Hale, for reasons unknown, and it got her killed, whether it happened in Florida or not," I said. "I don't know how much the reporter knew, but I believe he knew enough that it got *him* killed by someone who could only have been on Hale's side of this."

Quirk did not look tired. He never looked much older to me than he had when I'd first met him, but that happened a lot with me, I locked people in time. And something else had not changed with him: As often as I told myself I needed to get to the right side of things, when I did get there, Quirk was always waiting for me.

"I know why you're so engaged by the other stuff," he said, "and

I would be, too, if I were working this from your angle. But my agenda hasn't changed: I want to know who killed the reporter and thought they could get away with it in my town."

I nodded and drank.

Quirk said, "You think that paternity test is real?"

"If it's not, I need to find out why it's not, one of these days," I said.

"And you will."

"That confidence is why I have a soft spot in my heart for you," I said.

Quirk nearly smiled, just didn't get all the way there. Happened a lot.

"You know," I said, "we're more alike than you might think."

"Hey, just because you poured expensive hooch," he said, "doesn't give you the right to insult me."

"I take that back," I said.

"They can't possibly think they can scare you off," he said.

"Tony Marcus, however big his footprint is in this, knows that, obviously," I said. "But Estrella might not. He's probably used to getting his way in whatever way he wants to. And Giles came out of wrestling, where everything is a show and hardly anything is real."

"Wait . . . what?" Quirk said, frowning. "It's not real?"

"And Giles did send two of his bangers after me already," I said.

"Would Vic Hale send a couple shooters after you and threaten to do the same with somebody who might be his own son?" Quirk said.

"I can't see it, frankly," I said.

"Because his old man and you were friends?"

"There's that," I said. "And there's the fact that unless he's a complete moron, he knows who I am at this point."

"Which means enough to know that if he fucks with you, you will get up into his shit and never get out," Quirk said.

"There's also that," I said.

He held up his glass, which still had some Midleton in it, and twirled it around.

"Is there a possibility," he said, "that Estrella has some other agenda here, as yet to be determined?"

I shrugged. "Let me tell you about the very rich," I said. "They're different from you and me."

"Guy who wrote that probably could have polished off this bottle by himself," he said.

"And not just this one," I said.

Quirk finished his drink, walked over to the sink and rinsed the glass and carefully dried it and put it in the rack. He did the same thing after we drank whiskey in my office.

"Of all of them," Quirk said, "who's the most afraid that the whole house of cards could fall apart before the hand is played all the way out, including Hale?"

"When I know, you'll know," I said.

"Fuckin' ay," he said.

"Bill Parcells, who once coached our Patriots, said one time that when a game looks even, bet the team that needs it more," I said.

Quirk said, "So who needs this one more?"

"I do," I said.

"You always do," Quirk said.

"Always nice to be noticed," I said.

FIFTY-ONE

Nancy Bayless looked like Maggie Smith, just a lot younger version of Maggie than the one who'd showed up in *Downton Abbey*. I had never watched the series the way Susan had, and religiously. But had liked the movies after she dragged me to them, mostly because of Maggie, whom I saw as a great dame in all ways.

Bayless had called after I'd somehow managed to get a few hours of sleep, saying we could meet this morning if I didn't mind driving down to Cohasset on the South Shore, telling me without me asking that she'd moved down there after she retired to be closer to her youngest grandchildren.

"Of whom," she said, "I have many."

I said I would be happy to make the drive. She then asked if I liked donuts, saying there was a great place less than a mile from where she lived that had amazing homemade donuts, and we could meet there.

"Don't be a tease," I said.

So we did meet at Seabird Coffee & Co. on Main Street, where, she informed me once we were seated at our table, because it was Friday, the donuts were not only as tasty as ever, but free. She wanted to know before ordering if old-fashioned donuts were all right. I told her my general position on donuts was that there really were no bad options as far as I had ever been able to determine, and that I had extensive experience in the determining.

"Just so you know, I googled you," she said.

"On our first date?"

She smiled. It was a very nice and very genuine smile that made her look younger, despite her white hair and lines on her face that somehow seemed to suit her just fine, ones she wore exceedingly well. Her eyes were the color of sapphires.

"One of the pieces I read about you in *The Globe* said you fancied yourself a great wit," she said.

"Wayne Cosgrove wrote that in a column before he became editor," I said. "He's just jealous."

She smiled again. "He wrote that you *fancied* yourself a great wit, not that you actually were one."

"How witty of *you*," I said.

A plate of donuts was delivered to the table. She immediately broke off a piece of hers and dunked it in her coffee. A dunker. I thought I might be in love.

"Okay," she said, "why don't you tell me everything you haven't told me."

"You sound like some cops I know," I said.

"Kind of was one," she said. "My official title was chief nursing officer, after all."

I told her pretty much everything except Vic Hale's name because there was no need for her to know about him at this point, or ever. Further, I did not tell her that there was a murder investigation tied to my own investigation, just that the precipitating event for Daniel Lopez's trip to Boston had been the DNA result he'd found after his mother's death, one she had locked away and about which she had never told him, allowing the lie about his father having died in a border crossing to have sustained them both.

"Can I see the test, please?" she asked.

I found it on my phone, which I handed across the table to her. She reached into her purse for oversized reading glasses that nearly matched the color of her eyes and studied it, before handing back the phone.

"Looks authentic to me," she said, "even though the ID number has faded with the fog of time, as you've already pointed out to me. But if the young man has just graduated from college, it has to fall into a general period not long before the hospital closed down, when the tests still looked like that."

She carefully dunked another piece of her donut.

"The hospital was behind the times getting itself digitized," she said, "despite the fact that I had been pushing for it for years. But by the time the process had started it didn't matter, to my way of thinking. Too little, too late, because we were on our way out of business." She sighed. "Sadly, we just could no longer keep up with the bigger hospitals."

You always had to let them tell it their way. I could see, by her bearing and her tone, that she had probably overseen the units in her charge at the hospital like a commanding officer. And that we would almost certainly get to where she was taking us when she was good and ready for us to get there, and not a moment before.

"I was the chief in our last years at Stuart Medical," she said. "But there were several other nurses, I guess you could call them my lieutenants, who reported to me and ran different floors and units. I wasn't directly overseeing prenatal in those days and spent very little time on that floor, unless I needed to fetch a test result for some reason."

"Otherwise you had people for that."

She winked at me. "If you can't get them to get you things," she said, "what's the point of even having them?"

"I have a feeling that when you wanted something gotten, it got gotten in an expeditious fashion," I said.

"You got that right, brother," she said. "Anyway, after we spoke originally, I made some calls, about the general time frame of which we were probably going to speak. Just to refresh my memory." She narrowed the striking blue eyes just ever so slightly. "A memory that still works just fine, thank you."

"Never doubted it for a second."

"And when I did narrow it down, I came to the conclusion that the test was probably administered about the time that I was on a lengthy grandmaternity leave when my second daughter had her third child." She grinned. "Or maybe it was my third daughter and her second child, they were coming fast and furious in those days."

"Sounds like you might have been the most overqualified baby nurse ever," I said.

"Tell me about it," she said. "Anyway, I did some quick detecting of my own and managed to come up with a list of names that might have been involved in the process when this mother of yours showed up for her test. Even in those days, and particularly with unwed mothers, there were more of them showing up than you might think, speaking of fast and furious." She shrugged. "I hope that doesn't sound judgmental, from someone who came to all of that from another time."

"And a damn good time it is," I said. "Just curious: Would it have mattered whether or not Marisol Lopez would have had insurance?"

"Even if she didn't, she could have paid out of pocket," Nancy

Bayless said. "It wouldn't have been much more than a couple hundred dollars, as I recall."

"Would it have likewise mattered if the young woman in question had been to Stuart Medical previously?" I said.

"They came to us for their own reasons, and from all over the area," she said. "Maybe a friend had gone there. Maybe she knew one of the nurses, even one of the phlebotomists. But at least I've managed to compile a list of names that I remembered and that some of my old colleagues remembered, even knowing that it's only a partial, for both the nurses and the lab techs."

"How many, all in?" I asked. "I started with a much bigger list of my own of the staffing from that period."

"Around three dozen," she said.

"Do you have contact information for all of them?" I said.

She grinned. "Nope," she said. "You asked for names. And aren't you the detective?"

"My own memory fails me on that sometimes," I said.

She reached into her bag and came out with a list that looked as if it had been produced by a manual typewriter, the type looking pretty wonderful. Speaking of better times.

"Wait," I said, "you do have some contact info on that page."

She smiled again. "You asked if I had it for all of them," she said, "not some."

I snapped off a salute. "Yes, *sir*!"

She laughed.

"The nurses outnumber the lab guys about two to one," she said. "I have no idea how many of these numbers are current, there's simply no way of knowing."

I looked down at the list. "Most of the phone numbers seem to be local," I said. "And now that I've got names, I might be able to locate them all on social media."

"Why do I get the feeling that might be somewhat challenging for you, Mr. Spenser?"

"Hey," I said. "I've got people to get me things, too."

She pointed to a name at the top of the list. "It were me, I'd start with Karla Morelli," she said. "One of my top lieutenants, and my best. She took over most of my duties when I was on my grandma leave."

She asked then if I wanted to take the rest of the donuts with me. I said I'd be a fool not to, and waved for the check.

"Let me see if I understand this," Nancy Bayless said. "You're doing all this about a test that in all likelihood was on the level in the first place?"

"Yes," I said.

"Because the son wants to know," she said.

"Him and me both, sister," I said.

FIFTY-TWO

I had not yet told Susan about my car having been used for target practice the previous evening, preferring to tell her in person. It was, I knew, a form of avoidance, if only transitory.

Hawk had stopped by my apartment before I left for Cohasset and not long before the truck from Mike's Auto Repair on Route 9 with their small flatbed arrived to transport the Cherokee over there. When Hawk had finished inspecting the damage, he'd said, "Do not resuscitate."

He had then driven me over to the Hertz on Park Plaza and I had managed to rent an SUV for the drive to Cohasset and to use until either Mike's could save my car or I'd have to buy or even lease a new one.

When I got back to Boston from Cohasset, I parked in the alley near my office and gently patted the roof of the rental and told her she'd be safe here, despite what she might have heard about my previous ride.

Cassius was upstairs, working away. Before I'd left the coffee shop I'd taken a picture of Nancy Bayless's list of names and texted it to him, so he was already checking phone numbers and trying to find addresses to put with the names and scouring everything on the Internet, from TikTok, to Instagram, to LinkedIn, to what would always be Twitter to me.

"We're making progress," Cassius said.

"Slow and steady," I said.

"I've always believed that slow and steady went by the boards with overnight delivery," he said.

"Maybe at some point we could find a way to see if any of the nurses on this list made flights to any of the South Florida airports in the period before Marisol Lopez's death," I said. "That might be helpful."

"And might be a bridge too far even for me," Cassius said, "at least without credit card numbers."

"Just try to work as much of your magic as you can," I said.

"How long did stuff like this take you before you hired me?" he said.

"It's too painful for me to even think about now."

"We're sure that Daniel said it was a nurse friend?" Cassius said.

"If it wasn't a nurse," I said, "you have wasted a lot of time on multiple laptops and I just wasted a trip to the South Shore, even if I did bring back donuts."

I put the bag on the desk. He opened it and said, "They're all plain."

"When in Cohasset," I said.

Cassius said, "I've been wondering about something. If the nurse in question, whomever she is or was, had enough of a relationship with Daniel's mother to fly down to Florida to see her, wouldn't she have reached out to Daniel in some way after Marisol died, to pay her condolences or maybe even explain why she'd paid Marisol that visit?"

"I've asked myself the same question," I said. "But let's table that for the moment as we continue on the long and winding road to finding the right nurse."

"Long and winding road," he said. "That's some old song, right?"

I told him he was going to hell.

I called the number next to Karla Morelli, the nurse whose name Nancy Bayless had highlighted. It was no longer in service. But before we both left the office for the day, Cassius had indeed worked his magic and discovered that Karla Morelli-Bruton was now a surgical nurse at the Tufts Medical Center on Washington Street, not more than a mile away from where we were sitting.

I tried their switchboard first. They sent me to her unit. I ended up on hold for so long waiting for someone to pick up that I thought summer had ended. And called back.

This time somebody did pick up at whatever nurses' station to which I'd been transferred. I gave the woman at the other end of the line my name, identifying myself as a detective, which was technically true as well as completely misleading, and was told that Nurse Morelli-Bruton had just gone into what was expected to be a lengthy surgery. I told her my matter was hardly as urgent as that, gave her my number, and asked if I might possibly get a call back at her earliest convenience.

"Can I ask what the matter might be?" the woman said.

"Police business," I said.

Something else that was technically true.

"I'll be sure to pass the message along, Detective Spenser," she said.

"Preserve and protect," I said.

At that point, I was exhausted from all the time I'd spent the past couple days on the phone and somewhat nursed-out despite the help I'd gotten from former Chief Operating Nurse Nancy Bayless. I was about to head over to the Harbor Health Club and work out my frustrations on the heavy bag when Junior and Ty-Bop walked in.

Ty-Bop had what was so often a concealed weapon with him quite unconcealed at the moment, just showing me his, but I knew that was just him playing. Being a gun guy, I noticed right away that the gun in his right hand was a Glock 19M.

"Nice piece, Ty," I said. "You know that's the primary sidearm for FBI agents?"

He stared past me and out the window behind me to somewhere far in the distance, perhaps all the way to Neverland.

"You need to come with us without no lip or trouble," Junior said.

He was wearing the same porkpie hat he'd been wearing at Buddy's, and a dark blue Adidas warm-up suit, featuring pants that looked big enough to be a duvet.

"Without lip or trouble, would I even be able to maintain my sense of self?" I asked.

"Let's go," Junior said.

"Am I even allowed to ask where?"

"For a ride," he said.

FIFTY-THREE

There was a black stretch limo double-parked on Berkeley, though the length of the thing made me think that triple-parked might be more appropriate.

Junior opened the door on the sidewalk side for me before getting back in himself and behind the wheel. Ty-Bop was next to him in the front, riding shotgun. Or Glock, in this case.

Tony Marcus and Bill Jones, both wearing dark business suits, were next to each other, facing the front. I took the long seat behind Junior and Ty-Bop, stretching my legs out in front of me, just because there was more than enough room for me to do that.

"We couldn't do this in one of your offices?" I said to Marcus and Jones.

"I like to conduct business in the car, to tell you the truth," Bill Jones said.

"Like *The Lincoln Lawyer*?" I said.

"Who?" Jones said.

Sometimes even my topical references fell flat.

Junior eased the limo out into traffic and made the left onto Newbury.

"Happens that I do some of my best thinking in the car, too," Tony said.

I told them that when I tried it for very long, I'd get carsick.

Tony turned to Bill Jones. "See what I keep talking about with this motherfucker?" he said. "It's the lip gets him into trouble most times."

"I take it we're not going for tea this time?" I said, undeterred.

"Maybe we can stop somewhere and get you a to-go cup, we see how all this goes," Tony said.

"How what goes?" I said.

"You leaving Vic Hale the fuck alone, once and for all," Tony said. "Leave him alone and leave this deal we trying to close alone and just walk the *fuck* away."

"That does appear to be the prevailing opinion about me," I said. "From almost every imaginable direction."

"Told there was bullets coming from one of them directions the other night," Tony said.

"So you heard," I said.

"It happened around here, I heard," he said. "I didn't hear? Almost like it never happened."

"The person doing the shooting not only suggested that I walk away, he suggested I do that before I got shot and a friend of mine got shot along with me."

"The boy," Bill Jones said.

"I assume he'd prefer 'young man,'" I said, "now that he's about to enter Harvard Law."

"If he makes it," Jones said.

"Now you're the one threatening him?" I said. I smiled. "Don't let your lip get you into trouble."

"Just referencing the threat you just referenced," he said. "Just being lawyerly."

I looked out the window. We were crossing Mass Ave and about to get on the Mass Pike, heading west.

"Tony," I said, turning back to them, "we've known each other a long time, have we not?"

"Long enough for you to fuck some things up for me, in a manner of speaking," he said. "Something you are going to avoid doing this time around. One of the reasons why we taking this ride."

I nodded. "I know you, you know me, we know each other," I said. "So make sure you understand me when I tell you that young man is not to be touched. Not by the two of you or anybody else involved in this deal. Because if that should happen, then it will be more than your deal getting fucked up." I grinned. "In a manner of speaking."

"Lot of people have threatened Tony and me over the years," Bill Jones said. "And we're the ones still here, just as a point of fact."

"Same," I said.

I looked out the window again, saw we'd gotten off at the Watertown exit, making the big circle there and probably about to get back on the turnpike. Outside, at least, it was a beautiful summer day.

"Tony," I said now. "You couldn't possibly have set up this car date to threaten me, because you know better than that. So what's this really about?"

Tony smiled fully.

"Art of the fucking deal," he said.

FIFTY-FOUR

Tony told Junior to take the Copley Square exit when we were getting close to downtown. Then it was Bill Jones doing the talking.

"There are only a few people in Vic Hale's weight class these days," Jones said. "In his space, so to speak. Joe Rogan, of course."

"You're telling me that Vic Hale is set up to make Rogan money?" I said.

"We're not running with the big dog yet," Jones said. "Maybe next time around, though, if we get this done right."

"'We'?" I said.

Jones was the one smiling then. "Vic, me, and Tony," he said.

"Bill got his piece of Hale," Tony said. "I got my piece of Bill. Picture it like as one of them pie graphs."

The partition behind me went back down then, and Junior asked Tony if he was supposed to drop me back off at my office. Tony said to just drive around a little bit more, our meeting was almost over, and then he could kick my ass to the curb.

Jones then elaborated on what he knew of the terms of Rogan's new deal with Spotify, with its upfront minimum guarantees and revenue-sharing based on ad sales, and what he'd made spinning his show out to YouTube and Apple podcasts and more inside baseball that went completely over my head. But it was Spotify that was Rogan's home base, Jones said, the way Woody Giles and Brass Ones was Vic Hale's base, and had been for a long time.

"I tried to get Spotify into play with Hale, just to move the needle a little more in our direction," Jones said, "thinking they might be interested in having two kings of the world instead of one. And I did have another podcast company, up-and-comer called Monarch, in play until they dropped out, saying the money we were talking about was too rich for their blood."

"My man, being manly," Tony said. "Doing whatever it took to get a bidding war going."

"Except the problem was, there really wasn't one once Spotify and Monarch took their bats and balls and went home," Bill Jones said. "We knew it and Woody Giles sure knew it, which is why our numbers and his numbers suddenly weren't even close."

"But then the Good Lord smiled on us," Tony Marcus said, "as He's so often done, with me, anyways."

"And Mauricio Estrella came calling," I said. "Formerly the coffee king of Guatemala."

"Little man swinging his wallet like it was a great big dick," Tony said.

"Aren't they the same thing?" I said.

"With me they are," Tony said.

"And you're both telling me that Estrella would actually do something like this to *his* base, and in his own space?" I said. "You honestly believe he's serious about this?"

"As serious as his heart attack."

Junior had made his way over near the Esplanade, not far from the bust of Arthur Fiedler and the river and a short walk from my apartment. Maybe when we were done I could rub Arthur's head for luck, as I occasionally did before beginning a run or walk along the Charles.

"So it's down to him and Woody Giles bidding for Hale," I said.

"Like they two teams bidding up one of them free agents in baseball," Tony said. "Be still my fucking heart."

"So they're not looking to partner up?" I said. "I heard that was a possibility."

"No fucking comment," Tony said.

"Put it another way," I said. "Can Giles stay with him if they don't happen to partner up?"

"Our boy Woody might need outside help to do that, it plays out like that," Tony said. He smiled. "Which I might be able to set up for him, long as he don't care where the money be coming from."

"Wouldn't you be double-dipping at that point?" I said.

"You making a sundae," he said, "do it really matter where the scoops are coming from, long as it tastes good in the end?"

I felt my phone buzzing in my pocket and ignored it.

"Why are you really telling me all this?" I said.

"Just to give you background," Jones said. "And to provide context. And some perspective on why we don't want anything happening that might diminish Vic's brand before we cross the finish line, which we soon will, whether Woody Giles and Mr. Estrella do it hand in hand like people crossing the finish line at the Marathon or not."

He paused.

"Which gets to the real purpose of this meeting, at long last," Jones said. "We are willing to make a substantial cash offer to Mr. Lopez if he will walk away now. And just keep walking."

"I keep telling you guys this," I said. "He doesn't want money, he just wants to know who his father is."

"Who the fuck cares?" Tony Marcus said. "I still don't know who my old man was. And look how things turned out for me."

"Well, around jail time."

"Fuck you," Tony said, "and the white horse you rode in on."

"Is this the two of you making this offer," I said, "or did it originate with Vic?"

"Vic's position ain't changed," Tony said. "He says the kid's basically gotten paid his whole damn life." He gave a quick shake of his head. "For now, this is the two of us looking to make it happen in a more timely fashion."

"We are on the threshold of making the deal of a lifetime," Jones said. "For Tony, for me, for Vic. We are now in one of those dream situations where two men want the same thing and have pretty much bid up on it as far as they're going to go, unless one of them stands down. Now it's just a question of who wants it more if one of them *doesn't* stand down and they do end up standing together in a fluid situation like the one we have going. Estrella, he's used to getting what he wants, even if that means they don't find the body afterward."

"So I've heard," I said. "What about Giles?"

"Woody probably needs Vic and his show more," Jones said, "because without it he just goes back to being some guy out of wrestling who made one big score and used to be somebody before people stopped inviting him to parties."

"And you're telling me Vic Hale wouldn't hesitate to go to work for an immigrant, no matter how rich that particular immigrant is?" I said.

"Vic Hale will take the most money," Jones said.

"On account," Tony said, "that everybody a whore in the end."

"Daniel Lopez isn't," I said.

"Well, now," Tony said, "we about to find that out, aren't we?"

"Am I allowed to know the amount of money on the table?" I said.

"He can tell you when we tell him," Jones said. "But you might mention if his brain wandered into seven figures, it would be in the right neighborhood."

"And then he has to decide whether he wants to make a score of his own," Tony Marcus said.

"Like father, like son?"

I saw him shaking his head.

"Think about it, Spenser," he said.

As always, it came out "Spens-ah."

"If the boy do take the money to disappear," Tony Marcus said, "he'll really be favoring his mother more, now, won't he?"

FIFTY-FIVE

I needed to talk about this with Rita Fiore, now that the stakes were clearly about to be raised, and I knew that I couldn't be the one to answer for Daniel, not at these prices, and even though all I had was a ballpark number at the moment.

Benjamin Walsh said that Rita was in court this afternoon. I knew full well what Rita's price was as a lawyer, because she loved to tell me every time her hourly rate at Cone, Oakes was raised yet again. But I wondered now how much she would have been willing to pay to find out who her birth father had been.

Or if there was any amount of money that would have had her walking away from knowing for sure.

Tony Marcus and Bill Jones, only one of them Hale's representative of record, had made it clear that Vic Hale would go for the most money at the end of the day, and any loyalty he might feel toward Woody Giles would go right out the window at the same time, as highly as he seemed to grade himself on loyalty. But would a young man about to be a law student turn down a chance to make life-changing money of his own?

And even if it meant living out his life not knowing about Vic Hale?

I needed a good lawyer to help answer the question. But Walsh had told me Rita wouldn't be out of court for a couple hours at least. I still had not heard from Karla Morelli-Bruton, and wasn't sure if I ever would, or if she had even gotten my message at the hospital.

So now I made the trip to the Harbor Health Club that I had planned to make before Junior and Ty-Bop had paid me their visit. I went upstairs to the men's locker room, got my old Gleason's Gym sweatshirt with the sleeves cut off out of my locker, along with sweatpants and the ancient New Balance cross-trainers I kept there, Hawk having finally shamed me out of wearing my old high-top boxing shoes. Then I walked into the gym still prepared to take out my frustrations about my general state on the heavy bag. And if I couldn't rid myself of all my frustrations, I could at least knock a lot of them around for the next hour.

Henry Cimoli taped my hands and helped me into my gloves.

"You got that look today," he said.

"And what look might that be?" I said.

"We both know which one," he said.

"Oh," I said. "*That* one."

I started out with a power-punching drill, using the oversized clock that Henry had once used in a corner of the ring that was long gone, setting the clock for one three-minute round after another, planning to do five in all, planning to stop only long enough after the old-fashioned bell rang to set the clock again. Come for the boxing, get the cardio, too.

I jabbed in the first round, quickly working my way up to the hardest jabs I could throw. Left hooks in the second round, right hooks in the third. Then left uppercuts and right uppercuts, with all that I had, which today was a lot.

My wind was good, even the burn I began to feel in my arms and shoulders was good, as I imagined myself throwing hard rights and lefts at Vic Hale and Woody Giles and Tony Marcus and Bill Jones and Mauricio Estrella. One round for each of them, even though I realized I would have needed to stand Estrella up on a chair to get a clean shot at him. Wondering as I went along, and all over again, which one of them might have been willing to kill a reporter, even one of Estrella's reporters, to keep the sweetheart deal that Marcus and Jones had just described to me very much alive.

At one point Henry poked his head back in and said, "Yep. Definitely that look that I seen plenty of times before."

I was frankly a little bit surprised that I felt as strong as I did at the end of the five rounds, particularly how strong my legs were, perhaps because of all the walking I'd been doing. Or perhaps it was all the time I had spent chasing my own tail since Daniel Lopez had come to town.

I eventually moved into a few rounds of combinations before finally finishing off the hour with some footwork drills, a way of really testing how sturdy my knees were, especially the one that had been cheap-shotted by Woody Giles's man Deke.

I stood about three paces back from the bag, stepped forward, threw a punch. Stepped away again, moved back in, threw two punches next time. Left and rights. Then three punches in succession until I reached my arbitrary goal of ten.

Then I was done.

I sat on a bench and drank a liter bottle of water, showered, changed, got back into the rental. There was a message on my phone, almost like a Christmas miracle, from the boys at Mike's Auto Repair, saying that not only had the Cherokee made it through surgery, it would be ready for me early next week, barring any post-op complications.

Rita called when I was on my way back to the office.

"Young Benjamin said he spoke with you and that you said it was imperative that you speak to me as soon as possible," she said.

"That sounds so unlike me," I said.

"Yeah, right," she said. "So what gives, Mr. Impatient?"

"There's something we need to discuss," I said.

"Who's 'we'?"

"You, Daniel, me," I said.

"And what do we so urgently need to discuss?" she said.

"A possible plea bargain," I said.

FIFTY-SIX

We met at Foxhole, a small sports bar on Newbury that was so much more than that, one I didn't patronize nearly often enough, something that occurred to me every single time I did.

Hawk drove Daniel over there and joined us. Hawk had finally broken down and admitted that the safe house was in Auburndale, a little place he had purchased years ago. What he said was one of a couple homes away from homes for him, leaving it at that.

"Once again, good job with the driving, Hoke," I said when he and Daniel sat down at Foxhole.

"Here we go again with the Miss Daisy shit," he said.

"Sometimes I just can't help myself," I said.

"Something you treat like breaking news every time you *can't* not fucking help yourself," I said.

Rita was only about five minutes behind us, enabling her to make an entrance, an essential part of her playing the character of Rita Fiore to the hilt, and also an essential part of her most formidable skill set. Today she wore a fuchsia dress that must have dazzled the holy hell out of both the men and women in court if she hadn't changed since then, short and extremely formfitting, as just about everything except a hospital gown seemed to be with her. The heels seemed even higher than ever, the skirt even shorter than usual. All part of Rita being completely Rita. There were a lot of guys seated at the bar already, all of whom followed her with their eyes across the room as if their lives had just gotten a lot better.

She smiled like a happy little girl when she saw Hawk.

"My hero!" she said.

"Thought I was your hero," I said.

"Hey," she said, "there's no shame in being first runner-up. Like with Miss America."

"Tell that to the first runner-up," I said.

She ordered a dry martini with a twist. Daniel and I both ordered Narragansett lagers. Hawk ordered a bottle of Vintage Brut, but showed what I thought was remarkable restraint by choosing one that cost only $150 after Rita had announced she was buying.

"Zendaya came in here for a drink last year," Hawk said, "when the girl was filming a movie here."

"Zendaya?" Daniel said. "You're joking!"

"I should know who that is, right?" I said.

Hawk looked sadly over at Rita. "Don't even know why I make the attempt keeping the boy current."

"You think Zendaya is sexier than me?" Rita asked Hawk in a husky voice.

"Hell, no," he said. "But maybe she be first runner-up if for any reason you can't serve."

"My hero, times two," she said.

"Pushover," I said to her.

"As I keep trying to tell you," she said.

I waited until the drinks had been served before I took them through my conversation with Tony and Bill Jones.

When I finished, Daniel's first response wasn't "No fucking way" or something along those general lines.

Instead, he said, "How did you leave it with them?"

"I told them I would bring it to you, and to Rita," I said.

He drank some of his beer from the bottle. I did the same. Something about Narragansett still made me feel as if I were a young guy in Boston all over again.

"And they spoke of the offer being in the seven-figures range?" Daniel said.

"They did," I said.

"They absolutely have to be talking about that kind of money," Rita said to me, "or they wouldn't have wasted your time, or dispatched you to then go waste Daniel's." She smiled. "And without knowing what the number actually is? I'll get more out of them if it comes to that."

"On account of Daniel being the only one with the ability to turn Vic Hale radioactive," Hawk said.

"This would all be a lot simpler, for everybody, if we could get that asshat to submit to another DNA test," Rita said, "if that's the only way to prove conclusively that the first one was either right or wrong."

"You do decide that is the only way and decide he needs some extra persuading," Hawk said to Rita, "goes without saying that kind of persuading be one of the best things for me and my trusty sidekick."

"Here we go with the sidekick shit," I said.

Daniel sat there in silence, his index finger making slow circles around the opening to his bottle, as if he was not hearing the rest of us.

"Tell you what, and not that anybody asked," Hawk said. "It was me, I'd tell them I'm the one ready to play Let's Make a Fucking Deal, have Miss Rita here find out what the offer is and then jack it up, like she say she can. Then Daniel here can go off to Harvard with a filled-up bank account and set out to out-lawyer Miss Rita someday."

"Hey, no talking dirty," Rita said.

"Since when?" Hawk said.

"You'd really take the money?" Daniel said to Hawk. "Seriously?"

"Soldier of fortune," Hawk said, "especially if we talking about a small fortune here."

"You mean that, don't you?" Daniel said.

"Uh-huh," Hawk said.

"Not like I can judge," Daniel said. "It's exactly what my mother did once with Vic Hale."

I told him that a similar comment had been made in the back of the limousine by Tony Marcus.

"He happens to be right, as much as I hate to admit it," Daniel said in a quiet voice. "There's no escaping the fact that's exactly what she did."

I didn't tell Daniel Lopez what Tony Marcus had said about everybody being a whore.

"But if I do walk away," Daniel said, "that does nothing about getting justice for my mother, or for Ricardo."

"Doesn't mean we still can't get justice for them in the end," Rita said. "Because even if you walk away, Daniel, trust me on something: These two won't."

"But are you prepared to do it?" I said. "Even though it would probably mean never knowing for sure if he's your father or not?"

Now Daniel's voice wasn't much more than a whisper. *"I don't want him to be,"* he said.

He held up his beer bottle now and studied it as if there were a note at the bottom that he was trying to read.

"You want to know something else?" he said. "As much as he paid my mother, it wasn't enough."

He nodded, as if on the verge of ending some brief debate with himself.

"Maybe it's time for me to be the one to settle up with him," he said.

"They maintained that the offer was coming from them and not Hale?" Rita said.

"They did," I say. "But lawyers do lie on occasion, present company excluded, of course."

"Or not," she said.

No one spoke then. We all drank our drinks.

Finally Daniel turned to me.

"Tell them they can make their offer," he said. "But on one condition."

Somehow I knew what was coming. But let him be the one to say it.

"They make it to me in person," he said.

He paused and said, "And Vic Hale has to be in the room when they do."

FIFTY-SEVEN

I did not speak to Hawk again before he and Daniel were in the Jag and driving off. Rita then asked if I wanted to share an Uber with her, but I said I needed some air and walked back to my apartment.

I called Tony Marcus when I got there, was sent straight to voicemail, left a message, got a call back from him about fifteen minutes later.

"Daniel says he's willing to listen to the offer," I said, but then explained his terms.

"His terms got nothing to do with ours," he said.

"If you want this deal to happen," I said, "then you're going to need to try something new, at least for you."

"And what might that be?"

"Bringing people together for the common good," I said, "and not just your own."

There was a pause at his end. "Might take some persuasiveness," he said.

"Who better at the art of persuasion?" I said, and told him I'd wait to hear back from him.

At this point I decided I needed a real drink, and perhaps more than one, and decided that my best option on this night was the best scotch I had, Johnnie Walker Blue.

I got a highball glass out of my kitchen cabinet and put ice in it and then poured the Johnnie Walker over the ice before adding what I knew from experience was the perfect amount of soda, stirring it with my finger until I saw that the contents were the color of straw.

Then I took my drink back into the living room and opened the top of the Angels Horn turntable that Susan had bought me last Christmas for playing my old vinyls, replacing the turntable that was nearly as old as some of the records.

"I know I'm being an enabler by doing this," she said.

"Why do your psych words always make me hot?" I'd said after opening the box.

"Butterflies taking wing make you hot," she said.

I pulled out Sarah Vaughan's *After Hours* and then sat on my couch and drank my best scotch and listened to her ease into "My Favorite Things":

"Raindrops on roses . . ."

I drank to that, and to Miss Sarah, but before long was again thinking about what kind of money they might be prepared to offer Daniel Lopez to make him go away and how much he might be willing to take to do it.

If he wasn't bluffing.

Unless, of course, he was.

It still wasn't my place to tell him what to do, he was a grown-ass man, a lot more grown-up at his age than perhaps he thought he would be when his mother was still alive. Maybe in the end he would become just one more person in Vic Hale's orbit to strike it rich, take what would be blood money in so many ways, now more than ever with Ricardo Baez dead, too.

I drank more of my drink, feeling the scotch slowly making its way through me, spreading a familiar warmth. I had read once about the rate of alcohol absorption eventually matching the rate of metabolism.

Or perhaps it was the other way around.

I knew Hawk was right about the money, even if it meant Daniel making the whole thing transactional in the end. But it did not change the fact that it was up to Daniel to determine what he thought was right here, or wrong, what his own bottom line was.

I further understood that on some fundamental level, it should not be right for Vic Hale to just write another check, no matter what the amount, like it was one more get-out-of-jail-free card for him.

I had come to this, before the death of Ricardo Baez, wanting to do right by Daniel Lopez. But who was I to tell him not to put money into a bank account the way his mother had, in the interest of giving himself the best possible life?

Who was I to tell him how to live his life?

Better yet: Who was I to tell him to live it on terms other than his own?

I had lived my own life by my own terms as well as I could, trying to be on the right side of things as often—and as well—as I could.

I felt ice on my teeth then and went back into the kitchen and made myself another drink and came back into the living room. Sarah was into "Wonder Why" by then. I walked over to the picture window and saw that night had come fully to the city. I stared out at it and raised my glass. And drank. *Hello darkness, my old friend.*

I wondered what the conversation between Hawk and Daniel

had been like on the ride back to Auburndale, if Hawk had further elaborated on what he thought Daniel should do, had laid out the terms of his own existence, his own belief system, which was so similar to mine in so many ways, but vastly different in others.

I knew Hawk well enough to know that if it were up to him he would find a way to get Hale in a room and hit him in the face like he was back in the ring and draw blood from him that way, and take the blood sample to the nearest hospital and Daniel would give a sample of his own blood, and game over.

Then we would know.

But even if that happened, I would still not know who had murdered Daniel's mother and if it was the same person who had murdered Ricardo Baez, and if someone on Vic Hale's side of the negotiating table might be about to get away with murder.

Daniel Lopez had spoken in the bar, all of us feeling as if we were in a real foxhole with him, about finding justice for his mother and for his friend.

I drank more scotch and smiled as I definitely began to feel the effects of the rate of absorption, especially having not had dinner yet, walked away from the window and sat back down on the couch and picked up my phone off the coffee table and called Susan Silverman.

When she answered I said, "Let's not waste time here: What are you wearing?"

"A mask," she said.

"I'll be right over," I said.

"Sorry, not that kind of mask," she said. "The facial-cream kind."

"I've been drinking," I said.

I heard her giggle. "Okay, nobody moves, nobody gets hurt," she said.

"Not only have I been drinking," I said, "I have found myself wrestling with the kind of moral dilemma that finds me in need of a good therapist."

"Well, sir," she said, "if you'll call back during normal business hours, there are several in the area I'll be happy to recommend."

"I'm kind of being serious," I said.

"And despite my frivolous response," she said, "I kind of intuited that."

I told her then about the conversation at Foxhole, and how it had ended, with Hawk especially.

"Hawk is right," she said, "but I'm betting you already know that."

The music had stopped. My glass was again nearly empty. But I knew that talking to Susan was more therapeutic than either the scotch or Sarah Vaughan.

I told her my fears about Vic Hale or someone close to him getting away with murder.

Susan said, "There's a part of me that feels as if Vic Hale gets away with murder on a daily basis. It would make me physically ill if I thought for one minute that he might get away with it for real here."

"Hence my own dilemma about whether or not I think Daniel should take the money," I said.

I drank the last of the scotch, at least for now.

"So what is your professional advice, Doctor?" I said.

"That despite your concerns, this is Daniel's decision to make, and only Daniel's," she said. "But I suspect you already know that, too."

"He hasn't yet asked me what I think," I said. "What do you think I should tell him if he does?"

"You're allowed to tell him your own truth, without fear or favor," she said, "because in my experience it has always been one hell of a rip-roaring truth."

She paused and added, "But guess what, sweetie? He's smart enough to already know what it is."

"I love you," I said.

"I love you, too," she said. "Without fear or favor."

"What do I do if he does take the money and walk away?" I said.

I smiled as I pictured her in bed, with goop I was only rarely allowed to see covering her face, Pearl at her end of the bed, either a book next to Susan or some movie or television show frozen for the moment on her laptop.

"You allow him to take that money with both hands, no matter how reluctantly," she said. "Reluctantly for you or him or both of you."

She paused again.

"And then," she said, "you go crack this case and hopefully nail Vic Hale's balls to the fucking wall."

FIFTY-EIGHT

Karla Morelli-Bruton called in the late morning from Tufts Medical, saying she had some time to talk before what was shaping up to be a busy surgical afternoon.

"Full disclosure, I called Nancy Bayless and she gave me her personal background check on you," she said.

"Did she open with ruggedly handsome, or charming?" I said.

"Neither," she said.

"Is there a chance we could meet in person?" I said. "I promise not to take up too much of your time, I know how crazy things can get at a big-city hospital."

"Firsthand experience?" she asked.

"Some," I said. "But the girl of my dreams watches a lot of *Grey's Anatomy*."

"I'll bet she's the type who thinks she could perform a tracheostomy if she had to?" she said.

"Totally," I said.

She asked where I was. I told her Berkeley and Boylston. She said she'd come to me, she could use a break from being in a big-city hospital. And that she could use even a short walk, as she hadn't been getting her running in lately, she was in training for next year's Marathon.

"Have you run it before?" I said.

"Bucket-list deal," she said. "Gotta do it once before I die."

Karla Morelli-Bruton didn't as much resemble a marathoner when she came through my door as a sprinter coming up and out of the blocks. She couldn't have been much more than 5'1" or 5 '2", runner's body, dark, curly hair, dark eyes, olive skin that spoke to the Morelli part of her, chock-full of energy and life and, I suspected off just one brief phone conversation, fun.

"I'm Karla," she said, shaking my hand, flopping down in a client chair and growling, "Coffee."

I told her I could manage that and made a cup for her and one for myself. After she tasted hers she said, "Starbucks Breakfast Blend, am I right? Kind of a coffee nerd."

"Then you left nerd school early," I said. "We only serve Dunkin' at this establishment."

"Sorry," she said, "after the string of days and nights I just had, I guess my taste buds are fried along with the rest of me."

I noticed she was wearing Hoka running shoes even more colorful than the ones Hawk owned, the blue in them matching up quite nicely with her hospital pants and shirt.

"Nancy Bayless speaks quite highly of you," I said.

"Sisterhood of the Traveling Scrubs," she said. "She's one of the best people I've ever known, and probably the best nursing officer of all time."

"You miss working with her?" I said.

"Miss her, miss that hospital, crazy and understaffed as it was," she said. "Like the kind they'd make a TV series out of. I'm a Milton girl, born and raised. All I ever wanted to be was a nurse, and the only hospital I ever wanted to work at was Stuart Medical, where I actually was born." She smiled. "Then they up and shut us down."

She had already finished her coffee. Smiled at me then and reached out with her mug. I took it and refilled it and handed it back to her.

"It's been suggested by those who know and love me that me being caffeinated almost seems redundant," she said.

"I hear you," I said, and smiled back at her. "They'll only take my hot coffee away when they pry it out of my cold, dead hands."

"Nancy said you were kind of funny," she said.

"Kind of?" I said.

Then I said: "Since you know why I reached out, can we now get to me asking if you can help me?"

"The good news," she said, "is that I'm almost positive which nurse on the staff would have handled the test you showed Nancy, if you and Nancy have the time frame right, which I assume you do."

"Do I even want to know what the bad news is?" I said.

"Doesn't matter whether you want to or not," Karla said. "You're going to hear it anyway."

I waited.

"The nurse in question is dead," she said.

It was as if all that fun had come out of her at once.

"How long ago?" I said.

"Not long," Karla said.

"How?" I said.

"They say she shot herself," she said. "But I happen to believe that is a hot, smoking load of crap."

FIFTY-NINE

The nurse's name was Olivia Briggs.

Karla said that Olivia was a few years younger, but that they had shown up at Stuart Medical in Milton at around the same time. They had become friends almost immediately, Karla looking out for her the way some of the older nurses, starting with Nancy Bayless, had looked out for her.

"It was clear from the start that she was a solid nurse," Karla said, "even as scared and nervous as newbies could be. But what also became clear after a few months is that her real problems weren't with the work."

"You mean personal problems," I said.

"I mean a drinking problem," Karla said, "even as a kid."

"Pretty sure there's no legal age for that," I said.

"It's why, in the end, she only lasted about a year," she said.

"But just backing up," I said, "you seem pretty certain that she was involved with the test I'm investigating while she was still around."

"Not pretty certain," she said. "*Am* certain. Because I distinctly remember her saying she had to get it done as quietly and quickly as possible for a friend of hers."

"Male or female friend?" I said.

"Just that it was a friend," she said, "and that she wanted to be the one to handle the test."

"So it would have been her and then somebody at the lab?" I said.

She nodded. "It would be harder for me to determine who handled the samples at the lab," she said. "A lot of people were coming and going at that point, because the handwriting about the hospital was on the wall, we all knew it was more than rumors that the place was going out of business. So there was a lot of turnover. That old thing about not being able to tell the players without a scorecard sometimes."

Karla said that from what little Olivia Briggs told her about her personal life, the younger woman was in a sketchy relationship at the time. Eventually, whether because of the bad boyfriend or because of the progression of what Karla believed was clearly alcoholism, Olivia quit before she was going to be fired, thinking that would help her down the road if she ever hoped to get another job in nursing.

"I once quit being a cop before I got fired," I said, "but it didn't have anything to do with drinking."

"Let me guess," she said. "Problem with authority?"

"How did you guess?" I said.

"Sometimes," she said, "a good bedside manner involves getting a quick read on people."

She tried to stay in touch with Olivia Briggs after Olivia had quit Stuart, but hadn't heard from her for years until a couple months ago. She called to tell Karla that she had been sober for two years, a personal best, had finally put her life and her career back together, moved up to Vermont and gone to work for a private-duty nursing service in Manchester. She sounded happy, Karla Morelli-Bruton said, and at peace, if you could determine something like that off a phone call.

"Then she died," she said. "It was pretty awful, single bullet to the head, uncapped bottle of Grey Goose in the room with her. Maybe she knew she was going to drink again, but killed herself instead before she did. But you know something? Only Olivia knew."

"People have been known to fall off the wagon," I said. "Or consider falling off, in this case."

"Well aware," she said. "My mother used to say she could stop drinking anytime she wanted, she'd done it plenty of times before. But she finally did stop through the grace of God, started going to AA, was on fire with that and her religion, lived out her own life happy and at peace. The last time I talked to Olivia, it was like that. I told her she sounded like my mother, but that it was a good thing."

"Did Olivia leave a note?" I said.

Karla Morelli-Bruton shook her head. The dark eyes were on me now, and suddenly on fire.

"Somebody killed her and staged it to look like a suicide, including putting the bottle there," she said. "The woman I talked to on the phone that day absolutely did not take her own life now that she finally had one."

"Do you remember the exact date when they found the body?" I said.

She gave me the date.

It was right after Marisol Lopez had been shot to death in Miami.

"I drove up to Vermont when I heard, I was just so *freaking* pissed off," she said. "Told them what I just told you, that there was no freaking way. The chief of police up there was a good guy, but told me that as hard as they looked, they hadn't been able to find a single shred of evidence that a murder had been committed, or that a killer had set it up to look like suicide."

The dark eyes still on me.

"So what do you think?" she said, everything about her tone challenging me.

"I think maybe it really was staged," I said.

"Are you saying that because you really believe that, or because you want to get me out of your office?" she said.

I smiled at her again. "Are you a religious person?" I asked.

"I used to think about becoming a nun until I discovered boys," she said.

"Aren't you guys taught that faith means believing without seeing?" I said.

She managed another smile of her own. "Or something along those lines," she said.

"Well," I said, "I believe that somebody might very well have killed your friend. And I want you to have faith that if it did happen that way, I'm going to find out who did it."

She whistled softly.

"Maybe my prayers have been answered by coming over here today," she said.

"It's a full-service agency," I said.

SIXTY

Tony Marcus called to tell me that the sit-down Daniel Lopez had requested would have to wait a couple more days, because a sit-down for Vic Hale and Bill Jones and the YouTube TV people in Northern California had been moved up suddenly, and they'd flown out there from Boston this morning.

"Are you fading me on this, Tony?" I asked.

"I wouldn't waste my time fading you if I didn't think the meeting was gonna happen, I'd just tell you to go fuck yourself," he said. "Again," he added.

"The longer this takes," I said, "the better the chance the young man might change his mind."

"With the amount of money about to change hands?" he said. "Now who's fading who?"

I then called Chief Jesse Stone in Paradise and asked if he might possibly know the chief up in Manchester, Vermont.

"And here I thought you were calling for crime-stopping tips," Stone said.

"Yeah, yeah, yeah," I said. "*Do* you know the guy?"

"What, you think all us small-town coppers are in a special club?" he said.

"Can you help me out here, or are you just looking to bust balls today?" I said.

"I can't do both?" he said.

He was an ex-boyfriend of Rita's and, after she'd been shot, he eventually helped me catch the guy behind the hit. Stone was very good, the way Quirk and Belson were very good at this kind of work. A great cop, really, small-town or not.

"Guy's name is Pete Ciccone," he said. "A pro. I worked with him a couple years ago on a thing that took me up to his neck of the woods. And I do mean woods."

"I'm thinking about taking a ride up there on a thing I'm in the middle of," I said.

"The kid and the dead reporter?" he said.

"You've been talking to Rita," I said.

I heard him chuckle. "With Rita, listening is generally a more accurate description."

"Whatever happened to attorney-client privilege?" I said.

"Rita says it doesn't count with pillow talk," he said, "even when there's no pillow. And that I am a member in good standing with the law enforcement community."

"You two thinking about starting up again?" I said.

"Maybe when I have my strength," he said.

"Something happen to you?"

"Yeah," Stone said. "Rita."

I asked if he would give Chief Ciccone a heads-up that I was coming up there to ask about a victim named Olivia Briggs.

"How'd she die?" Stone asked.

"Gunshot wound to the head that a friend of hers doesn't believe was a suicide," I said.

"Any proof the cops up there might have that it wasn't?" he said.

"Nope."

"Any proof that you might have that maybe the cops up there don't have?" he said.

"Nope."

"Sounds like a day at Paradise Beach," he said.

"Or a walk through the wood," I said, "dwarfed by trees lining my way." I paused and then said, "Want to know who wrote that?"

"Gotta run," Jesse Stone said.

SIXTY-ONE

I made my way to Fresh Pond Parkway and then Route 2 and finally to 91 North. WAZE had said that the trip would take slightly under three hours. It didn't bother me because I was in no rush to get up there, thinking this might turn out to be a fool's errand, with me as the fool.

I liked being in a car, even when it was a rental. And did good thinking on long car rides, despite what I'd told Tony Marcus and Bill Jones about car sickness.

At this point in my life there was a better chance of me becoming a classical pianist than my knowing how to sync up some of the music on my phone with a rental car's sound system. So I just put the phone in the console and cranked up the speaker as loud as it would go and listened to the playlist that had some of my favorite female vocalists on it, in formation:

Ella and Sarah and Carol Sloane and Diana Krall and, to make myself feel slightly more current, Becca Stevens and Lizz Wright and Jane Monheit. You go, jazz girls.

I finally took the Brattleboro/Bennington exit, then VT 30 to 11. Pete Ciccone, Manchester's top cop, had told me it would save time if we just met at Olivia Briggs's cabin.

After two false turns even using WAZE and finally driving carefully on a narrow dirt road at the end, I found my way to what looked to be a cozy two-story house, the exterior a somewhat darker shade of the fir trees in the woods around it. There was a gravel driveway that reached all the way to the road. I could see an SUV with POLICE MANCHESTER on the side parked there, and a stone walk leading to the front door, where Chief Ciccone stood waiting for me.

He looked to be on one side of fifty or the other, and seemed as if he might've played some football at some point in his life, he had the build for it, and still looked to be in very good shape.

I shook his hand and he said, "Stone said I'd be fine with you as long as I didn't make any sudden moves."

"He only thinks he's funny," I said. "I *know* I'm funny."

"He said you'd say something like that," Ciccone said.

The place was even more quaint inside than it was outside, a second-floor loft you needed a ladder to access, fireplace and old-fashioned wood-burning stove, bookcase underneath the loft, a lot of needlepoint pillows that didn't look store-bought on the chairs and sofa.

Ciccone said the only thing different now from when they'd found Olivia Briggs is that they'd cleaned the blood off the floor, after she must have slid down there off her couch.

"The body wasn't starting to mummify yet, it was too soon for that," he said. "ME said she'd only been dead a couple days before the people at the nurse service got worried."

"Any bruising?" I said.

"No," he said.

"Signs of a struggle?" I said.

"Same answer," he said. "One shot through the temple. Gun was still on the couch."

"She was right-handed?"

"According to the other nurses, she was," Ciccone said.

"I'm told there was no note," I said.

Ciccone said, "Nope."

"Drugs in her system?"

He shook his head.

"Just the one bullet gone from the chamber?"

He nodded.

I looked around the interior of the house in the woods where Olivia Briggs had lived out the last moments of her life.

Alone.

Or not.

"You believe she did herself in?" I asked him.

"Going off the evidence, I got no choice, whether I like it or not," he said. "People at her work told me about some of the AA meetings around town they thought she attended, but when I tried to talk to people after those meetings? Even the ones who remembered her told me the confidentiality didn't stop after a person died. The best I got was from one guy who just said it made no fucking sense to him, her whole life had turned into a serenity prayer. You never knew for sure if somebody was going back into the bottle. But he just didn't believe she would've, the way she was working the program."

"People are able to hide depression," I said, "before you hear about something like this happening."

"Going off the people I canvassed," he said, "she not only would've had depression hid, she would've had it buried somewhere halfway up the mountain."

"Did you talk to her sponsor?" I said.

"I finally managed to get a name. A woman. And even that took some doing, no shit. I get the anonymous part, but I get the feeling it would be easier to get intel out of the CIA."

"She willing to talk to you?" I said. "The sponsor?"

"Not even a little bit," he said. "The only thing she told me before she hung up on me was that Olivia would have reached out to her if she felt like she was about to have a slip."

"What about family?"

"Parents dead," he said. "No siblings."

"Boyfriend or girlfriend?" I said.

"Not that anybody knew about," he said. "From everything I was able to piece together, she worked the program and worked as a nurse and came back here at night."

Olivia's prints were all over the place, he said, and prints from the housekeeper who came in once a week. And a local plumber, and a handyman who the housekeeper said kept the woodstove up and running. There were a few footprints around the house, nothing unusual. I'd seen for myself there was a stone walk leading to the front door.

"She have a car?" I said.

"A Corolla," he said. "We still got it, but nothing helpful inside."

"Surveillance cameras?" I said.

He snorted. "Oh, sure," he said, "we've got instant replay up here, too."

"Sorry," I said. "Dumb question. I'm quite adept at them once you get to know me."

"Don't be sorry," he said. "This whole thing just pisses me off, and royally. She'd become one of ours up here, which makes this personal for me. Here was somebody whose drinking tried to wreck her goddamn life and she wouldn't let it in the end." He gestured at the rattan chair. "And now she ends up like this."

I said, "What kind of gun?"

"A .22," Ciccone said. "Wasn't registered to her. No serial number."

"So it wasn't legal," I said.

"No, sir," he said.

"So how does a nurse get her hands on a piece like that?" I said.

"Maybe she knew somebody who knew somebody and wanted to have one living alone up here," he said, "and didn't want to go through the process or the paperwork, even though up here it's pretty easy to get one, you don't even need a permit as long as you're of age."

"So it came from the same place a lot of guns come from in this country," I said.

"Somewhere," Ciccone said, finishing the thought for me.

I took another look around.

"The housekeeper come in after it stopped being a crime scene?" I said.

"Nope," he said. "This is pretty much how we found it after we found her."

"So Olivia Briggs tidied up like this right before she put a bullet in her head?" I said.

He sighed.

"I got eight full-time sworn officers up here," he said. "Four dispatchers. But we're pretty good at what we do and none of us found anything to indicate it was something other than it looked like it was, even if you don't believe it's what it looked like it was and neither do I."

"Not hard to stage something like this, you know what you're doing," I said.

"Sneak up behind and pop her, probably wearing leather gloves," Ciccone said. "Put her hand on the gun after, fire another round out the door so there's powder burns on her hand, put a bullet back in the chamber so there's only one missing."

"Find anything in the woods where the other bullet might have ended up?" I said.

"Nope."

He took me through the rest of it, told me he'd gone through her phone records and credit card receipts and her bank account and couldn't find anything that would point to a suspect in there. He said he couldn't get into her laptop without a password, and nobody at work seemed to know what it was. She had no social media presence.

"I'll say this, though," he said. "For somebody who did have a problem with the bottle, she'd done a pretty good job of not blowing through her money."

"Nest egg?"

"Slightly over a hundred grand," he said. "Looked like she had what she had in some kind of money-market thing, for a long time."

"How long?"

"Long," he said.

"Will?" I asked.

"A treatment center for teenagers over in Johnson gets it all," Ciccone said.

We walked back outside and he locked the door behind us and stood on the front porch and looked around at the woods.

"You ever get tired of looking at the trees?" I said.

"You ever get tired of looking at the ocean?" he said.

We began walking toward our cars.

"This part of something else for you?" he said.

"I could take you through all of it," I said, "but it would just give you the same headache I've got."

I looked around at all the tall, pretty trees.

"But my gut is telling me it might be connected to a couple other murders," I said. "One in Miami, one in Boston."

"Your gut ever wrong on the big stuff?" he said.

"I used to say that it was wrong about as often as the Sox won the World Series," I said. "But I've had to revise that, for obvious reasons."

I started to get into the rental and stopped with my hand on the door.

"Hey," I said, "were you able to put names with the numbers she called recently?"

"Most," he said. "I've got the file on my computer back at the office. But I didn't see anything that jumped out at me. Most of the calls were local, and there weren't a hell of a lot of those. She might have been the last person who didn't spend her life, at least when she still had one, on a phone. Or taking pictures of herself for Instagram every time she stepped outside this cabin."

"She didn't have more than one phone, then, I'm guessing," I said.

"Just the one we found in her bedroom," Ciccone said.

I walked back over to him and gave him my email address and he put it in his own phone and said he'd forward whatever he had.

We shook hands one last time. He asked if I was going to spend the night, because if I was, he could recommend a couple good inns, and places to eat. I told him I'd considered it, but was just going to head back.

"I absolutely fucking hate the idea of somebody getting away with murder on my watch," he said.

"Know the feeling," I said.

Ciccone grinned.

"Jesse Stone said that whatever it is you're into, his money's on you," he said.

"Hero worship," I said.

SIXTY-TWO

It was past ten o'clock when I was back at Marlborough Street. When I parked behind my building, I had my .38 in my hand before I got out of the rental. Fool me once.

When I was upstairs, I made myself a fried-egg sandwich with cheddar cheese on sourdough bread and spicy Wickles Pickles on the side and opened a bottle of Samuel Adams Summer Ale and watched the Red Sox postgame show on NESN, having listened to almost the whole game on the drive home. They had won again. Six in a row. At least somebody was on a roll these days.

I checked my home laptop to see if Pete Ciccone had emailed me Olivia Briggs's phone records, or anything else he thought I might want to see. He had not. Probably in the morning. I knew he'd stay with this, too. He was the type, no sign of quit in him that I had detected, just his gut telling him the same thing mine was.

I was even more convinced than I was when I'd left for Vermont that Olivia Briggs's death was a piece—perhaps an essential one—of a much bigger and more complicated story, one that had begun a long time ago when Marisol Lopez had come into Vic Hale's life and into his home and finally into his bed.

And then, from what I now knew, Olivia Briggs's life had first intersected with Marisol's at the hospital in Milton, and almost certainly again when the nurse had gone down to Florida to visit her.

Now both were dead.

I opened another bottle of beer and was about to sit down at my desk with a legal pad and make a couple of lists, one with what I knew and the other with what I thought I knew, just to see all of it on the page in front of me as a way of organizing jangled thoughts, when there was a knock on my door.

No one had buzzed from downstairs so that I could get them through the front door and into the building.

I had placed the .38 on one of the small side tables in the living room. I picked it up now as I walked across the room and looked through my peephole to see who my visitor was at this time of night.

When I did, I stuck the gun into the back pocket of my jeans and opened the door.

"Is this a bad time?" Mauricio Estrella said, and then walked past me and into my apartment as if he owned the place.

Perhaps out of force of habit.

SIXTY-THREE

He stopped in the middle of the room and looked me over. "So how was Vermont, Mr. Spenser?"

It got a smile out of me, one I couldn't hold back.

"You had me followed?" I said. "Was it Heckle or Jeckle or both?"

"I'm sorry," he said.

"Hector or José?" I said.

Now he smiled. "I have many people whose job it is to help look after my interests, and after me," he said. "Though perhaps none of them is as formidable as your Mr. Hawk, I will grant you that."

"So you have been following me," I said, "and not just tonight."

"I make it my business to know as much as possible about all of the others at the table," he said.

"I don't have a seat at the table," I said. "I see myself more as an interested third party."

"Or, and even more accurately, a persistent pain my ass," he said.

"Well, to be fair," I said, "not just yours."

I motioned for him to take the couch. He did. He was wearing a black polo shirt and beige linen pants and suede loafers without socks.

"Would you care for a drink?" I said.

"I have tried to limit my alcohol intake after a health scare from a few years back," he said. "But have also made a lifestyle choice not to abstain completely. Do you have vodka on hand?"

"I have a bottle of Tito's in the freezer," I said. "Would that be acceptable?"

"Even though you appear to have it on ice, I would prefer to have it *over* ice, please," he said.

I went into the kitchen and poured his drink and a glass of Jameson for me. I handed him the vodka and sat across the coffee table from him.

"Salud," he said.

"To our health," I said.

He smiled again, more thinly this time, hardly anything changing in his face, certainly not in his eyes.

"Your health, perhaps," he said.

"Not yours?" I said.

"Mine is not the one in jeopardy at the present time."

"Not to be a bad host," I said. "But if you think mine is, you haven't done the homework on me you seem to think you have."

"Fair enough," he said. "I don't wish to argue with you. I walked over here tonight from my hotel so the two of us might have a civilized conversation, in the hope that I might reason with you at the same time."

I drank some of my whiskey and waited. It was his show, for now, anyway.

He drank some vodka. "I want to reason with you one last time to stay the fuck out of my business," he said.

I smiled at him again.

"It's funny you mention that," I said. "Because somebody essentially told me the same thing the other night before putting my car in front of a firing squad."

He offered the same thin smile.

"Tell me something I don't know," he said.

SIXTY-FOUR

I thought he looked inordinately pleased with himself. So I waited to give him any kind of reaction.

"So you sent the shooter?" I said finally. "That wasn't very neighborly."

He shrugged and sipped a tiny bit of his vodka. It was like watching Susan Silverman drink.

"Whether I did or did not is frankly irrelevant at this point," he said.

"Tell that to the guys at Mike's Auto Repair on Route Nine," I said. "And by the way, and even though it's irrelevant at this point, how did you get up here without buzzing me from outside?"

Estrella shook his head as if I'd insulted him, or at least disappointed him.

"Heckle and Jeckle, as you call them, are quite resourceful in getting someone's full attention," he said.

"Why are you really here?" I said. "You could have said what you wanted to say over the phone."

"I prefer to do business in person when possible," he said. "To look the other man, or woman as the case may be, in the eyes. And have them look into mine when I tell them my truth."

"Or face consequences," I said.

I thought of Susan having referenced my own truth.

Estrella sighed and showed me the same sad face.

"My own truth, in this case," he said, "is that I firmly believe that your interests regarding Vic Hale and my interests are actually aligned."

"I find that difficult to believe," I said.

"Whether you do believe me or not," he said, "believe this: We both want to take the man down."

"You certainly have an odd way of showing it," I said.

"Perhaps so," he said. "But I have my reasons as to why we have all of us arrived at this juncture. Or fork in the road, as you will. And you need to know that all the king's horses and all the king's men aren't going to stop me from the resolution with Vic Hale that I seek."

"And *you* know that all of the king's horses and men couldn't put Humpty Dumpty back together again, right?" I said.

Another smile. Another neat sip of vodka. At least I didn't have to worry about the man getting drunk, not at this rate.

"I frankly always have wondered what the king's horses had to do with anything," Estrella said.

"I never said that I wanted to take Vic Hale down," I said.

"Oh, please, Mr. Spenser, that is exactly what will happen if you help young Mr. Lopez prove that Hale is his father," Estrella said. "It would be impossible to contain information like that in the modern world, keep the world from learning that the young man is in fact the product of a union between Hale and the kind of person he now wants hunted down like a dog."

He placed his glass down hard on the coffee table.

"I was that kind of illegal once," he said.

My apartment was quiet for several moments until I said, "You entered this country illegally? That's not what your bio says."

"You should know by now that you can even buy the past you desire for yourself if you have enough money," he said. "And I do."

He took in a lot of air and exhaled loudly, like a sound that should have come out of a much larger man.

"I hate that man," he said. "He is the one who is a dog."

"And yet you are negotiating for his services," I said. "You need to explain that to me."

"No," he said.

He held up a hand.

"And please don't waste my time or your own asking me again."

I studied him even more closely then, the hardness of him, the certainty, even the arrogance. I had spent so much of my adult life, too much, in the presence of two kinds of people: those who were tough and those who wanted you to think they were.

The little man sitting across the table from me was tough enough. He drank some of his drink and I did the same.

When he was ready he said, "I know much about you. But I do not know you well enough to share more than I have already shared with you this evening about my plan."

"But you obviously have one," I said. "And even though you are of the opinion that we share the same goal with Vic Hale, you are unwilling to share that plan with me, which seems somewhat counterintuitive."

He leaned forward, smiling again. "You look like a thug, sir, but do not speak like one."

"Wouldn't *ruggedly handsome* be more appropriate?" I said.

Maybe I could at least get him to buy into that.

"I need you to stand down until I close this deal in my favor, which I will," he said. "Then you and the boy can do whatever to him that you want."

"He's not a boy," I said. "He's a young man. And not to sound like a thug here, neither of us needs your permission to go at Hale as hard as we want and whenever the fuck we want to."

"My way is better," he said.

"Then tell me what it is."

"No," he said again.

It was clear that he liked saying the word much more than hearing it.

He said, "Clearly, someone whose interests are aligned with Vic Hale's killed one of my people. Or had it done. Perhaps it was Hale himself. Nothing else makes sense to me, and why I need you to let me handle this in my own way." He nodded, as if in agreement with himself. "I assure you it would be in your best interest and the young man's best interest. And I can assure you further that on the other side of this, I would make it worth his while, and your own."

"But what if I'm the one who says no?" I said.

He had somehow finished his vodka, even with ice still in the glass. He set it down gently this time.

"I really have done an extensive background check on you," Estrella said. "And understand that you only kill as a way of not being killed yourself."

He stood.

"But please don't confuse your own value system with my own," he said.

I stood, too. My size did not appear to intimidate him any more tonight than it did the first time we met.

"You really now have been warned for the last time," he said. "Thank you for the drink."

Then he made a brief shooting motion at me with his thumb and index finger and left me standing there, trying to decide whether or not I'd just been hit.

SIXTY-FIVE

Tony Marcus called when I got to the office the next morning to tell me that Vic Hale and Bill Jones would likely be back tonight from California, and that Bill Jones would try to set up the meeting Daniel had requested with Vic Hale within the next couple days.

"I will relay that to my client," I said.

"Thought the boy was Rita's client, not to make too fine a point of things," he said.

"You know how we roll," I said. "What's hers is mine and what's mine is hers."

"Not what she says," Tony said, "'specially with the rolling-around part."

"Gotta ask you something," I said. "Isn't this a little early for you to be up and about?"

"Used to be," he said. "But now I got me one of them Oura rings, monitors my sleep and whatnot. So I got some solid wellness going for me."

"Did not see that coming," I said.

"Tell the boy take the fucking money and run," he said, and ended the call on that pleasant note.

In the interest of my own wellness, I decided against going for donuts this morning and just stayed with coffee. I opened my email and saw one from Chief Pete Ciccone, with a couple attachments, and was about to open them when I heard the bygone-days ringtone I'd had Cassius put on my iPhone, just more nostalgia from me for Ma Bell.

The very modern screen read UNKNOWN CALLER, but I threw caution to the wind and answered anyway.

"Spade and Archer," I said.

"It's Woody Giles," I heard. "I need to see you."

"Let me check my book," I said.

"Can you stop dicking around for once?" he said. "This is important."

"Talk to me."

"I will when I see you," he said. "I can come to you, you want."

"Are you at your office?" I said.

"Yeah."

"I'll come there," I said.

"How soon?"

"Walt Whitman said we should live in the eternal present," I said.

I heard him sigh rather loudly. "You really can't stop dicking around, can you?" he said.

"And on that cheery note," I said, "I'm on my way."

SIXTY-SIX

When I was once again seated across the big desk from Woody Giles, he said, "Let me get right to it."

I grinned. "Good," I said. "Don't you just hate people who dick around? I know I sure do."

He rubbed his temples as if a headache had sprung up, just like that. He was wearing a soft-looking sweater with a hood in back, which I always thought made guys his age look silly. Or guys of any age, for that matter.

"This meeting is a bad idea," he said.

"And yet you made it sound as if there was much for us to discuss," I said.

"I don't mean this meeting, funny guy," he said. "I mean the one between Vic and the kid. Jones and Marcus might have signed off on it. Vic still might. But I didn't. And I'm the one trying to make him richer than he already is."

"So you're aware of the unholy alliance between Jones and Marcus," I said.

"Keep your friends close," he said, "and the rest of that shit."

He asked if I wanted coffee. I said I was fine. He reached for a tall glass next to him filled with something the color of seaweed. Probably part of his wellness program.

"So no moral alarms have sounded about both you and Vic being associated with a known gangster like Tony Marcus?" I said.

Giles laughed.

"Both Vic and me had that kind of alarm disabled a long time ago," he said. "You've probably noticed that Vic has a little trouble with brown people. Different story with Black guys, at least in Marcus's case. Sometimes I think he's calling the shots with Vic's career more than Jones is."

"Tony's never been much of a delegator," I said. "So why do you think the meeting between Vic and Daniel is such a bad idea?"

"Because even if they do meet, the kid still isn't going to get the closure he's up here looking for," Giles said. "He won't know what he wants to know and what Vic doesn't give a shit one way or the other about knowing. The best thing for the kid is to get paid and get lost."

"Do you know how much money we're talking about with Daniel?" I said.

"A lot," he said. "And you know why? Because I don't need more problems with this thing now that I've got that fucking Guatemalan breathing down my neck and giving me one head fake after another."

"Mr. Estrella seems to be of the opinion that he's going to be the last one in the room," I said.

"Let the little prick think that way," Giles said. "He's not taking Vic away from me and he's not taking my company, just because they're pretty much the same thing. In the end I'm gonna win and he's gonna lose unless he wants to do things my way."

"Is that what this is really about?" I said. "Not wanting to give up the belt?"

"Not to some coffee-beaner who looks like he belongs in *Scarface*," he said.

I smiled. "Hey," I said. "If you do lose Vic, maybe you could start a podcast of your own."

He shrugged. "What can I tell you?" he said. "I am who I am."

"And that's all that you am," I said.

"More poetry?"

"Popeye the Sailor," I said.

"You and the kid just need to get the hell out of my way and let me close this deal," he said.

"It's what people keep telling me," I said, "almost daily."

"You get the kid to take his cut and I'll cut you in, too," Giles said. "I figure it will be a hell of a lot more than the kid is paying you."

"He's not paying me," I said.

"Hey, you know what they say about the sucker at the table," he said.

"You really think that Hale will stay with you in the end?" I said.

He looked down at his hands and started fiddling with the big diamond ring.

"Vic's a greedy bastard like we all are," he said. "But he prides himself on loyalty. Giving it, getting it. He thinks you're disloyal, you're dead to him."

"Literally?" I said.

"Huh?"

"Nothing," I said.

"So we clear?" he said.

"Unequivocally," I said.

"You'll get the kid to call off the meeting?"

"I didn't say that," I said. "I was just pointing out that you have made yourself abundantly clear."

"Do this right and everybody wins," he said.

"But either you or Estrella will lose," I said, "unless you do somehow end up in business together."

"It won't be me losing," Giles said. "Either way."

"I'm curious about something," I said. "You ever think about the reporter who died?"

"Never," he said. "To me, the old joke about lawyers applies to reporters, too: One dead one is a start."

I was around the desk before he even processed what was happening, grabbing him by the front of his sweater, pulling him up and out of his chair, and then putting him against the wall with all his big-guy pictures on it, rattling the frames of many of them as I did, even though none fell.

Giles was a big, broad man. I was bigger, and stronger. My face was now close to his. This wasn't pro wrestling now. This was real, and he knew it.

"What the fuck," he said.

"That reporter was worth a hundred of you, Woody," I said. "And if I could write a check to bring him back, I would. But I can't."

I grabbed more of his sweater and pulled him toward me and then shoved him back into the wall. His face was red now, and he was having a difficult time breathing.

"I . . . had . . . nothing . . . to . . . do . . . ," he said, struggling to get words out.

Far as he got.

"But somebody in this thing did have something to do with it," I said.

"Wasn't . . . me," he said.

We were still nose to nose.

"I don't like anybody involved in the deal of the century, not a single one," I said. "I don't like you, I don't like your goons, I don't like Hale, who might be the biggest goon of all. And I'm tired of all of you thinking that just writing checks solves all the problems in the world."

I let go of him then, and finally stepped back, if not very far.

"I do hope, however, that I've now made myself abundantly clear," I said.

Giles stayed where he was against the wall, as if afraid I might misunderstand even the slightest movement on his part.

When I got to his door, I turned around.

He still hadn't moved.

"And lose the hood," I said. "It makes you look like more of an asshole than you already are."

SIXTY-SEVEN

Cassius Moore had asked if I minded him spending quite as much time in my office as he had lately. I told him I did not, that I liked having him around, not that he should let that *get* around.

"It might harm my lone-wolf persona," I said.

"Wait, you have a lone-wolf persona?" he said.

Cassius was there when I got back from Woody Giles's office. I asked what he was doing and he said, "Surfing the Net."

"Now who sounds old?" I said.

He got out of my chair. When I took his place he said, "You okay?"

"Fine," I said, too loudly and too quickly.

He cocked his head slightly, curious. "I sense that you are not being completely honest with me right now," he said.

"Well, you got me there, kid," I said, and then took him through the quality time I had just spent in Giles's office.

"Big picture?" Cassius said. "If he's still got his teeth, it sounds as if he got off easy."

I leaned back in my chair and laced my fingers behind my head, and then told him everything I had learned in Vermont about the late Olivia Briggs, no longer our missing nurse.

"She has to be the one," I said.

Cassius nodded. "So she was there at the beginning with Marisol," he said. "Now, twenty years later, Marisol is dead and she's dead and Ricardo Baez is dead, presumably for asking questions about everything that did start with the nurse and patient twenty years ago."

"While some of the people involved with the man who is or isn't Daniel Lopez's father are about to strike it rich," I said. "Including, at least in scale, Daniel himself, if that's the way he plays it in the end."

Cassius got up and fixed himself a cup of green tea. When it was ready, he chose to spare me today with what a rich source of antioxidants the tea was.

"But to be fair," he said, "if anybody does deserve to get paid here, it's Daniel, that's the way I look at it."

"Because he's the one who's lost the most," I said.

"May I speak freely?" Cassius said.

"When have you not, kid?"

"You seem pretty frustrated Daniel might take the money," he said. "And I think that frustration is one of the reasons you just bounced Woody Giles around, and not just because of what he said about reporters."

I sat back up in my chair and got my sneakers off my desk.

"Sometimes I feel as if I'm watching an armed robbery taking place," I said. "With three dead bodies left behind already."

I remembered then that I still hadn't opened the two attachments from Pete Ciccone. I did that now. Saw that one was Olivia Briggs's most recent credit card statements, and one was a record of the calls she'd made from her cell. Before I studied them closely, I first printed them out on my cartridge-free Epson, having finally abandoned my old HP at Cassius's urging, even though I tried not to look when he took it away.

"It was time to let go," he'd said after having the Epson up and running.

The new printer also did scanning and copying and pretty much everything except make pitching changes for the Sox.

I handed Cassius his stack and took my own and went through the credit card statements first, just because they were on top.

A few minutes later I said, "And there it is."

"There what is?" he asked.

"JetBlue flight from Logan to Fort Lauderdale a few days before Marisol Lopez was shot to death at that ATM," he said.

"The Vermont cop didn't mention that?" Cassius said.

"I didn't tell him the entire backstory about Marisol and her nurse friend," I said. "Just that all three deaths might be related."

"At least we do have our nurse," Cassius said, "even though she's gone."

"The nurse who paid Marisol a visit and left her at least unsettled, according to Daniel," I said. "Even if his mother never got the chance to explain."

"But why?" Cassius said

"Why did Nurse Briggs go down there or why was Marisol somewhat undone after she left?" I said.

Cassius grinned. "You pick," he said.

"Play it out," I said. "Twenty years after that DNA test, Olivia Briggs decides to pay a visit to one of the testees. Who then ends up dead, in what was supposed to look like one more random South Florida killing, but one we now believe was anything but. Then shortly thereafter it's the nurse who dies in what was supposed to look like a suicide."

"One you believe is anything but," he said.

"Curiouser and curiouser," I said.

"Isn't that what Alice said after she went down the rabbit hole?" Cassius said.

"She beat us down there," I said.

It was all right in front of us with the printouts. The flight down. The flight back the next afternoon. Airport hotel. Three Uber rides while Olivia Briggs was down there. Even parking at the Logan airport garage.

I was about to go over Olivia's call list, but Cassius, not surprisingly, was way ahead of me.

He whistled and said, "Whoa."

Then he was circling one of the calls before he started tapping away on his keyboard.

"What?" I said.

"A few days after our Nurse Briggs made her trip to Florida, she also placed a phone call to the 781 area code, and a woman named Kate Musgraves-Tebbets, whose name I just put with the number."

"Isn't 781 the northern suburbs here?" I said.

"Woman lives in Lincoln," Cassius said.

"And this has caught your attention why?" I said.

"Because I thought I might have recognized the name from Nancy Bayless's list," he said. "And as it turns out, I *did* recognize it, because the former Kate Musgraves worked in the lab at Stuart Medical when Marisol Lopez had the DNA tested for her and the father and her baby."

He came around the desk and put his copy down in front of me and showed me where he'd circled the number in red.

"Boom," I said.

"Maybe our luck is finally starting to turn," Cassius Moore said.

"Better late than never," I said.

I picked my phone up off my desk and called the number.

She answered on the second ring.

"This is Kate," she said.

I had decided not to overload her with too much backstory. So I kept it simple, giving her my name and telling her I was looking into the death of Olivia Briggs, and had a few questions about a prenatal test that Olivia might have conducted two decades earlier for a young Guatemalan woman.

There was a long pause at her end until Kate Musgraves-Tebbets finally said, "Which test? The first one or the second one?"

SIXTY-EIGHT

We agreed to meet at the deCordova Sculpture Park in Lincoln, a place where Susan and I had occasionally enjoyed weekend picnics over the years.

Nearly 40 percent of Lincoln was protected land, and I'd always felt that the museum here and the park at deCordova, which featured nearly fifty pieces of sculpture, were worth protecting as much as any place like it in the Boston area. There were also cafés on the grounds and shady lawns and walking paths.

Kate Musgraves-Tebbets and I found a bench that looked out at Flints Pond.

She was close to six feet tall by my estimation, long blond hair and longer legs, wearing jeans and sandals and a white Lacoste polo shirt. She was pretty, with pale hazel eyes and a faint tan that seemed to go well with the rest of her. She told me in the first few minutes we were together that she had one son at Tufts and another who was a senior in high school.

Her husband, she informed me, was an orthopedic surgeon at Mass General.

"What can I tell you," she said. "Just when I thought I'd gotten away from hospitals, they pulled me back in."

"You make them sound like the Mob," I said.

"Don't tell my husband," she said.

When we had taken our seats on the bench, she said, "It's so awful about Olivia. I just happened to see the story about it online."

"Were you good friends when you were both at the hospital in Milton?" I asked.

"Yes," she said, "just because we were more than acquaintances. I was only there about a year and a half, Olivia a little less than that."

"You worked in the lab," I said.

She laughed. "I was a glorified paper pusher," she said, "until I thought I could be doing a lot more with my life."

"And moved on to what?" I said.

"Eventually to the best job I ever had or really wanted," she said. "Being a mom."

I asked if she might possibly remember a young Guatemalan immigrant named Marisol Lopez from that time.

"Only because Olivia seemed so invested, I guess that's the right word, in her tests," she said.

"She say why?"

"Just that she was doing a favor for a friend by helping her find out who the father of her baby was," she said.

"Something worth finding out," I said.

"You *think*?" she said. "I asked if the Lopez woman was the friend and she said something about friend of a friend." She absently ran a hand through the long hair. "It was such a long time ago. But I do remember Olivia pressing me on seeing the results as soon as the lab had them."

There was one canoe out on Flints Pond, two people in it, making slow progress away from us across the water.

"You said there were two tests," I said.

She nodded. "I remember that the first one wasn't a match, and Olivia seemed upset about that, though she wouldn't explain why. Then she was back like two days later. Same mother, young Marisol. But a sample from someone else who might have been the biological father."

"You get a lot of fast do-overs like that?"

"Some," she said. "But again, I wasn't around long enough to know how normal or abnormal that was."

She sat there in silence then, before turning to me, and said, "But that's not the whole story."

She ran her hand back through her hair and sighed.

"The name of the potential father was the same for both tests," she said.

"But the second one was a match," I said.

"Sure was," she said.

She stared down at her hands now. I noticed a simple gold band. She wore no other jewelry. She had long, pretty fingers, too.

"I'm a good person, Mr. Spenser," she said. "And I consider myself an honest person. I raised my kids to believe that character is doing the right thing when no one else is around to see you do it. But in this case, I wasn't that person."

"You let it go," I said.

"I knew it was wrong," she said. "I pulled Olivia aside and told her I couldn't falsify records. But she swore that she only changed the name on the second one to protect her friend. What she called a victimless crime."

"She tell you why?" I said. "Or give you the guy's real name?"

She shook her head. "Just that she'd pay me to give her a pass," Kate said.

Everybody gets paid.

"May I ask how much?" I said.

"Five thousand dollars," she said. "It doesn't sound like much. But to me at that time it was a lot."

"So you took the money and shut up about the tests," I said.

She nodded slowly, staring out at the water and perhaps all the way back to that time in her life. We both watched a red-tailed hawk begin to dive and then think better of it and rise back up into the air and disappear to the east.

"She left not long after that, before me," she said. "I heard that she'd gone off to rehab, because I could see drinking was an issue with her. And I did my best to put that moment behind me. I just assumed that it wasn't just a friend she was trying to help out, but a boyfriend. But who knows?" She shrugged. "I hadn't thought about it all that much for years until she called a couple months ago and asked if she could come to see me."

The hawk had come back. Or maybe it was a new one.

"She told me how long she had been sober," Kate said. "And told me it had taken her a long time, a very long time, to get to the fifth step of the Alcoholics Anonymous program."

"Admitting to God and another human being the nature of your wrongs," I said.

"You're in the program?"

"Just in a long-term relationship with a Harvard shrink," I said.

"She just apologized for paying me the money, even if nobody made me take it," she said. "And asked me to forgive her, which of course I did."

"Sounds like a liberating moment for both of you," I said.

"More for her than me," Kate said. "She told me that day she'd finally gotten up the courage to tell the mother the truth, that Marisol had been living a lie without even knowing it was a lie. Olivia had put Hale's family name on both the tests to protect her boyfriend. She said the boyfriend needed Marisol to believe someone other than him was the father."

"But you didn't know it was Vic Hale at the time?" I said.

"I didn't know that's who this Halqvist guy really was until Olivia came to see me," Kate Musgraves-Tebbets said.

She turned to me, the hazel eyes almost becoming translucent.

"She told me that she wanted both of them, her and the mother, to make things right," she said. "Only now she's dead."

"So is Marisol Lopez," I said.

SIXTY-NINE

I called Susan when I knew she was finished with patients for the day and said, "I want a big old bone-in ribeye steak tonight, and don't try to stop me."

"What girl could possibly turn down a truly lovely dinner invitation like that?" she said.

"Capital Grille, seven o'clock?" I asked.

"I may have a big slab of beef myself," she said.

"Stop with all your sex talk," I said.

She dropped off Pearl the Wonder Dog at the apartment and we proceeded to take a long, leisurely walk in the twilight, eventually making our way down Boylston. The Capital Grille had moved a block over to Boylston from Newbury several years earlier, into a bigger space. But it was still all about great steaks, one of the best martinis in town, side dishes so good they could be main courses on their own, and a terrific bar.

Susan tonight wore a black cotton sweater and white jeans she'd recently purchased at Madewell after she'd dragged me there with her while she tried on variations of them.

"You still rock white jeans with the best of them," I said.

"Are you referring to how my ass looks in them?" she said.

"Perhaps," I said.

"Is that why you keep dropping a few paces behind me?" she said.

"It is!" I said.

We got a table in the main dining room underneath the portrait of Red Auerbach. We both ordered martinis.

"No white wine?" I said.

"Date night," she said. Then winked. "And for your information that *is* sex talk, sailor," she added.

Our drinks were delivered. We both tasted them. And for me it was as always with an icy-cold martini like this, one of those bells that now and then rings, right before a trip to the moon on gossamer wings.

I then told Susan about my conversation with Kate Musgraves-Tebbets.

"So what if Vic Hale isn't Daniel's father?" Susan said. "If it's Daniel's intention to get paid, wouldn't he want the money before he found out, just to hedge his bets?"

"We still don't know if he wants to get paid," I said. "He's being very cagey about that."

"Thinking like a lawyer already," Susan said.

"We still can't find out for sure unless Hale agrees to get tested," I said.

She had another taste of martini. "I sometimes forget how good these are," she said.

"I've rarely had a bad one," I said. "Even with gin."

"Gross," Susan said.

"What if I go to Hale before his meeting with Daniel takes place, if it does take place, and tell him about what went on with the tests lo these many years ago?" I said. "And admit that he might have been right about it all along?"

"Then he gets what he wants," she said, "right before he gets even more of what he wants when he signs his new contract."

She looked at me with eyes dark and deep. Frost had been writing about the woods being dark and deep, and promises to keep. But then the old boy had never looked into Susan Silverman's eyes.

"If it plays out that way," she said, "how would you feel?"

For some reason I thought about Olivia Briggs.

"God grant me the serenity to accept things I cannot change," I said.

Susan smiled then, and somehow made plucking an olive out of her glass and eating it seem like the most suggestive thing in the world.

"Since when," she said, "have you ever accepted things you can't change?"

Before I could answer, I felt my phone buzzing in my pocket. When I took it out, I saw that the incoming message was from Tony Marcus.

Hale got a place on Crystal Lake.

Tomorrow night. Nine o'clock.

Shoot you the address in the a.m.

I apologized to Susan and hit him right back.

Who will be there?

And didn't have to wait long for his response.

You. Him. The boy.

Before I put the phone away, I saw that he wasn't through, the little bubble things were still moving, meaning one more text was incoming.

Fuck me on this and you the one be dead.

He didn't include a smiling emoji.

We called an Uber to take us back to my apartment. I told Susan I would take Pearl out while she prepared herself.

"Prepare myself for what, exactly?" she said, and the look on her face was one of wickedness and mischief, and maybe of her own promises to keep. "I need details, man."

"That we lie down because 'tis night," I said.

"Sounds like a plan," she said.

And as we both discovered when I got back, it was a damned fine one at that.

SEVENTY

Frank Belson called when I was on my way to the office in the morning and asked where I was.

"You mean right now?" I said.

"Fuck you," he said.

"Where are *you* right now, Lieutenant?" I said.

"Outside your office," he said.

I told him that if I'd known he was coming I would have brought the frosted donuts with sprinkles I knew he secretly liked.

"Already got 'em, hotshot," he said.

He had, in fact, brought a small box. The one he took out had pink frosting on top. And sprinkles. I grabbed a Boston Kreme and then made us both coffee. Breakfast of champions.

Without preamble, he was talking about Ricardo Baez.

"Whatever notes the reporter had," Belson said, "I can't find them for the life of me. And, trust me, I've looked."

"Means they can't be found," I said.

"Yet," Belson said.

"Maybe being secretive when he was working on something was what made him so good," I said. "And from what I read, he was very good. I keep thinking that the things I've found out about Daniel

Lopez since he got to town, maybe Baez already knew before both of them got to town and kept it secret from both of us. And those things probably got him killed."

Belson ate some donut and drank some coffee.

"We rely on cell phones so much these days, my line of work," he said. "They almost turn into a crutch, they're so easy to track shit. But he left his in his hotel room the night he died, and when I finally had it in my hands, there had been no incoming or outgoing calls for a couple days before he got shot. And no files stashed away on it."

"Could he also have had a burner?"

"Probably had a lot of them," he said. "But if he had one up here, it wasn't with the body."

"My only thought is that he thought he might have a solid lead on who killed Daniel's mother," I said.

"Or maybe he found out something, maybe apart from the kid maybe being Hale's kid, that was going to sink the big mucketymuck deal Hale's got going," Belson said. "Maybe even for Baez's boss."

Belson took me through it. The deep dive he'd made into Baez's online profile. A trip to Miami to talk to his friends and colleagues. Hotel video. Street cams all around The Lenox.

And had repeatedly come up empty.

"Nada," he said. "Still a clean fucking hit."

He leaned back in the client chair and studied me with hooded eyes that looked sleepy but I knew were anything but. As long as we'd known each other and as often as we'd worked together, when Belson looked at me like that I was willing to confess to almost anything.

"I finally did manage to get into The Lenox's phone records," he said. "You ever try to do that? Lemme tell you, it stinks out loud. But there was only one call he made from his room once he checked in, and it was the day he died."

"You know who he made it to?"

Belson said, "You know a guy named Lee Chase?"

"Yup," I said. "Vic Hale's badass bodyguard."

"Him," Frank Belson said.

SEVENTY-ONE

Hawk and I ran the steps at Harvard Stadium together today, my first time back there since my encounter with Bobby and Deke, those two scamps. I was a little more tired than I preferred when I got to the top, and going downhill put even more strain on my knees. But I powered through, more out of vanity than anything else. Or entirely out of vanity. Just because Hawk wasn't showing any strain at all. But then he never did.

When we'd finished and were toweling off on the home team's bench, Hawk said, "Good to see you not ready for the home yet."

"Thanks, homey," I said.

I told him about Belson's visit, and how before leaving Frank told me he'd questioned Lee Chase, who didn't deny that he had spoken to Ricardo Baez, but said it had been only long enough to tell him to back the fuck off with questions about Vic Hale and Marisol Lopez.

"He admitted to Belson that he told Ricardo that if he tried to make trouble for Vic, he'd be making a lot more for himself," I said. "But Frank said Chase had an alibi for the night of the murder. The Glass Slipper over on Lagrange."

"Strip joint?" Hawk said.

"I believe they prefer *gentleman's club*," I said. "But yeah, plenty of people saw him, including one young lady for an extended stay in the VIP room."

Hawk smiled. "Belson get a name?" he said. "Maybe I should conduct a further interrogation."

"Doesn't sound like your style," I said.

"Depends on who wants to feel like a VIP," he said.

We sat in the sun, me with a towel draped over my head, both of us hydrating like crazy. By now Hawk knew all about the meeting with Hale and Daniel at Crystal Lake tonight.

"So if Hale ain't the baby daddy, who is?" Hawk said.

"I keep thinking it could be somebody who was working for Hale at the time in question, or with him," I said. "So I did some checking, and the people who have been with him the longest are this guy Chase, the producer, his lawyer. And the ever-popular Woody Giles, because I believe it was around that time that the radio show became a podcast, for fun and profit."

"You see one of them tapping their meal ticket's girl?" Hawk said.

"If they did," I said, "they would still be extremely motivated to keep that a secret."

"Maybe we figure out a way to get samples from all of them," Hawk said. "Could make it a game show. *Who's Your Daddy?*"

I took some of my water and poured it over my head.

Hawk said, "Sometimes I think you want to find out who the boy's daddy is more than he does."

"Don't you?" I said.

"Fuck it," Hawk said. "And fuck Vic Hale, and fuck anything might benefit his ass in the end."

"Even if I'm the one who somehow ends up doing at least some of the helping?" I said.

Hawk shrugged. "If the ass fits," he said.

I turned to look at him, completely at rest now, his breathing as regulated as it had been on the steps, what sweat there had been on his face and gleaming head long gone. He did not appear tired. Was not old or young. Just Hawk.

He turned to look at me then. "You got to let this go after tonight," he said, "whatever gets said between Daniel and Hale and whatever, ah, accommodation they reach. It's between them after that. And on them."

"What about the reporter?" I said.

"If Belson can't get whoever did it, then maybe that person can't get got," Hawk said. "But you need to be out of the Hale business. We put bad men down, you and me. But what we never do is cut them no slack."

"He did take care of Daniel and his mother for all those years," I said.

"To save *his* ass," Hawk said. "Right thing, wrong reason."

"But still the right thing," I said. "And more than that if he's not the father."

He stood then and said we should take a cool-down walk before we left. So I got up, too, and we made our way slowly toward the end of the field where CRIMSON was written in the end zone, before making the turn and then walking up the other sideline.

He was smiling again, as if he'd just come off the field after making a big play.

"Problem with you, on account of all the Boy Scout you still got in you, is that you still got lines you won't cross," Hawk said. "But sounds to me, just listening to you, that the little Guatemalan don't have issues like that he needs to work through where Hale is concerned."

"No lines," I said, "and no moral ambiguities."

"Ain't exactly no justice, no peace, is it?" Hawk said.

"No," I said, "it ain't."

SEVENTY-TWO

I was at my apartment, waiting for Hawk to drop off Daniel Lopez before I would drive Daniel and me to Newton, when Pete Ciccone called from the Manchester PD.

"Good news," he said. "Well, maybe good news. I got Olivia Briggs's AA sponsor to agree to talk to me. I took one more run at her and convinced her that I'm now more convinced than ever that Olivia didn't kill herself."

"You think she might know something that can help us?" I said.

"From the people I've talked to, she's the one who was closest to her," he said.

"Good luck," I said.

"Her name is Hannah Stovall," Ciccone said.

"When are you seeing her?" I said.

"I'm on my way to meet with her right now," Ciccone said.

I told him I was on my way to a meeting myself and would likely have my phone turned off while it was going on, but that he could text me or leave a voice message if he came up with something, and I would get back to him as soon as I could.

"It still could be dicey, getting something out of her," he said. "Something else I've learned about AA is that getting a sponsor especially to reveal stuff really is like getting a priest to talk about something he heard in confession."

"Bless me, Father," I said, and then went outside to wait for Hawk and Daniel.

Crystal Lake was a natural great pond not far from Centre Street in Newton, and also not far from where Vic Hale's Newton estate was. Maybe if I got the chance, I could ask him why he needed a home away from home this close to his other home.

I had once worked another case for a client who had an expensive home at the lake, just because none of them were cheap. There was a small swimming area, a bathhouse, a small park. Maybe Hale got tired of being behind the walls of his fortress, or being as close to the studio where he did his show. Whatever the reason, it was good being Vic, and had been for a long time. Not bad for the son of a punched-out clubfighter.

Daniel said little on the drive over there, just concentrated on reading me the directions to the address on Lake Avenue that Tony Marcus had provided.

Todd Jakes's Tesla was parked out front when we arrived. He was standing next to it, prepped out as usual in a sweater, a white tee underneath, khakis, sneakers. Maybe it was like a uniform for guys his age trying to dress younger if they still couldn't be younger.

"You must be Daniel," he said, extending a hand. "I'm Todd."

"Vic's producer," I said.

To me Jakes said, "Spenser." We shook hands. "You don't give up, do you?" he said.

"Hardly ever," I said.

"Sorry," he said, "but Lee Chase said I should pat you down."

I looked down at myself. Black T-shirt that I thought fit me rather nicely. Denim carpenter jeans. Red Wing boots. Not stylish. Just functional, in the extreme.

"Do I get to pat you down first?" I said. "I mean, fair is fair."

"You think I'm armed?" Jakes said. "Seriously?"

"I don't," I said. "But neither am I, unless you count being armed with the best of intentions."

He gave me a long look and finally said, "Follow me."

SEVENTY-THREE

Vic Hale, wearing the same Everlast sweatshirt he'd been wearing the day I met him at the Fens and the same kind of loose-fitting jeans, was waiting for us in the foyer.

Jakes said, "I'm still willing to sit in if you want, Vic."

Hale shook his head. "I got this," he said. "If I decide after that I want to go back over to the big house, so to speak, I'll call and you can come back and get me. Or Lee can if you got somewhere to be."

We heard the Tesla pulling away about a minute later.

I wondered how Hale would play it with Daniel, but not for long.

He reached out with a meaty hand and said, "I'm Vic. Nice to finally meet you."

Daniel took his hand. "Daniel Lopez," he said.

Hale looked at me. "I know I said you could come along," he said. "But you're free to leave, too."

"I'd prefer Mr. Spenser stays," Daniel said.

"Mind me asking why?" Hale said.

"Because I wouldn't be here without him," Daniel said. "And I'm basically the one who called this meeting."

"Well, all righty, then," Hale said, and led us into a spacious living room, a huge picture window to our right, looking out at the water, wood beams on the ceiling, fireplace, two long leather couches facing each other across a butcher-block coffee table that looked sturdier than the Soldiers and Sailors Monument. The wall to our left featured a screen that looked as big to me as the one in the outfield at Fenway.

"I know this place isn't that far from my other place," Hale said, answering my question for me before I chose to ask it. "But I feel like I can come over here and get away." He chuckled. "From myself, sometimes."

He took one couch and Daniel and I took the other.

"Not looking to piss you off here," Hale said to Daniel. "But you look like your mother."

"So I've been told."

"She was a good person," Hale said.

I noticed Daniel make fists with hands resting on his knees.

"I have to tell you, Mr. Hale, that she was a good person who would have hated the things you say on your show," Daniel said. "I feel the exact same way."

"You and a lot of other people," Hale said. "But in fairness to me, an awful lot of people *don't* feel the way you do about the things I say." He paused. "But did you really come here tonight to talk politics, kid?"

"I'm not a kid."

"Didn't mean it as an insult," Hale said.

"You do that to me and people like me on a daily basis," Daniel said.

I saw Hale arch his back slightly. "You have a right to your opinion," he said. "Same as I have a right to mine."

I noticed a framed photograph of him with his father behind him, Tommy Hale looking like a giant next to the little boy.

"Listen," Hale said then. "I tried to do right by your mother and by you. My father pushed me to do it and so did people I trust, even if my lawyer wasn't one of them." He turned then and looked up at the picture of him with Tommy Boy Hale, maybe for backup. Then back at Daniel. "I guess in my own fucked-up way, I loved her."

"Don't say that," Daniel snapped, the words sounding like the crack of a whip. "If you really loved her you wouldn't have sent her away when you found out she was pregnant."

Hale suddenly stood up, as if we might be done here. But he just said, "Anybody want a beer? I could sure use one." As if wanting to at least momentarily get around a subject that was going to be squarely between the two of them even if they talked until the end of time.

Daniel and I both shook our heads. Hale walked out of the room and came back with a bottle of Harpoon Ale. He drank some of it and remained standing, like maybe this was showtime now.

"Not gonna lie," he said to Daniel. "A lot of what I do on the show, it started out as an act. But then all of a sudden people were paying attention to me. And even though it shocked the shit out of me, my audience just exploded on the radio, before I started doing the podcast. Just like that, I was the loudest voice in town, even one as woke as this one is supposed to be."

"Then my mother was in your life," Daniel said.

Hale drank more beer. "And then she was pregnant, and even though I never believed I was your father, sorry, I knew how it would look." He sat back down and placed the bottle on the table in front of him. "I figured the right thing for everybody was for her to just go away."

"More for you than for her," Daniel said.

I could see Daniel fighting with himself to remain calm, even if he'd relaxed his hands.

"Guess you got me there," Hale said.

"And now," Daniel said, "after all the money you paid her in my lifetime, you're willing to pay me to go away."

Hale nodded. "You go away and I sign this deal and then when the contract ends, I go away, too."

"Really?" I said. "And do what?"

"Not this," Hale said.

If he was acting, he was doing a very good job of it. Or maybe everything was an act with him.

He finished his beer, wiped the back of his hand across his lips. "We'll get to what kind of money I'm talking about in a minute, by the way," Hale said.

"I haven't said I'm willing to take it," Daniel said.

"No, son," Hale began, then quickly stopped himself. "No, *Daniel*, you haven't. But like you've already been told, it's a lot. And if you give me your word you'll never talk about me and your mother, I'll add one more sweetener on top of the money."

"What's that?" Daniel asked.

"I'll take the test," Vic Hale said.

It was as startling in the moment as if he'd broken the beer bottle over his own head. Daniel and I looked at each other. Then Daniel looked back at Vic Hale.

"And what if it says you're not my father, like you say?" Daniel said.

"You still get to keep the money," Vic Hale said. "The way I look at it, you've earned it and, trust me, there's gonna be more than enough to go around."

He picked up the beer bottle then, and saw that it was empty.

"Then we'll both know, once and for all," he said.

SEVENTY-FOUR

Hale looked directly at me then.

"You can go ahead and be the one to set it up, you can even pick the hospital," he said. "My people aren't gonna be happy, but we need to put this behind us once and for all."

I turned to Daniel. "You good with this?"

"It's why I came up here," he said. Then he turned back to Hale. "But before we go any further, I need to ask you to your face if you had anything to do with Ricardo Baez's murder."

I looked over at Hale and saw the confusion on his face, as if Ricardo Baez's name had stumped him.

"The reporter," I said to Hale. "And Daniel's friend."

Hale didn't hesitate.

"I swear *on* my father that I know nothing about that," Hale said. "You can mark me as lousy all you want for the things I say, but there's things I won't *do*. Or ask somebody else to do."

"You better hope I don't ever find out you're lying about that," I said.

"You won't," Hale said.

To Daniel he said, "You ready to get down to business?"

"Before we talk about money," Daniel said, "I would like to talk to you about my mother, if you don't mind. About a part of her life that I didn't even know had existed."

Hale shrugged. "I got nowhere to be," he said.

I stood up.

"This is between the two of you," I said. "Why don't I take a walk and, Daniel, you can text me when you and Vic are done?"

"That'll be fine," Daniel said. "Thank you."

When I was out of the house and walking around it and down toward the water, I saw a missed call from Pete Ciccone, and a message from him, one that had come in after I'd silenced my phone on the ride to Newton so I wouldn't forget later.

I think I know who it is.

I stopped and held up my phone and stared at it.

He could be referring only to the person who he thought killed Olivia Briggs. Unless he was referring somehow to Daniel Lopez's father, now that I had finally explained Daniel's circumstances to Ciccone.

I tried to call him right away but saw that there were no bars showing on my phone.

Tried to text him back, but it wouldn't go through.

The night was clear, and relatively quiet, except for the occasional sound of a night bird, or a car from the other side of the lake. There was a full moon lighting the night sky. I held up my phone and began to walk around the edge of the water.

I tried Ciccone again.

Call didn't go through.

I kept walking, hoping for at least one stinking bar to appear on the phone and at least give me a shot.

Still nothing.

No text from Daniel came in as I walked.

I wondered what Philip Marlowe would have done when he didn't have enough bandwidth. I wondered, and not for the first time, what had happened to the good old days when all a private detective needed was a gun and a glass of whiskey and a good dame.

I happened to have all of those things, none of them doing me any good at the moment whatsoever.

Kept trying the call.

I didn't know how many times I tried or how long I'd been out here, and I had started to think I might have to wait until Daniel and I were out of this dead zone and headed back to town, when the call went through.

It wasn't much of a connection. I felt I had been transported back in time to the days of "Can you hear me now?"

But I could hear Pete Ciccone and he could hear me, and it was enough of a connection for Ciccone to tell me all he had learned from Olivia Briggs's sponsor.

It was a lot.

Before I began walking back to the house, I was able to make one more call.

SEVENTY-FIVE

I waited until I saw the headlights in the distance making the turn toward the house off Lake Avenue. Only then did I walk back through the front door, having not bothered to knock.

Hale and Daniel were where I had left them, facing each other from their respective couches.

They both looked over at me, surprised, perhaps, that I was back so soon.

"I didn't text you," Daniel said.

"I know," I said

I walked across the room and sat down next to him.

"This couldn't wait," I said.

"What couldn't wait?" Hale said.

"There's no need for you to take any kind of paternity test, Vic," I said. "You were right all along, going all the way back. You're not Daniel's father."

"I don't . . . I'm not sure I understand," Daniel said.

"You're about to," I said. "So is Vic."

In the next moment, Todd Jakes was the one walking through the front door.

"Daddy's home," I said.

SEVENTY-SIX

Jakes looked at me before quietly shutting the door behind him.

"You said when you called that Vic needed me to get back here right away, that it was urgent," Jakes said.

Now Hale was the one looking at me.

"What the hell is going on here, Spenser?" he said.

"Take a seat," I said to Jakes.

"I'm good where I am," he said. "What the hell *is* going on here?" He shook his head. "You really don't quit, do you?"

I let that one go. Already asked and answered.

"You want to finally tell your boss the truth, or shall I?" I said.

"The truth about what?" Jakes said.

"The truth about you once having had a sexual relationship, for at least one night anyway, with Marisol Lopez," I said, "and then doing everything possible to cover that up, starting with having your girlfriend switch those DNA tests so that Vic and Marisol would think he was the father."

"So, wait, you're taking the word of a drunk?" he said.

"We both know Olivia is dead," I said, "because you killed her. And now you're the one who's dead."

"I don't have to listen to this shit," he said. "And neither should you, Vic."

I said, "And then when your old girlfriend told Marisol what she'd done all this time later, and that it was time to make things right, Marisol must have reached out to you, now that she knew what you'd done all those years ago, and that you were the real father. So you went down to Florida and killed her, and came back and killed Olivia, too, thinking she was one last loose end."

Jakes ignored me and looked at Hale.

"You can't possibly be buying into this fever dream, can you?" he asked Hale. "This is me, Vic."

Hale shook his head, and then did it again, as if trying to clear it, squeezing his eyes shut and then opening them.

"My old man said Spenser was as honest and straight-up as anybody he ever knew, even as a kid," he said to Jakes. "Why would he start lying now?"

"Well, he is," Jakes said, "the same way he lied to get me back here."

Jakes turned his attention back to me.

"Who filled your head with all this crazytown bullshit?" he said.

"A loose end you never considered," I said. "Olivia Briggs's AA sponsor. Olivia told her everything about switching the tests, though she got you to believe she'd done it alone. Then she paid off the person who helped out of the money you'd paid your good friend Olivia to keep quiet." I shook my head. "Hush money upon hush money upon hush money."

Daniel Lopez finally spoke then, in a voice so soft it barely made it across the living room to Todd Jakes.

"You?" he said.

"Enough," Jakes said then.

When I shifted my focus back to him, he had the gun out.

"You should have patted me down, smart guy," Jakes said to me.

SEVENTY-SEVEN

I remained completely still now that the balloon had gone up.

"A lot of people know we're here," I said to Jakes.

"But all of the people who could support your cockeyed theory about things are dead, aren't they?" he said.

"Well, there's a very smart cop up in Vermont," I said.

"Who will never find me after tonight, because no one will," Jakes said. "And Spenser? If you try anything, I will shoot you first."

I wasn't watching him then. I was watching Vic Hale, remaining quite still himself, as if still trying to process the scene in front of him and everything he and Daniel had just learned.

"You?" he said to Jakes, echoing Daniel, even more wonder in his voice. "You and *Marisol*?"

Jakes shrugged.

"That part of it is true," he said. "It happened and I'm not proud that it happened. She even said afterward she didn't want it to happen. That I'd forced her that night." He shrugged. "She said, I said. But it didn't change that it had happened." He paused, but kept the gun steady out in front of him, no tremor to his hand that I could see, no nerves. "But when the first test, with that swab she got off you just so she'd know, wasn't a match, I realized I was the one who was fucked if you found out. I told Olivia not to say anything until we did the second test, with my swab." He took in a lot of air, let it out. "And then, yeah, Olivia switched them for me. And got paid handsomely to do it. Spenser's right. It *was* my hush money, just not nearly as much as you paid Marisol."

"Why are you telling us all this?" Daniel said.

"Because he plans to kill us," I said quietly. "Get rid of us like he got rid of every other loose thread, or so he thought. Including a reporter who was pulling on them harder than anybody."

"Shut up," Jakes said to me. "Or I really will shoot you first."

I saw Daniel open his mouth and close it.

Hale said, "You pushed me to pay her off, have her go away, as hard as my old man did."

"You never should have let her into your house!" Jakes screamed then.

"The cops might not be able to put you in Miami, or Vermont," I said, keeping my own voice calm. "But I heard tonight they can put you at Savin Hill Beach the night you shot Ricardo."

I was lying, but Jakes had no way of knowing that. And I needed to keep him talking. And keep him from using what I could clearly see was a Glock.

"You really plan to kill us all?" I said to Jakes. "And then what? Leave without getting paid, after getting this close, and after all you did to get here?"

He turned, just slightly, in Hale's direction, the gun now pointed directly at him.

"I did you a favor by getting her out of your life, whether you want to admit that or not," he said. "You think she wouldn't have told about the two of you eventually? Hell, even after all you paid her, she probably would have written a book." The gun in Jakes's hand was still steady. *"I was protecting you as much as I was protecting myself!"*

What happened next happened before I could do anything about it.

"You sonofabitch!" Vic Hale roared, and then Tommy Boy Hale's son was charging at Todd Jakes, coming up and off the couch like he was coming at him across the ring, bull-rushing him and getting his arms around him, trying to pin Jakes's arms to his sides, the gun between them.

Too late.

The gun went off.

And then Hale was staring down almost sadly at the blood already beginning to show through the EVERLAST on the old boxing sweatshirt as Jakes stepped away from him and wheeled to put the gun back on Daniel and me.

But as Hale dropped to his knees and then fell over forward, Daniel was off the couch, not going for Jakes or the gun but going for Vic Hale.

"Daniel . . . no!" I shouted.

Then I was rolling off the couch, and down behind the big coffee table and pulling the .38 out of my ankle holster.

Jakes tried to pull Daniel up and use him as a shield, but Daniel spun and before Jakes could get another shot off, I put three bullets into him from my crouch, all three grouped like I was on the range, all center mass, the .38 more than accurate enough in close quarters like these.

Jakes was on his back then, and the gun had fallen away from his hand by the time I closed on him, knowing he was dead even before I reached down and checked for a pulse.

As I knelt next to him I said, "You should have patted me down, too."

SEVENTY-EIGHT

I had Daniel use Vic Hale's landline to call 911 while I tried to stop Vic Hale's bleeding with towels Daniel had found in a downstairs bathroom.

"Why didn't he just kill me, too?" Daniel said, while I continued to press hard on Hale's chest wound.

"Maybe he didn't think he needed to," I said. "Or, who the hell knows, maybe even he couldn't do that to his own son."

We heard the first sirens then, either ambulance or cops, I still had a hard time telling the difference.

"You need to go," I said to Daniel.

"What?"

"Leave," I said. *"Now.* You were never here. Just go out the back door and walk around the lake until you get yourself far enough away from here and then hope you can find enough cell service to call Hawk. Or just keep walking until you do."

Hale's breathing was becoming more shallow. He had lost a lot of blood. I spoke to him and told him to hang on, but he did not respond. I kept pressing hard on his chest with the towel, certain he was dying.

Daniel stared down at him.

"Before you came back," he said, "he said that I might not want to hear it, but it was too late for him to change."

"And maybe never will," I said. "Now, get out of here."

He did. Then I tried to keep the sonofabitch on the living room floor alive until the EMTs arrived a few minutes later.

As soon as they did, I left them alone to do their work and then I was the one using Vic Hale's phone to call Frank Belson.

SEVENTY-NINE

Vic Hale survived eight hours of surgery needed to repair the damage done by the bullet fired into him at close range by Todd Jakes's gun, and the fragments left by what should have been a fatal tear through his internal organs but in the end was not, if barely.

"Like one of those cockroaches could survive a nuclear attack," Hawk said.

I elected not to tell Hawk that one of the EMTs on the scene at Lake Avenue had told me before they wheeled Hale out of there that if I hadn't done as well as I had with the towels he almost surely would have died on the living room floor before they got him into the ambulance.

Over the next several days while Hale recuperated at Newton-Wellesley Hospital, Bill Jones handled all media inquiries and was all over the media himself, saying what a blessing it was that Vic Hale had survived, what a tragedy it was that his friend and long-time producer had obviously had this kind of psychotic break, and that his client would give his own version of the events at his house when he was back on the air, because it was his story to tell.

When asked how the shooting and Vic's near-death experience

might affect the negotiations over a new contract, Jones said it would be inappropriate to even discuss that while Vic was still in the hospital.

"But stay tuned once he's risen all the way up like Lazarus," his lawyer said, and with a straight face.

Daniel had spent the last several days looking for a place to live in Cambridge in the fall, Susan helping him when she could. There had even been the suggestion from Hawk that Daniel and Cassius Moore might share a place, thanks to the big fat raise I'd given Cassius for the great J-O-B he'd done for me from the time Daniel Lopez had come into my life.

It was two weeks after the shooting that Vic Hale announced he would return to the airwaves, the expectation being that he would produce record streaming numbers across his various platforms, and with all the ships at sea, when he did. And he teased that there would be an even bigger announcement about *All Hale* forthcoming.

Susan and Hawk and Daniel and I had gathered at Susan's house on Linnaean Street to be part of the audience for Hale's first show back, Susan having cleared her afternoon schedule. We had all ordered box lunches from Potbelly.

"We're doing takeout just so you don't have to prepare an elaborate lunch for the rest of us," I said to Susan, knowing she had rarely ever produced an elaborate lunch on her own.

"Shut up," she said.

Hawk chuckled.

"That goes for you, too," she said.

"Didn't say nothing," he said.

Susan smiled sweetly at him. "My ass," she said, and before I could chime in on the subject of her ass, as she was certain I would, she pointed back at me and said, "Don't even think about it."

The often lurid coverage of the shooting at Hale's house had portrayed Jakes as someone about to be fired, even though I knew that not to be true. But it fit the narrative Bill Jones was masterfully leaking to various news outlets and websites, that sadly there had clearly been "signs" that they had all either ignored or missed about Jakes's fragile mental state.

I made no public comments myself other than to tell the reporter from *The Globe* who contacted me that I had been meeting with Hale that night because of a case unrelated to events there that I described, and with a straight face myself, as "tragic."

"Still say you should have let the man bleed out," Hawk said now.

"How do you know I didn't?" I said.

"Haw," he said.

"Even you have to admit Hale might have done one true thing by rushing Jakes the way he did," I said. "And maybe saving Daniel's life and mine in the process."

"Or maybe, and more likely, his only thought in the moment was getting the gun away from Jakes and using it on *him*," Susan said.

"Nevertheless," I said brightly.

"You look at it," Hawk said, "what did the man really lose in the end other than a few weeks of work?"

"He did nearly die," I said.

"And the world would have been a damn better place he did," Hawk said.

We heard the Rolling Stones singing "Start Me Up" then. And there was the image of Vic Hale, looking thinner than he had a couple weeks ago, still looking pale despite all the makeup I was sure he had on, sitting behind the desk and microphone I recognized from the day Todd Jakes had taken me to the studio. Now he was back in that studio. Business as usual.

"He's baaaaack," Hale shouted.

When the music finally fell away, he leaned forward and the camera came in closer on him.

"Let's get right to it," he said. "Just in case anybody out there in Vic Hale's America has been wondering if you were going to get a kinder and gentler version of me now that I've stared death in the eyes . . ."

"Kill *me* now," Hawk said.

". . . you can fuggedaboutit," Hale shouted.

His voice was so loud that I wondered why he didn't just open a window.

"The fight goes on," he said. "The enemy is still at our doorstep. The infidels are still poised to storm the barricades at our borders, despite all America has done to stop them. It's still us against them, and even a bullet can't stop me from continuing the fight *against* them, because this will always be our country and not theirs . . ."

"I've heard enough," Susan said, and pointed the remote at the television as Vic Hale's face disappeared and the room went mercifully silent.

"He told me the truth that night," Daniel said. "He really can't change."

He shook his head.

"And Hawk's right," Daniel said. "He wins. We lose."

It turned out we were wrong about that.

EIGHTY

Vic Hale was only back on the air for one week.

At the end of it, and before what he said would be only a brief sabbatical, he announced that he had signed a five-year personal services contract with Mauricio Estrella's parent company, Libertad Media, and that even though Estrella was based in Miami, Hale would continue to do his show from Boston.

"Different owner" is the way he described it. "Same team. And same voice."

He added this before signing off:

"My friend Mr. Estrella is an example of the way you're supposed to come to this country and pursue the American dream. He just did it the right way."

That was on Friday.

On Monday, Mauricio Estrella issued a statement that he was removing *All Hale* from his streaming services, from YouTube TV. From everything. It was, of course, news that rocked the media landscape.

Susan and Hawk and Hawk's new friend Emma, whom we'd finally been allowed to meet, were having a celebratory dinner about all of that at No. 9 Park in Beacon Hill. Daniel had already returned to Miami to start packing up, as he wanted to be in Boston well before classes started at Harvard.

Rita, I had discovered, had a date of her own with the law professor from Miami who'd put her together with Daniel in the first place. And, Hawk had informed the rest of us, Cassius had a date himself with one of the fitness instructors from Emma's club.

"Hawk assured me I have nothing to worry about with Cassius, that he's a complete gentleman," Emma said.

"Told her it was just like the girl be hooking up with me," Hawk said.

"At which point I *did* start worrying about Cassius," Emma said.

Emma had the figure of a runway model and a face that even Susan agreed was breathtakingly beautiful. Emma and Hawk were sharing champagne, insofar as Hawk ever shared much of his champagne. Susan had white wine. I was spoiling myself with a cabernet both delicious and expensive called Caymus.

Hawk raised his glass and the rest of us raised ours.

"To the little Guatemalan dude," Hawk said, "for doing Hale like this."

"Freezing him," I said.

"Uh-huh," Hawk said. "Like they do with a damn kicker at the end of a football game."

We all drank.

"That was the plan Estrella wouldn't tell me about," I said. "His own deal with the devil. He was willing to pay Hale crazy money to shut him up, and shut him down, for as long as he can. He hates him that much."

"Diabolical," Susan said.

"You *think*?" I said.

The news had broken this morning. In the end, Mauricio Estrella had been even more badass than I had suspected.

"People get canceled all the time," Estrella said in a brief statement. "Now Vic Hale has been."

Hale and Bill Jones responded immediately, saying this was a clear violation of Hale's right to free speech. An hour later, Estrella's lawyers were more than happy to release not only the financial details of Hale's deal with Libertad Media, but all the fancy and detailed non-compete and play-for-pay language they had baked into it about not only current media, but future media, for the entire length of the contract. Hale got his money in the end, just lost his bullhorn.

"Balls to the fucking wall," Susan Silverman said.

Emma reached over so Susan could bump her some fist.

"Couldn't have put it better myself," she said, "speaking as a proud Haitian American."

"God *bless* America," Hawk said.

"Maybe God's," I said, "but not Vic's."

"I don't mean to throw cold water on the conversation, and I'm certainly no lawyer," Susan said, "but isn't there some way that Hale could seek injunctive relief of some kind?"

"He'll certainly try," I said. "But when I spoke to Estrella, he told me his lawyers were better than Hale's. Or maybe anyone's. And said he'd been certain all along that all Hale and Jones and our dear friend Tony Marcus cared about was that he, Estrella, had blown Woody Giles right out of the water with his offer."

I drank more Caymus.

"He says that he might not be able to tie up Hale in court for all of the next five years," I said. "But the little guy sure seems dead set on trying."

"And doesn't care about the cost?" Emma asked.

"I asked him about that," I said. "And was told that whatever it cost him, it would still be a bargain."

"What they call fuck-you money," Hawk said.

I said, "The first time I sat down with Hale he told me that he'd bury Daniel if Daniel tried to make trouble for him. Now Estrella is trying to bury him."

"In a way," Susan said, "Estrella is doing what Vic Hale did with Marisol a long time ago: paying him to go away."

"Just not quietly," I said.

Susan turned to me.

"I need to ask you something," she said. "Is this enough for you?"

"You know, I've been asking myself that same question all day," I said. "And I guess the best answer I can give you is the same one Redford gave Newman at the end of *The Sting*."

"Refresh my memory," she said.

"No, it's not enough, Suze," I said. Then I grinned. "But it's close."

ACKNOWLEDGMENTS

As always, my gratitude goes out to David and Daniel Parker, who allow me to do this kind of work in a world their father first imagined.

Esther Newberg is the literary caretaker of that world, and Tom Colgan, the pride of Archbishop Molloy, is such a pro's pro as my editor.

Of course, Ivan Held is the capo di tutti capi.

I could not write these books without the generosity and wisdom of John Fisher, Chief of Police, Bedford, Mass.

Ziggy Alderman, Nancy Alderman, Peter Gethers are all there from the start, every time.

Finally, and from the heart: My thanks to Taylor McKelvy Lupica, my first reader and still my most trusted one.